PRAISE FOR CAROLYN MILLER

Praise for the Original Six series

"I LOVE THIS BOOK!! I love the uniqueness of the characters - we don't see too many hockey player heroes which is a true shame because THOSE KISSES!!"~ *CARRIE BOOTH SCHMIDT, Reading is my Superpower blog*

"I loved the dialogue and the hero and heroine, the very authentic and real challenges they faced and the unique setting and hockey slant." ~ *RACHEL MCMILLAN, best-selling author*

"A touching romance set on the breathtaking shores of Canada's Lake Muskoka. Sarah and Dan are so vividly drawn they practically leap off the page! Their sweet, slowly evolving friendship deepens into the kind of lasting love Christians long for. A must read!" ~ *MEGHANN WHISTLER, award-winning author of The Billionaire's Secret*

"I have been waiting for TJ's story and am so glad it's here! It's perfect...This is truly a story about loving the unlovable and the blessings that come as a result." ~ *GOODREADS review*

"There is nothing like a wonderful redemption story where someone changes their life and becomes a better version of themselves. It is a good reminder to me that God offers incredible grace to all of us." ~ *GOODREADS review*

"Carolyn Miller keeps on turning out these beautifully written, tender hearted books!... There was humor and brilliant bantering conversations, heart stopping romance, as well as exciting descriptions (and sometimes dangerous passages of play) of hockey games. Well worth the late night/early morning read!" ~ *KAYE'S REVIEWS & NEWS*

"A sweet love story that continues the Original Six Hockey series by Carolyn Miller. The setting of Montreal with the Gardens and all the French woven throughout was delightful!" ~ *GOODREADS review*

"I am emerging out of my book hangover after reading *Checked Impressions* by Carolyn Miller....The romance, humor and themes of identity are so enjoyable and make for a great read!" ~ *BECKY'S BOOKSHELVES*

"Adrenaline, chemistry, romance, and lots of wooing!... You do not have to be a fan of sports or even knowledgeable in hockey and short track to appreciate *Love on Ice*." ~ *GOODREADS review*

"Carolyn Miller scores another win with *Love on Ice*, the second book in her Original Six Hockey series. I absolutely loved the faith thread in this story. It's message that success does not lie on what we do, but who we are is powerful." ~ *GOODREADS review*

"*The Breakup Project* is a fun, charming, and faith-filled contemporary romance with adorable characters set in the competitive North American ice hockey world. Highly recommended." ~ *NARELLE ATKINS, Author of Solo Tu & Her Tycoon Hero*

MUSKOKA SHORES

CAROLYN MILLER

ALSO BY CAROLYN MILLER

<u>The Original Six hockey series</u>

The Breakup Project

Love on Ice

Checked Impressions

Hearts and Goals

Big Apple Atonement

Muskoka Blue

Muskoka Shores

Muskoka Christmas

Muskoka Hearts

<u>Northwest Ice hockey series</u>

Fire and Ice

<u>Trinity Lakes collection</u>

Love Somebody Like You

<u>The Independence Islands series</u>

Restoring Fairhaven

Regaining Mercy

Reclaiming Hope

Rebuilding Hearts

Refining Josie

Historical:

MUSKOKA SHORES

CHAPTER 1

 as there anything more special than watching a man look into his bride's face with that deep look of promise and devotion?

Serena Williamson released a soft sigh. Well, maybe if it was Dwight looking at her like that, instead of Toronto's hockey star Dan Walton gazing enthralled at his redheaded Aussie bride. She rubbed the empty space on her ring finger.

"And do you, Daniel, promise to take Sarah as your lawful wife, to love and protect her, for as long as you both shall live?"

"I do."

Shivers rippled up her spine. As the assistant event coordinator for the Muskoka Shores Resort, she'd witnessed many weddings over the years, but few had made her heart throb like the intensity of this moment.

Pastor John McPherson asked his niece Sarah Maguire the same question, and again something twisted inside. Envy? A yearning for Dwight to look at her with just a quarter of the awe with which Dan regarded Sarah? Although she knew both of them from church before, she—along with the vast majority of the congregation—had been surprised to learn the true state of their relationship a few months ago, when John and Angela had announced from the pulpit Dan and Sarah's engagement.

In her role as wedding coordinator she'd met with the couple once, their busy schedules and time overseas limiting opportunity for an in-person consultation, but in that time, she'd sensed the depth of their commitment. There was something precious between these two, so much she just *knew* this marriage would work out. Some couples were not so assured, seemingly more devoted to a day of extravagance than lifelong dedication to each other. She bit her lip. She shouldn't judge. That was what her job entailed, after all, giving couples their dream day. But still, she couldn't help but be glad that these two were so forthright about including God in the midst of their promises to love and cherish each other all the days of their life.

Sarah's ivory gown glittered in the afternoon sunshine, the floral lace enhanced by subtle crystals, the A-line shape and sweetheart neckline perfect for her slender figure, the spaghetti straps and light veil perfect for today's heat. Dan filled out his navy suit to perfection, and with his blush-colored tie and rose and gum-leaf boutonniere he was sure to fill a million Pinterest boards as the epitome of a handsome bridegroom. But more than their clothes, it was their joy, that deep sense of love and devotion, that really spoke to Serena's heart. Maybe it was the fact they were both committed believers, or that she'd gleaned from some of the things Sarah had said last year a little of the tragedy and triumph of her story, but Serena sensed this marriage was going to thrive.

Bible readings followed: Sarah's sister, Dan's friends Boyd and Beau Nash, another of the hockey stars in attendance. The nuptials had garnered a huge amount of media attention, forcing the resort to employ extra security to keep the ceremony and celebrations private from those wanting to make a quick buck from selling photos online. Fortunately the lakeside location of Muskoka Shores meant only guests could access the resort's chapel with its picture windows overlooking Lake Muskoka.

Serena quickly scanned the guests, but everyone possessed similar smiles to the one in her heart. She'd personally met each person as they'd entered the venue, doing her best to not fan-girl over the likes of famous hockey players such as Brent Karlsson and his wife Holly, Beau and his wife Maggie, Mike and Bree Vaughan, or the other members of Heartsong Collective, the worship group Sarah was part of, whose songs stocked Serena's personal playlists. Muskoka Shores had hosted celebrity weddings before, but few had tugged at her heartstrings the way this one did.

The service continued with a message from Pastor John—advice to be each other's biggest cheerleaders, to keep God at the center of their love—then prayers were prayed, then the moment everyone waited for: "You may now kiss the bride."

Dan's smile of delight tugged fresh longing—had Dwight ever looked at Serena liked that?—then he cupped Sarah's face with both hands and leaned down to kiss her, in a long tender moment that seemed meant for movies.

Laughter and applause met them as they finally broke apart, Sarah's ecstatic smile echoed on Dan's face, his look holding something of his wonder and joy at what had happened.

As they slowly made their way down the aisle, pausing as they were met with hugs and kisses from family and friends, Serena shifted from her discreet position to the exit, joining Alexa Reddick, the photographer, whom she'd worked with a number of times before.

"That was so beautiful," Alexa murmured, before snapping another candid shot.

"Probably the best wedding I've seen," Serena admitted.

"Right? It was like you could feel the love," Alexa said. "I think every picture is going to be amazing. But it helps when they're both good-looking, and with the rain clearing up from yesterday. How lucky were they with the weather?"

"Another answer to prayer, for sure," Serena said.

Alexa nodded, moving into position to capture the jubilant bride and groom.

The next half hour would be taken up with photographs, then they'd all move to the reception venue, the Bala Ballroom, with French doors opening onto the terrace that overlooked the lake. She checked to see the waiters were ready with the hors d'oeuvres and champagne, giving them a discreet thumbs up before moving back to check over the reception room one last time.

The team had done a beautiful job, the creams and white décor perfectly complemented by the striking floral arrangements the bride had requested, combining cream and pale pink roses with ruby red waratah flowers, gum nuts and eucalyptus leaves. The rustic posies suited the relaxed yet elegant table settings, the gleaming glassware awaiting the toasts, the gold-edged dinner plates ready for the meal already scenting the air. Everything was going according to plan.

Guests soon trickled in, swelling the room in a happy hum of excitement. Even Dan's family seemed to have finally relaxed, the smile on his mother's face looking more genuine than any of the previous times she'd met Helen Walton.

Serena moved among them, helping guests find their seats at the round tables, directing people to the washrooms, or the table for gifts and the guestbook. Snatches of conversation drifted to her ears.

"…so happy for them!"

"She's so beautiful. I loved her hair up like that."

"Elle est si belle," Beau's French Canadian wife agreed.

"Did you see his expression when she walked in? I thought my heart would melt!"

"I still can't believe she's that singer." Bree Vaughan rubbed her belly. "Do you think she'll have time for an autograph?"

"Didn't you ask her the other night?" a petite Aussie—Holly Karlsson—asked.

"I meant to, but we got caught up talking about little Ethan, and baby number two."

Serena suppressed a smile as she moved to check the cake. It seemed funny to have NHL wives as awed by the status of the bride as she was. But even though many of them had spent several days at the resort beforehand, checking out the facilities, spending time with the happy couple either on the lake with their husbands and families or getting pampered in the spa, it seemed that vacation time always slipped away too fast.

The cake stood ready, its two layers of cream-frosted red velvet and chocolate mud cake decorated with more of the floral garlands showcasing flowers from the bride's homeland. She straightened the knife, then turned as the volume in the room increased.

"Miss Williamson." Austin, one of their newer servers, drew her attention to the door.

She caught the eye of Luke Walton, the groom's older brother who was acting as the emcee today. He nodded and joined her near the entryway.

"It all looks amazing," he said, glancing around.

"We always aim to please."

"Pretty sure you've succeeded. Hey, here they come."

She stepped back as Luke grinned at his brothers: Sam Walton, acting as Dan's best man; and the man of the hour, Dan Walton, Toronto's top defenseman, and brand new husband. Dan held hands with Sarah, who stood, still beaming with joy, while her sister, clad in emerald-green, supervised her daughters who'd made the cutest little flower girls in history, their balletic movements and artistic scattering of rose petals down the aisle drawing more than a few chuckles and smiles.

Sarah caught Serena's eye, mouthing a thank you. Serena gave her a thumbs up as her own smile deepened. Thankfulness grew in her heart that the arrangements had flowed so easily. They might've been the most relaxed couple she'd ever dealt with, but it had still been a rush to get everything ready. The cancellation that had opened up this opportunity for Dan and Sarah had only occurred two months ago, a 'miracle' as Sarah's Aunt Angela had put it when Serena had met with her and the groom's mother to discuss arrangements. Serena's smile dimmed. One couple's decision to call off their long-standing engagement might not be considered miraculous by them, but still. Angela was right. Today was going perfectly.

She motioned for Luke to move to the small podium and gestured to the swing band to pause the music as he announced the arrival of the matron of honor and best man, before introducing the bride and groom to raucous cheers and applause.

They entered the reception room, their smiles drawing renewed anticipation. One day. Soon. She and Dwight would look as happy as Dan and Sarah did, whose grins lit up their faces as they walked, hands clasped and held high, past their cheering guests to the bridal table at the front of the room. She couldn't wait.

"Excuse me? Miss Williamson?" Serena turned to Austin, whose fresh face looked up at her expectantly. "Are we ready for serving?"

Serena glanced back, noting the bridal couple was now seated. She caught Luke's eye and nodded. He stood again and made some comments before asking Sarah's father to pray the blessing as everyone bowed their heads.

Serena nodded to Austin, and with the ease of a well-oiled machine, the bridal meal service began. Her lips curved. This afternoon was going to be another wonderful event; she could feel it. Of course, it helped when the bride and groom weren't too fussy and were happy to keep things simple.

But simple didn't have to mean basic. She stood in the corner as the July sun poured through the windows, bouncing off the chandeliers and crystal glassware, catching the golden highlights of the bride's beautiful hair. Sarah was a radiant bride; it was no wonder her new husband seemed unable to take his eyes off her.

Serena recalled the first time she'd met her, just over a year ago at the church in Muskoka Shores, when Sarah had been keeping her distance from everyone in a totally different way to Dan's reserve with his fans. Over the months she'd grown more relaxed, her personality taking on a sparkle, and her vivacity had helped as she'd led the music team at church, something sorely needed. Her return to Muskoka a few days ago had seen Sarah slightly foggy from jet lag, having come all the way from Australia, but her warmth, enthusiasm, and genuine appreciation suggested she wasn't liable to Bridezilla moments like some.

Serena patted her hair to check her French twist was still smoothly in place as she glanced around the room again. Everything seemed to be going fine. Meals were being exclaimed over, and those who weren't eating yet were laughing, smiling and posing for photos. The rich smells of beef and roasted vegetables filled the room, chasing away the delicate perfume of the roses that centered each table.

"Everything looks beautiful, Serena. You've done an amazing job."

Serena turned to see her boss, Joanne Seymour. The worry lines in Joanne's forehead had smoothed out for now. "The team's done a great job."

"Don't sell yourself short. I've only heard good things." Joanne's lips widened. "And that's helpful with such high profile guests." She winked. "It's not every day we have so many NHL players in one room."

Serena kept the smile pinned on as she discreetly adjusted

the buttons on her too-tight suit jacket. Something she and the resort's event manager had always disagreed on. It shouldn't matter whether the client was high profile and rich or how many followers they had on social media. Every couple deserved to have the best wedding reception possible, and it was Serena's goal to give them a magical time they'd never forget.

Joanne patted her on the back. "But then you always aim to please, don't you?"

"You know me." Serena's heart twisted. Joanne didn't mean to sound condescending. And it *was* true. It wasn't just part of her job description; since she was a child, she'd been told she was a people pleaser. It meant she'd earned a reputation as someone who was prepared to go the extra mile to make everything work out well for the bride and groom. It had proved a challenge sometimes, when the resort was simply unable to meet some of the more bizarre requests certain Bridezillas seemed to demand, like the bride who'd wanted confetti cannons that shot chocolate candy—in the height of summer. Serena winced, imagining the stains. Fortunately, she'd managed to avoid too many awkward confrontations over the years.

She eased back on her heels, shifting her weight as Joanne left and the next course was served. The smell wafting from the kitchen made her stomach growl. Oh well. The candy bar in her desk drawer would have to suffice until she could eat later. She made a quick exit to her small, cramped office, found her lifesaver of a chocolate bar and inhaled it in two bites. And frowned. The chocolate hadn't taken the edge off her hunger at all. She needed another one. Or five. But she didn't have time to hunt now. She had to get back. If any time during a reception was problematic and ripe for her soothing touch, it was during the speeches. Alcohol and good times made for looser lips than normal, not that much alcohol was being served at this wedding, but still...

She hurried back, panting slightly at the effort. Ugh, she was so unfit! Her black skirt cut into her midsection and she tugged it down. The suit usually did a good job of creating the slimming effect her less-than-svelte figure needed, and amidst all the glamorous guests she didn't want to appear frumpish. She couldn't apologize for loving food, and one of the best parts of her job involved the taste testing of new menus. This role had fallen to her since Joanne had become increasingly absent with her mother's illness, and Alphonse, the resort's French-trained chef, had certainly appreciated Serena's appreciation of his food. But the ensuing curves didn't bother her too much, and Dwight didn't seem to mind. Any time she made a disparaging remark about her looks, he was always quick to encourage her, assuring her he preferred her voluptuous curves to what he called "stick insects" like her friend Hope.

Poor Hope. Serena's housemate was a physical education teacher who worked at the same high school as Dwight. Hope never seemed to be able to hold a boyfriend for longer than a month, which was surprising, as Serena had always thought Hope was attractive, in a really-skinny, model kind of way. Poor Hope. If she didn't find someone soon, she'd be stuck on the shelf forever, and she'd never find love like Serena had with Dwight.

Serena dragged her thoughts back to the job at hand as Luke stood and smiled at the guests. "Are we all having a good time?"

Serena caught herself starting to nod then smiled at her foolishness. The afternoon was going perfectly.

LATER THAT EVENING, after yet another successful event, Serena pulled out from the resort's tree-lined drive onto the highway heading home, slightly earlier than normal, happy that the rest of the team were able to finish up for her. It had been a good day. Serena smiled at the memories: The cutting of the cake, then the playful way Sarah smeared Dan's face with icing. Dan and Sarah completing their bridal waltz, eyes only for each other. Watching other guests dancing: TJ Woletsky's surprisingly smooth moves, Jai Mullins caressing his wife's baby bump as they slow danced, Brent Karlsson dipping his wife to her gurgle of laughter. Sarah, throwing her arms around Serena just before they left, exclaiming, "Serena, thank you so much. Today has been a dream come true!"

The open affection had drawn Serena's laugh of surprise. "I'm glad you've enjoyed yourselves."

"We couldn't have done it without you," Dan had said, pressing a kiss to his new wife's brow. "Thanks again."

"My pleasure. Congratulations to you both."

"I still can't believe you managed to pull everything together so quickly," Sarah said, her head tilted on Dan's shoulder. "It's worked out like a dream."

"God is into miracles," Serena said.

"That's so true," Sarah said, her eyes on Dan, their smiles for them alone.

Serena recognized her cue to leave, and inched away when Sarah called, "If ever there is anything either of us can do, please let us know. You have my number."

"Thank you."

She'd nearly scoffed at the thought that a person she followed on social media—along with thousands of others—might actually be willing to help her. When would that ever happen? But Sarah hadn't exactly been shy about promoting her love for the resort and area, to the extent that #MuskokaShores was trending today. God bless her.

Serena's heart still skipped at the way Dan and Sarah had stared at each other, their secret smiles hinting at the almost tangible attraction pulsing between them. She chewed her bottom lip. She couldn't wait for Dwight to look at her the same way on their wedding day. How much longer would she have to wait? She and Dwight had known each other since they were seniors in high school and had been good friends for years before starting to go out three years ago. He said he loved her, he knew she loved him, so the next logical step had to be an engagement, right?

She overtook a minivan towing a trailer with two jet skis, no doubt heading home after an action-packed day on the lake, then settled back in her seat as the small silver Mazda zoomed through a darker stretch of forest, lit with the last golden rays of sunset. As much as she loved making other people's dreams come true it would be nice to personally experience being the happy bride. She'd already picked out her dress and planned her wedding down to the flowers (red roses and pink lavender) and canapés (retro-inspired ratatouille tartlets – tasty, yet not too salty). All that remained was for Dwight to pop the question, so she could fill in the date on the invitations she'd already started designing on the computer at home.

Serena rounded the corner then slowed as the township's lights glowed. This time on a Saturday night in peak summer season was notorious for tourists. The resort took its name from the nearby town of Muskoka Shores, whose population swelled every summer from hundreds to thousands, along with the traffic congestion such tourists always longed to escape yet helped create. She passed The Coffee Blend, the town's best coffee shop, then through the town center with its quirky stores designed for tourists: a chocolatier, a vintage toyshop, the 'Nuthouse', the ice-creamery, each storefront decorated with twinkling lights and some still serving the last of tonight's summer customers. It wasn't any surprise people loved visiting this town. She turned and took the back streets to her own stretch of residential. Two corners. One. She sighed. Almost home. Almost time to kick back and relax after another super successful day. She was so glad tomorrow was a Sunday, and the start of her regular two days off. It had been a long week.

Her heart skipped a beat as she noticed Dwight's car parked out the front of the house she shared with Hope. He'd said he'd be out somewhere with workmates tonight. She smiled. He must want to surprise her. How romantic! She killed the lights before parking beside his Pontiac, gathering her handbag as she took care to quietly close the car door. Let the surprise be on him.

She tiptoed up the garden path before silently unlocking the front door, placing her handbag on the entryway table as she paused. The living room was filled with glowing candles. Her expensive, special frangipani-scented candles. They'd been lit for a while because wax was spilling onto the table, dripping onto the varnished floors. Serena frowned. How long had Dwight been waiting for her? And where was he, anyway?

"Hello?"

There was no reply. She stood waiting for the big bear hug that Dwight usually equated with romance but it didn't come. She sniffed the air. Intermingled with the delicate tropical scent was the savory tang of—her mouth watered—pizza. Mr. Healthy had ordered pizza?

She took another step then noticed the pizza box dumped on the floor, the lid open, with one slice of Supreme staring forlornly up at her. What? Unease slid through her and she started moving through the dim house. Maybe something terrible had happened and Hope knew where Dwight was. The door to Hope's room was slightly ajar, and with a sudden sense of foreboding, Serena pushed it open.

And gasped.

Dwight and Hope lay entwined on Hope's bed, their passionate kisses unlike any Serena had experienced. They were clothed at least, but this barely registered as she stared in horror. She blinked, but the image remained the same. She swallowed bile, summoning up strength to speak.

"What are you doing?"

Dumb question, but the lip-lock broke apart, two faces turning to her, but only one wore guilt.

"S-Serena! You're home early!" Dwight stammered as he inched away and tried to sit up.

Serena placed a hand on the doorframe for support, trying to force air into her lungs. "Not early enough, it seems."

"Wasn't tonight the wedding of your famous celebrity couple?" Hope asked, slowly buttoning her shirt, as if she hadn't just been busted making moves on Serena's boyfriend.

Yes, but—

"Did you see Karlsson? Was Mike Vaughan there?" Dwight asked.

"I'm sorry"—wait, why was she the one apologizing?—"what has that got to do with this?" Serena pointed to the bed. Nausea swilled her insides.

Hope shrugged as she fastened the last button, her gaze unapologetic. "It was bound to come out eventually."

"Eventually? What do you mean eventually?" Was this a bad TV drama? She didn't know the lines but already had a bad feeling how this episode was going to end.

"You don't think tonight's the first time we've been together, do you?" Hope's insincere smile made Serena's skin crawl. "We've been together for years."

"Years?" And what did she mean by 'been together'? That didn't mean what she thought it meant, did it? Not when Dwight had always said he respected her decision to wait until marriage. Had the two of them—? No. No, *no*. "I don't believe you."

"Fine. Don't." Hope pushed her fingers through her long tawny mane.

Serena looked at the tumbled bedclothes, the flickering candles, as the hopeless truth made air suddenly hard to find. Her grip on the doorframe tightened as the world grew dizzy.

Dwight eased off the bed. "Serena..."

She blinked and he came into focus again. "Dwight, I don't understand."

He looked at her like a deflated puppy as Hope moved to stand beside him, flicking her dyed blonde hair over a scrawny shoulder.

"What did you think would happen, Serena? You spend your life fussing over others at the resort or at church, and you leave a good man like Dwight at loose ends. Of course he's going to find you boring and want a little excitement in his life."

Hope's words stung like acid. Serena turned to Dwight, her eyes filling with tears. "You…you think I'm boring?"

Dwight stood there. "Serena, I'm—"

"Renie, someone's got to tell you," Hope interrupted. "Come on, it's time you faced it. You're fat, you're unfit, and you're never going to change. You've got no direction. Face it. You're boring. You've got nothing to offer anyone."

Serena flinched, each word a slap. Fat? Boring? Nothing to offer anyone? Who was this woman masquerading as her friend? She dragged in a deep breath. "How dare you?"

Hope's lips curled up. "Easily." And she leaned over to give Dwight a big kiss on the lips.

Serena's mouth sagged, her neck, her face suddenly impossibly hot, as lightheadedness swept her again. This couldn't be happening. This had to be a bad dream.

Hope turned back, her head leaning against Dwight's shoulder. Serena suddenly saw the likeness, the matching lean runner physiques, the matching veneers of friendship she'd believed to be true. She covered her mouth. How could she have been so gullible? How could they treat her like this? Was nice just another word for stupid? A million memories flashed, melding into heat that banded tight across her chest, igniting into a blazing anger that burned through the fog of confusion.

Hope opened her mouth. Serena took a step forward, palm outstretched. "Shut up, Hope."

She turned to Dwight. "I can't believe you did this. And you pretended to be a Christian too!" Emotion roared, leaking out her eyes, trickling down her cheeks, and she angrily swiped it away. "You are such a... such a—" What could she say? If only she had a script. "Get out. Get out of my house and get out of my life. I'm sorry I wasted so many years on you!"

Dwight inched toward her. "Serena, I'm—"

"Pathetic, a fool, a user, a hypocrite." The words were finally there. "Get out, Dwight. I don't ever want to see you again. And you," Serena's eyes narrowed at Hope. "You've got ten minutes to get your stuff and get out too."

Hope didn't look so cocky anymore. "But—"

"I said shut up!" Serena yelled. "You're beyond belief! I take you in, you pretend to be my friend, you live in my house, and then you go steal my boyfriend?" Serena breathed to steady her voice from its high-pitched screech. "Get out. Get your things out of my house now. And don't you *ever* speak to me again."

The arrogant tilt to Hope's face faded, as if she was starting to realize just what she'd done. The house was Serena's, an unexpected legacy from her grandparents' will five years ago. Serena had always loved visiting their quaint and cozy home and had relished gently restyling it with a subtle Hamptons vibe. Hope paid a nominal rent, but with no binding contract, Serena had never been too strict on enforcing when Hope had paid, something Hope had taken advantage of more than once. Seemed that wasn't the only thing of Serena's she'd taken advantage of. But the upside of no legal document was that Serena didn't have to give Hope any notice before kicking her out.

"Come on, Serena. You can't do that."

"No?" Disbelief at Hope's nerve massed within until red spots danced before her eyes. "What did you think I might do? Throw you a party? How dare you tell me what I can and can't do in my own house? When you, you..."

As Hope continued to stand there, Serena suddenly moved to the set of drawers, opening them, then tossing the contents at Hope. "I said, get your stuff out of my house. So get out! Now!"

Her scream finally mobilized Dwight and Hope into action. Dwight edged his way from the room while Hope frantically stuffed clothes in her bag. The furniture was all Serena's, and as she stood there watching, she realized what the house would be like in the next few days. Empty. Alone. Just like her life. No-one to share it with.

Pain worse than when she'd broken her arm as a kid threatened to overwhelm her, so Serena turned on her heel and moved to the kitchen. Grabbing a large plastic bag, she moved to the kitchen, stuffing it with all the health foods Hope had bought, along with her stupid Garfield mug Serena had always hated. She threw it into the bag where it made a satisfying crack.

Next, she moved to the bathroom. "You've got five minutes!" With energy borne from rage she grabbed another plastic bag and shoved Hope's toiletries and medications in it. She filled it with a couple of towels from the cupboard, some ugly Hope-bought cushions from the lounge, and one of Hope's trashy Staci Everton books. Glancing down she saw the discarded pizza box. She tipped the cheesy slice in on top of the towels before moving swiftly to the front door and throwing the bag onto the lawn. Petty? She was just getting started.

Breathing hard now, she ignored the across-the-road neighbors who'd been sitting outside enjoying the balmy night and now sat watching the crazed antics of Miss Boring. She smiled grimly. Not tonight she wasn't, anyway.

Dwight slid out the front door, car key in hand. "I'm really sorry—"

"Don't." She shook her head. "Just don't." She strode back in, catching sight of the guttering candles. The supremely expensive frangipani soy candles Dwight had given her on her last birthday. Tears filled her eyes. She picked up a melted yellow mass and ran back outside. "Hey Dwight."

He turned around.

"You forgot something."

She threw it—hard—and almost cheered as it banged against the freshly waxed car. Petty? Yes. Satisfying? One thousand percent.

"Rena! Look what you did!" He crouched next to the wax-spattered door panel.

"Look what *I* did? Don't you dare go there."

She ran back inside and scooped up two more of the traitor's candles then ran outside again, throwing them as he stared at her in shock before quickly getting in the vehicle, gunning the engine and disappearing into the night. Good riddance.

Heaving out a frustrated breath she stomped back inside. "You've got one minute!" She swiftly scanned the room, trying to find any lingering evidence of Hope. Nope, nearly all traces of Hope were gone.

Hope appeared with a couple of suitcases, hefting a plastic bag of shoes, with several health magazines and books spilling out the top. "Serena, I think—"

"I don't care what you think." Serena kept her voice low and level, like she did when dealing with her Minimites Sunday school class. "You've already told me enough of what you think. Just get out. If there's anything else of yours I find it'll be on the front lawn tomorrow morning. Now leave."

Hope looked at Serena. "I'm sorry—"

"No, you're not!" Anger shrieked again. "You're just sorry you got caught. I hate you, Hope! I hate you. Don't ever speak to me again!"

Serena was for once glad for her extra bulk as she pushed Hope out, scooping up the shoe bag and throwing that on the lawn next to the other bags. Bras and underclothes glowed white on the dark lawn. Hysteria bubbled up. The neighbors had never had it so good.

Hope was scrabbling around in the dark trying to find her car keys. Serena strode over to her. "Give me my house key."

Hope sullenly handed over the spare key to Serena's house then started loading her bags into the backseat.

Serena watched her for a moment, before stomping back inside and slamming the door, throwing the lock. As she stood, her chest heaving with adrenaline, the rage that had dictated her actions in the last ten minutes slowly ebbed from her veins. How had her day turned so bad so quickly? Was this even really real?

Vaguely, she heard Hope's car start up. Her lip curled. Dwight didn't even have the decency to help Hope out, not that Serena cared. She didn't know where Hope was going to sleep tonight either. Most of the town's accommodations were booked pretty heavily in the peak summer season. Maybe she'd stay with Dwight.

Her stomach shuddered, and she raced to the toilet and vomited, releasing her stomach's contents, wishing she could so easily release the pain.

She clasped either side of the porcelain bowl. How could she have ever trusted Hope? How could Hope have pretended to be her friend? How could Dwight pretend he enjoyed kissing her when he'd obviously been doing a lot more with Hope? Her insides heaved again.

Later, kneeling in the shower, crying in frustration and rage as the warm water pulsed over her shoulders, she could still hear the accusations fly: You're boring. Fat. Have no direction. Nothing to offer anyone.

She might never want to hear Hope's words again, but they continued to swim around her brain: *Boring. Fat. No direction. Nothing to offer.* In other words she'd be alone forever. Unwanted. Ugly. Stuck. Naïve. Hopeless. A doormat.

She pushed her heavy graying blonde hair back from her face. If only she could have a do-over of the past twelve hours. The first part had been so wonderful, the latter half just hellish. That night as she lay wide-eyed in bed, begging God to help her sleep, she wondered what her future would hold. Anything had to be better than this.

CHAPTER 2

*S*leep didn't come. The next morning after lying in bed with the night's horror roiling through her brain, Serena forced herself to focus. Today was…Sunday. Which meant church. A groan escaped. Maybe she could cancel leading Sunday school and stay in bed all day. Surely that box of chocolates she'd been saving for a special occasion would help her feel better. Even if this occasion sure didn't count as special, it still counted as a moment requiring some TLC, right? And people would understand her no-show, especially after knowing whose event she'd been working on the night before. If anyone would understand it'd be John and Angela. They'd likely not be there, anyway, considering they'd been so involved yesterday, and were likely catching up with Sarah's family, and—

Oh. Wait. Her heart grew heavier. Trudy, the church's secretary and children's church coordinator, was away this weekend, and with so few helpers, Serena really would be needed, especially considering vacation season meant more tourists would likely attend services. Great. She rolled over, arm splayed out across the mattress. *God, please help me. I don't want to go. I've got nothing to offer. No capacity whatsoever. I need You.*

She closed her eyes, but her whirling thoughts barely paused, and she sucked in an unsteady breath. She might have no capacity, but that wouldn't stop the kids from showing. She'd just have to pretend she was fine, then get out of there quick before any questions could be asked.

She dragged herself to the shower. Managed hair, and makeup—way more than usual, to hide her red-rimmed eyes. Their puffy nature demanded glasses instead of her usual contact lenses. No way did she want her eyes drawing any more attention than they usually did. Kids at school used to tease her and say her eyes' slight almond shape and deep green color looked like cat's eyes; to this day Serena still wasn't sure whether it was a good thing or not. She dressed, avoided break-fast—as if the roiling in her stomach could be satisfied with food—then drove to church.

How could the world look the same after what had happened? How could people clutch coffees and smile—worse, laugh!—as if the world hadn't changed? Why was she going to church today of all days?

"Because you're a stickler for the rules," she'd heard Hope say before, when she'd protested why Serena felt it necessary to attend church after one of Serena's Saturday night soirees went later than normal. Serena had always thought regularly gath-ering with other believers on Sunday was a good thing, a time to encourage and be encouraged, and up there with being responsible, with being trustworthy. But maybe it just meant boring. Able to be counted on, sure, but counted on to be else-where, oblivious, while others sneaked around behind her back.

Bile rose again, and she breathed deep while collecting her thoughts. *Get it together.* She couldn't break down today. She *wouldn't* break down today. At least, not this morning. Not before church, anyway.

Willing the tears away, she parked, drew in a deep breath, and slowly exited the vehicle. Was it wrong to pray that Dwight and Hope wouldn't be here today? She rolled her eyes at herself. As if she'd ever see them in this church again.

"Hi Serena!" Jenny Wells, her former high school English teacher, now retired, called from across the parking lot. "How are you?"

Serena faked a smile she hoped counted as answering the question. "The more important question is how are you?"

"Still going strong," her husband Mitch said proudly.

"I'm glad." Mitch and Jenny had experienced a rough few years, between the death of their eldest son and Jenny's second bout of breast cancer. "I've seen you a time or two at Pilates at the resort."

"I love it," Jenny said with a grin. "Hey, are you on Minimites today?"

When was she not? Serena nodded, snatching at the excuse provided. "I'd better go set things up." She waved a hand in farewell and escaped to the room in the church basement, thankful for the chance to get away, to sort out the materials today's activity required. Simple tasks. Basic things. Things she could control. Unlike—

No. Don't think about him. Or her. Or—

"Please God, let the kids behave today," she prayed aloud, as much as to give her brain the memo to think differently as anything else. It triggered a few other prayers for the children to hear Godly truth in today's lesson, for blessings on their lives and on their families.

Fifteen minutes later she was being wrapped in a hug by little Jemima Taylor. "Miss Serena! Guess what?"

"What?"

"We got a kitten!"

"Really? How wonderful. Tell me all about it."

As Jemima shared excitedly about her family's new kitten, Serena's thoughts wandered. Maybe that's what she should aim for. Kittens. Be a cat lady. Cats could be trusted to be loyal, right? Or was that dogs?

Somehow she managed to make it through the lesson, thankful that the story was one she'd given before. Somehow she managed to keep it together okay, although Jemima noted something was wrong with their usually bubbly teacher and gave her a hug, which only sparked more tears Serena desperately tried to hide.

Rachel, Jemima's mother and one of Serena's good friends, drew her aside as their time ended. "How did the wedding go yesterday? Damian was so excited to hear about all the hockey players, he'll probably be wanting to chew your ear off today as soon as you get to the main service."

Great. Yet another reason to delay getting to the main service, and then to exit as soon as she could. She faked a grin, released a shaky breath. "It was good." Her smile relaxed into genuine. "It was perfect, actually. Sarah was beautiful—"

"I bet she was."

"And Dan was—"

"Hubba hubba, am I right?"

Dismay filled her. Was nobody loyal anymore? "You're married, aren't you?"

"Doesn't mean I don't have eyes."

Rachel winked one of those eyes, but Serena's consternation only grew. What, even her friends couldn't be trusted to stay true? She turned to clear up the mess of papers, her lips pressed together. What did that say about Serena, that she couldn't pick loyal friends?

"Dan is so hot. Sarah is a lucky girl."

Dismay at her friend's lack of faithfulness to her own husband faded at Rachel's last comment. Sarah was a lucky—a blessed—girl who'd nearly lost her life in a car accident several years ago, or so she'd heard Angela once say. Sarah had never been too forthcoming about that, and Serena had never pushed to find out more.

"They were so blessed by the weather, weren't they?" Rachel continued. "I thought for sure Saturday was going to be as wet as Friday, but it cleared up and was just lovely. The perfect Muskoka day."

"Sure was."

"Hey, are we on for another soiree soon?"

"One day," she promised, collecting the kiddy scissors and sticky tape and placing them in their respective plastic baskets. She couldn't even think about hosting another dinner party any time soon. Not when she wasn't sure which friends she could trust. And especially not when she couldn't even start processing how she was supposed to explain the humiliation of what had happened last night. She drew in another shaky breath and prayed Rachel would go away.

Rachel, however, did not seem to be listening to God. "Rena, are you okay?"

"Sure." Her neck prickled, like it did whenever she lied. She kept her eyes on the table.

"Hmm." Rachel stood in the door for a moment longer. "Well, I guess I'll see you upstairs."

"Mm hm."

Serena nodded, keeping her attention on her task until footsteps indicated Rachel had moved away. She let out a breath, wondering if anyone would notice if she left. Then she could hop back into bed, find those chocolates, and eat herself into a food coma that just might dull enough of the pain to help her survive another day.

A creak in the hallway outside suggested someone else wished to speak to her. *Please, Lord, help me keep it together.*

"Oh, Serena!" Angela McPherson's voice drew Serena's head up. "How are you holding up after yesterday?"

Another fake smile. "Fine."

"What a beautiful day it was."

Another nod.

"I know Sarah and Dan were so moved by all the special touches. You went to a lot of trouble."

"That's what we do."

"You're a real blessing, you know that?"

A savage pain creased her chest. No, she wasn't. She was a fool. A fat, boring, gullible fool. She nodded, anyway.

Angela's head tilted slightly. "Are you coming upstairs? The service is about to begin."

"Uh, sure."

Angela flashed a smile. "I told John not to preach too long, because I want to catch up with my family some more before they head back to Australia. See you up there soon."

She didn't wait for an answer, obviously assuming Serena would do as Serena had always done and do the right thing. *Boring,* an evil thought whispered. *So dull and predictable.*

No, she shook her head at herself. "I'm not boring," she whispered, working to control the slip-slide of emotions. If anything she sensed the need to be upstairs, that she desperately *needed* to hear whatever John was preaching about in his sermon today.

Once she judged herself emotionally steady enough, she trailed up the stairs and slipped into the back row among some tourists. At least she wouldn't be expected to converse much beyond trivialities back here.

She stood through the worship as if in a trance, her body automatically going through the motions while her brain felt like it was struggling through quicksand, unable to hold any coherent thought for more than a few seconds, before another painful memory of the night before slipped in to undermine her. The world had gone tipsy-turvy, tilting crazily, and nothing seemed normal anymore.

How could she have been standing here singing with Dwight just last week, and now discovered the depths of his deception?

How could she pretend God's grace was enough? She mouthed the words, but it too was a sham. Was everything about her life fake? Which of her friends were trustworthy? What even was real anymore?

After the time of worship, John gave the announcements. Images on the big-screen from yesterday's wedding drew a collective sigh from the congregation. Something was said about John and Angela taking some time off, which meant there'd be a new assistant minister arriving with his family soon who would be officially inducted in a couple of weeks.

Serena half listened as she thought about the next few days and who she would need to tell about the break-up. Her friends, church family, her parents, her sister in Vancouver. Everyone had expected Dwight and her to be together forever, they'd seemed like such a great match. *Seemed* like. Emotion clogged her chest, her throat, her nose. This was going to be such a shock to everyone.

John's sermon was on faithfulness, the message a stark reminder about the lack of faithfulness in this world. Tears burned, then started to trickle out of her eyes. She swiped them away, hoping her glasses hid some of her anguish, then held herself still, barely breathing, as if the effort of taking a deep breath would shatter the illusion of calm that she was desperate to portray. Eventually the sermon finished and the concluding song meant they were released.

Serena nodded stiffly to the people around her, her fake smile still in place, as she stood to leave. She was almost at the door when she felt a light touch on her shoulder.

"Serena, dear, something is definitely not right." It was Angela again.

At the look of caring in her eyes, Serena's filled with fresh tears, and her bottom lip began to quiver. She bit it to stop the emotion spilling over for all to see.

"Come with me."

Serena followed her mutely, head bowed, avoiding eye contact with the congregation she'd known for years, people who loved her and cared for her as she did for them. The minister's wife led her to her husband's office, thankfully vacant, gently guiding her to the lounge, before sitting down next to her.

Serena leaned forward, her face in her hands as if to stuff the tears back in, but they wouldn't be stopped. The silent trickle of tears grew into quiet sobs. How could he? How could she? She felt prickly with shame and humiliation. Angela rubbed her back, probably praying quietly like she normally did when confronted with these types of situations. Serena had seen her in action before.

Serena sucked in a shaky breath. "I'm so sorry. You have a family gathering to get to."

"As far as I'm concerned, you're family too. They can wait, but you can't."

The kindness in her words drew fresh emotion, and Serena placed a hand over her mouth. Oh, if only she could hide away. If only she could eat herself into a chocolate-coated oblivion.

"Is it Dwight?"

Serena nodded. Somehow she managed to calm herself enough to admit the truth. "I came home early last night from the wedding and"—it still seemed unbelievable—"and found Dwight kissing Hope in Hope's bedroom."

"Oh, my dear Serena." Angela's hug tightened.

That simple act of love and support gave courage to continue the story. "They…they've been hiding this for months. M-maybe even years." She struggled to recall all the horrible details. "I kicked Hope out. Threw her belongings on the front lawn." The memory drew a small curl of satisfaction at the bottom of her stomach.

"Good girl."

Serena lifted her gaze to encounter Angela's snapping blue

eyes. She was used to the ministers preaching love and forgiveness, not looking like this.

"You've done exactly right. People need to be held accountable for their actions. And if you've given your hospitality, your time and money to help someone who calls herself your friend, then you have every right to show them the door if they betray you. Christians aren't doormats."

That's right. *I'm* not *a doormat*, she told herself fiercely. But the moment of courage was quickly swamped by raw pain. "I just don't understand. Why did they do this to me?" Serena's voice quaked almost an octave higher than her usual speaking voice. The tears began to flow in earnest as she sobbed out her hurt. Angela handed her some tissues, and kept rubbing her back, waiting as the tears began to subside.

The door opened. Serena flinched, ducking her head as John drew inside. She looked down at the floor, trying to surreptitiously wipe away the remnants of her grief and get her ragged breathing back under control.

"Oh, there you are, my dear. Everyone is wondering where my better half has disappeared to. I think some of them want you to spill the beans from yesterday."

"You'll need to tell them I'm busy and can't be disturbed. Serena has had some tough news which we don't want broadcast to the world." Angela glanced at her. "We would like two cups of tea, though. Strong, with milk and a sugar for Serena. Thanks, hon."

With a sympathetic smile at Serena, John left, closing the door quietly behind him. His wife shifted herself on the lounge, gently clasping Serena's hands in hers.

"Serena, you may never really know why this has happened—"

"Hope said it was because I was boring and fat." A jagged spear of pain ran through her.

Angela shook her head. "People say things in the heat of the moment that aren't always true."

Serena stared blankly at the well-worn carpet. *But it is true. I am overweight, I don't have ambition, I must be boring. But at least I'm not a man-stealer.* She frowned. Never. *Ever.*

"Knock, knock." John reappeared with the promised cups of tea.

"Thank you, darling."

Serena stared into the steam before taking a careful sip as he exited again.

Angela put her cup down. "But you do need to know that we love you and will always support and care for you. Anytime you need to talk, please do so. Don't isolate yourself with your pain. It never leads to good things."

Serena nodded half-heartedly. She hated being this vulnerable and exposed, but she knew she couldn't afford to block everyone out. She'd seen others do that and noticed how withdrawing had only made things spiral further out of control.

"Who else have you told?"

"No one." It was still too raw, too new, too humiliating.

"I think you should tell your folks. Even though they may be away they'd want to know if their youngest daughter was hurting like this."

Serena nodded. Her parents were currently halfway through a four-year stint as missionaries in India teaching English. When they'd left, Serena had thrown herself into her work and her relationships with Dwight and her other church friends, hosting regular gatherings like her weekend soirees. She liked her life. She liked her small town. Sure, it wasn't hugely exciting, but life had seemed pretty good, until Hope's poisonous words had cast doubt. Recent events had certainly made her life more dramatic at least. Her lips twisted and she struggled to hear the minister's wife conclude.

"Serena, sweetheart, know that we will always be here for you, that we're praying for you."

"Thanks," she whispered.

"And please don't let this cloud your view of men. God obviously has someone better lined up for you. Remember, He is always working things out for good."

Serena nodded. God might be, but it sure didn't feel like it right now.

SLEEP WAS A FUNNY THING. Too little and Serena felt edgy. Too much and she felt like a slug. But on those rare golden days when she managed to get it just right, she felt a million dollars. Or maybe that was the effect of the prayers of Angela and John. Whatever. Her return from church on Sunday had seen her crawl into bed, exhaustion chasing her to deep, dreamless sleep. She'd woken the next morning feeling ready to face the world, only to discover half a dozen missed phone calls and concerned messages from her friends.

But before she could figure out how to respond to Anna, Jackie, and Rachel, she had a very important call to make. One she didn't really know how to explain, but hey, God might help her frame her humiliation in a way that didn't sound quite so humiliating.

She clicked on the Zoom link emailed to her and fussed a little with her makeup and hair. There was no need to worry them more than absolutely nec—

"There you are!" Her mom's voice held such sunshine Serena's defenses dropped. "We missed chatting with you earlier."

As they usually did for their Sunday call. Time zone differences meant it was Monday night in India now. Still, this was the perfect segue to explain. "Sorry about that. I fell asleep."

"That's right. You had that amazing wedding, didn't you? How did that go, honey?"

"Great. Really good. It was actually the most perfect wedding I've ever been to." And she'd been there foolishly wishing, hoping, that one day she too would have Dwight look at her the way Dan adored Sarah. She bit her lip to stop the tremble.

"Oh, you'll have a wonderful wedding, too," her mother assured.

Serena shook her head, her mouth filled with words too hard to say.

"Oh, don't give up, hon. He'll propose one day. Dwight is a good man."

"No, Mom. He's not." She swiped at a tear that had dared escape. Great. Now she'd be in for twenty questions.

"Honey? What is it? What's happened?"

Somehow Serena found enough grit to admit what had happened. Her mother's gasp said she was as shocked as Serena had been, which was something at least. Maybe she wasn't so completely stupid and naïve if he'd been able to fool her parents too. As for Hope…

"I can't believe it! To think we used to babysit her! Oh my goodness, Serena. I'm so sorry."

She smeared her damp cheeks. "That's why I didn't answer yesterday. I told Angela at church, but then had to race away." She managed a wobbly smile. "I might've scared a few people there with all my tears."

"Honey, it's perfectly okay to be upset. In fact, I'd be upset if you weren't upset! This has to be devastating for you."

She nodded, glancing down where her phone blinked a new message. Anna. Again.

Her mother continued with her sympathy and righteous outrage, until Serena felt herself teetering on the edge of hopelessness again. Why was it that some conversations left her feeling empowered, like yesterday's with Angela, and others left her wanting to crawl back under the covers? Maybe it was the child in her wanting to return to the security blanket of her pre-teen years.

"…and I'm so sorry your father isn't here to hear this too. I'll get him to call as soon as he gets back from the meeting, okay?"

"No, Mom. It's really okay."

"I don't know that it is." Her mother's brow pleated. "Would you like us to come see you?"

"No! No, you have your work to do, and I'm a big girl. I'll cope."

"Well, maybe you'll consider coming to see us again. You know we'd love to have you."

"Thanks." But visiting her parents in India was fraught with other dangers. She'd been smothered by their good intentions before. "I have some other weddings I'm committed to this summer, so I'll have to see how I go. Maybe later in the year," she hedged.

"Well, you know we can't wait to see you again. This," her mother gestured between the screen and herself, "is a hundred times better than a phone call, but still not quite the same as being in the same place."

She nodded. Sometimes it seemed her mother was as skilled as Hope in the art of manipulation. She gritted out a smile she hoped looked partway convincing, then bit back a sigh of relief as her phone flashed with an incoming call.

"I better take this." She held up her phone.

"We'll be praying for you, honey. Love you."

"Love you, too."

She offered a smile and ended the Zoom connection then stabbed the phone to accept the call. "Anna. Hi."

"You're alive!" her best friend since high school exclaimed. "I swear, I was about to do a drive by and make sure you weren't lying on the floor, frothing at the mouth or something. Are you okay? You normally don't go an hour without replying to a message."

Was that because Serena had no life, and what little she had was often handled virtually? She shook away the disconcerting thought. "I'm okay." She would be. One day. Maybe.

"Are you sure? You raced out of church yesterday before I had a chance to say hello, and then Rachel said you didn't seem yourself, and I…" Her words trailed away, then she gasped.

"What?"

"Oh no. Serena, are you at home?"

"Yeah."

"Is Hope there?"

"Nope." Her lips twisted. "No Hope here."

"Oh my goodness. Okay, I'm going to have to let my boss know I'll be late for work. This is an emergency. Don't go anywhere."

"What is it?"

"Don't panic. Everything will be fine. See you soon." A second later she muttered, "I'll kill him."

A skin tingle suggested someone Anna might like to kill. Her cousin. AKA Dwight.

But how could *Anna* know? Surely he hadn't done the unthinkable and had Hope stay at his place last night. Would he? A quick scroll through social media saw no updates in his relationship status. She couldn't check Hope's after blocking her as a friend last night, but she wouldn't put it past her…

Ten minutes later the front door was being pounded. Serena opened the door to meet Anna, Rachel and Jackie, who all surrounded her in hugs, their murmurs of sympathy welling fresh tears.

"Why didn't you say anything?" Anna asked a short time later, as they drank to-go cups of coffee from The Coffee Blend. A selection of pastries lined the smoked glass coffee table, their promise of sugar-laden comfort teasing her to escape into her beloved fat-and-sugar balanced carbohydrates.

"It was all too new, too shocking."

"I can't believe Hope has put it on Facebook, trying to make out she's the victim." Rachel shook her head. "What a—"

"Easy," Jackie said. "Don't climb into the cesspool with Hope. She's not worth it."

"Tell you who's not worth it is my cousin," Anna raged. "I'm going over there tonight to give him a piece of my mind. Aunty Dawn and Uncle Eric will be so disappointed. I know they've never liked Hope."

"I don't want to think about her. Or him," Serena said.

"Have you told your folks?" Jackie gently stroked Serena's cold hand, much like Serena imagined she did at the retirement home she worked at. "What did they say?"

Serena explained about the earlier Zoom call. "Mom wants me to visit."

"Maybe you should."

"I can't. Not right now. I've got several big weddings still to come this season."

"Maybe after that, then," Jackie said.

"You want to get rid of me or something?"

Jackie shook her head. "Not at all. You know we want what's best for you. But it might be good to do something that helps clear your head."

But traveling to India and filling it with unfamiliar sights and sounds and smells wouldn't heal a broken heart. Distract it, maybe. For a time. Until reality had to be faced again.

"She's right, we want what's best for you," Rachel chimed in, sighing as she pushed to her feet. "Hey, I better go back home and get the rug rats to preschool—Damian has a late start today —but Rena, if there's anything I can do, you know you only need to call."

"Thanks."

With a squeeze goodbye she left, her departure soon followed by Anna, who regretted having to leave, but added, "My boss will kill me if I'm any later again this month. But hey, don't you worry, I'll make sure that cousin of mine gets what is coming to him."

"That's the Christian spirit," Jackie murmured, which drew their shared laughter.

"Seriously? You want Serena to just forgive and forget?" demanded Anna.

"You know forgiveness is not so much about releasing the offender as it is about setting free the person who has been wronged."

"Thank you, Pastor Jackie," Anna said, with a roll of her eyes at Serena.

Jackie meant well. It's just Serena didn't need her meaning well *quite* so soon.

But later, as she settled onto the sofa with comfort foods aplenty—God bless her friends—to binge-watch old episodes of 9-1-1, Jackie's words kept stealing through her day. God didn't really want her to forgive Dwight and Hope, did He? Really? Surely He could wait a few days and understand a girl needed time to process, needed time to consider what her life would look like without two of the pillars she'd long imagined would always be there. The ridiculous TV storylines couldn't hold her attention. *Forgive. Forgive. Forgive.*

She shook her head, and shoved in another double row of chocolate, savoring the sweet taste as it melted on her tongue. No. Forgiveness was for the weak. For those who basically begged to be trodden on. And she was done with being nice. Done with being a doormat. Done with being naïve. And she'd never trust a man or let him break her heart again.

CHAPTER 3

"Thanks for all you've done, Joel. We're gonna miss you, bud."

Joel Wakefield gave the teenager a hug. "I'll miss you, too."

This had been such a great church family to be part of over the last four years as he'd completed further study, but it was time to move on. Toni had gone to bed already, and the last of the guests were collecting their belongings and now-empty platters and giving farewell hugs.

"Joel, we can never thank you enough for what you did for our Christopher. He was such a mess before you came along."

"You and I both know that was all God."

"Who used you," Chris's mom insisted. "Take care of yourself and keep in touch."

"Yes, ma'am."

She gently swatted his arm at the "ma'am" then released him to talk to some friends nearer his age.

"We'll be praying for you, that the new church works out well, that you make some friends soon, although they'll never be as good as us."

Joel laughed at that comment, but he'd been deeply touched

by the support he'd received from the congregation ever since the announcement about his new posting as an assistant minister had been made. In his years as a youth minister here, he'd begun a program with some of the youth's boys, teaming them with older male mentors who had encouraged the young men to steer clear of trouble whilst living for God. This had proved really successful, and he had so many of them wanting to keep in touch with him now.

How ironic though, that in striving to keep them out of trouble, he'd been oblivious to what was happening at home. At least Toni had agreed to keep the baby and come with him to the new church, several hundred kilometers north in a beautiful part of the world called Muskoka. It was a fresh start, and Joel prayed his sister would make the most of it. He'd had to be honest with the new church board about his sister's situation, and he'd been amazed that they actually practiced what they preached, encouraging him, and promising not to divulge the details about her story, but letting Toni share as necessary. They agreed that this was an opportunity for a fresh start for her, and people didn't need to be prejudiced before getting to know them.

He followed the last of the guests to the door, thankful for those who had assisted in this farewell party. As he leaned against the doorway and waved goodbye, his thoughts turned to the move tomorrow, and all that still remained to be packed. He had a few weeks before he needed to begin his position, but he was hoping to get things done quickly, as the house he was to move into was vacant as of this weekend. He hadn't told anyone about his early arrival, wanting a few days to settle in, do some stuff around the house and just get a feel for the town before putting his sister in the spotlight of the usual questions as people got to know them.

Yawning at the late hour, he moved to the bookshelves that groaned with the titles Toni collected. He grabbed a cardboard box and started shoveling books in: romance, crime, suspense, something about pirates? He squinted at the author's name: Staci Everton. Then tossed it in to join the rest. Ever since their parents had died three years ago in a car accident, Toni had become even more of a bookworm, closeting herself from reality for hours on end. He'd thought it had been a good sign to see her finally getting out and about, gaining some new friends. Until he'd realized just what these new friends were into. His sister might have more artistic skill in her little fingernail than he had, period, but her new artsy associates seemed to focus their energies on other aspects of creativity, proving to be equally creative with their understanding of the law as they were about respect for marriage vows. Yes, Toni had made her choices, but nobody had dreamed just what a price she would ultimately pay.

Joel finished the bookcase, another yawn escaping as he glanced at his watch again. It was time to call it a night. He glanced around, the living space cluttered with furniture and labeled boxes. There wasn't much more he could do, anyway. God bless the ladies from church who'd volunteered to clean the place tomorrow. A couple of friends had promised to help finish the packing and load the hired van early in the morning, and it was probably best he preserve some energy for what would likely prove a huge day. So Joel locked up, switched off lights, headed to the bathroom then to bed.

THE NEXT DAY DAWNED BRIGHT, with that tell-tale early morning warm mugginess that always led to a stinking hot day. Now, if they could get things underway before the heat caused too many more problems...

Matt and Wade were true to their word, bringing fresh muscle and decisiveness to a situation that sometimes this past week had felt impossible to finish. As he carried and loaded and completed a myriad of other tasks, Joel prayed this position in Muskoka would really work out. He didn't want to have to face moving again for a really long time.

"How're you feeling?"

Matt's kind question to Toni drew the usual non-reaction as she lethargically pushed herself up out of the dining chair. With less than two months to go until her due date she was looking pretty rotund these days, with the energy levels to prove how uncomfortable she was feeling. She headed to her bedroom without a word or glance at Matt. Joel still wasn't sure if it was shame or fear that made her withdraw whenever his friends were around.

Joel's lips flattened. "Maybe one day."

Matt shrugged in resignation. "Maybe."

Joel only hoped that was true.

By early afternoon the cleaning had commenced, the truck was loaded, and Toni's car was filled with haphazardly packed clothes and kitchen items.

With last hugs for the faithful church ladies, Joel joined Toni in her car and reversed, offering a final wave. Concern for his sister's tiredness meant he'd arranged to drive Toni in her car, Matt was driving Joel's F-150, and Wade would drive the hired truck. The plan was to drive to Muskoka, unload, then the guys would travel back to Toronto tonight in order to return the hired truck in time to avoid the late return penalty. Toni had protested the driving arrangements at first, not wanting to relinquish her independence, but Joel could see as the day's heat took its toll just how fatigued she was. Even though she hadn't been able to do very much, the emotional strain the move was placing on her had affected her.

He glanced across at her now as she rested against a pillow, listening to her music with her eyes closed. *Thank You, God, that she decided to come with me, and didn't insist on driving herself.* Despite his headache, he gave a small smile.

Joel rubbed his thumping forehead, then fished around the central console for ibuprofen that he swallowed with a gulp of now-tepid water from his water bottle. *God, let this move be a fresh start, especially for Toni.* But mingled with the prayers was a churning sense of anticipation. God had good things in store, for both of them. He just knew it.

Several hours later they finally pulled up outside the Muskoka Shores realtor office. Threatening summer clouds banked up overhead, doing their best to smother the lake in darkness. It was nothing like when he'd visited a couple of months ago for his interview, when spring was showing its flowery gorgeousness throughout the town's parks and window boxes. Toni had only heard his descriptions of the pretty town and had been expecting a beautiful summer playground of lakes and trees, and this ominous start to their new life hardly filled them with hope.

"And I just need you to put your autograph here and here." Meghan Windsor, the cheery realtor, pointed to where Joel was to sign.

He obeyed, as the realtor began talking about all the benefits of their community. "...so many boutique stores, community groups and festivals."

"Festivals?"

"Yes. You've just missed our Canada Day festivities—we like to think we host the best celebrations in Muskoka—but the Cranberry Festival is in a few months. It's a great way to get to know people."

"And local churches?" Joel asked, swallowing a smile. Okay, so the evangelist might've left the city, but he'd never lose the evangelistic streak.

"Ah, we have a few."

"I've heard the community church is pretty good."

"Really?" Meghan's expression cleared. "Oh, right. That's the one Dan Walton goes to when he's here for the summer, right?"

"Dan...?" Joel feigned ignorance of the man he'd met several times.

Meghan mock-gasped. "You know, plays hockey for Toronto. Spends each summer in a big cottage nearby. Just married the niece of the local church minister last weekend. Oh!" Her eyes widened. "The community church."

"Maybe you should check it out." Especially seeing as she seemed a fan of Dan. Hey, whatever got them through the door.

Meghan nodded. "Maybe I will."

He grinned, shook her hand, and pocketed the keys, then made his way back out to Toni. She stared wide-eyed at the town's cute main street, complete with ice-cream soda shop, chocolate store, and more.

"It's not exactly the big smoke, is it?" he said, keying the ignition.

"Sure isn't." Loneliness washed across her face.

"Hey, it's gonna be okay. You're gonna be okay. You'll make friends."

"Yeah." Her rolled-eyes look screamed of skepticism.

Lord, help Toni make friends.

Prayers filled his heart as Joel drove to the house. This was a new start, for both of them. No more would they be defined by the past: their parents' deaths, his youth ministry work, Toni's unplanned pregnancy. Instead, they'd forge a new life, with new opportunities, new friendships. God was about doing new things, after all.

He glanced at the map then scanned the road signs. "We're on Poplar Drive."

After years of living in the city, Joel's preference had been for a house with water views, and when this older style, renovator's delight of a home on the water had come up, he'd snapped it up, thankful he'd never needed to touch his share of the proceeds from the sale of their parents' home, otherwise he'd never have been able to afford it. Toni's share of the estate was waiting in trust until she either turned twenty-five or married. Likely it was that promise of a certain level of wealth that had attracted Toni's fly-by-night friends, friends who had swiftly left her when push came to shove.

"Here we go. Poplar Drive. We're number...twelve." Joel stopped the car and they looked at their new abode. From the outside it was obvious that a lot of work would need to be done, given the peeling paint and overgrown shrubs and lawn. Inside wasn't much better, but years of supplementing his basic youth minister's wage by working odd jobs for building contractors meant he knew he could get the place up to scratch in the next few weeks. Fixing things was the call on his life, after all.

"So, are you ready for this?"

"Do I have a choice?" Toni muttered.

"Nope."

She rolled her eyes at him as he helped her from the car. Together they walked up the short concrete path then up the front steps to the little porch. With a grin, Joel turned to his sister, holding out the key. "Want to do the honors?"

"It's your house. You do it."

As the first spits of rain fell from the sky, he unlocked the front door, turning on the lights, thankful the electricity was connected as Meghan had said. They stood in the entryway looking down the short hall to the big windows out the back that showcased the lake in all its magic. Matt and Wade would be coming soon, but for the moment they just savored the quiet. The unfavorable weather had cleared the lake of pleasure craft, and for the moment peace reigned. Even the recalcitrant weather couldn't diminish the natural beauty displayed before them.

Toni walked through to the dining area, unlocking the glass doors that led to an outside room, screened on three sides. She took a deep breath. "This is beautiful." For the first time in a long time Joel saw her shoulders drop as she started to relax.

He walked over and wrapped an arm around her shoulders. "This will be great. You'll have more inspiration for your art, you'll be able to relax."

"Yeah, because there's nothing to do here."

Exactly. No drugs. No nightclubs. No partying until all hours of the night. Not that anywhere was perfect, but removing those temptations had to be better, right? "It won't take too long until you settle in."

"Right."

"Come on, kiddo." He tugged gently on one of her dark pigtails.

"Kiddo? I'm barely six years younger than you."

Sometimes it seemed a lifetime.

"Maybe you just say things like that when you're so old."

"Twenty-nine isn't old," he protested.

"Sure it isn't, Grandpa."

He chuckled, glad to glimpse a return of the sass she used to display. "You're mean."

"You know it."

He wrapped her in a hug and pressed a loud kiss on her forehead. "You're gonna love it, I just know it. I think God has brought us here for a few reasons, and fresh hope is only a part of it."

Toni threw him a sudden shrewd look. "What are you hoping for?"

Joel just smiled and shook his head. He couldn't explain the funny feeling he had. It just felt like God had something good coming his way.

They completed a tour of the rest of the house, opening windows to let in fresh air, checking the water ran clear, and discussing details of furniture placement as Toni drank in all the details. The four bedrooms would need new paint eventually, but with sturdy built-ins and newish carpet and blinds, they appeared fairly presentable. The bathroom and kitchen had tiles and fittings popular in the 1970s but seemed service-able enough.

"The building report said everything works," he assured. "It just looks old."

"You could call it vintage." Toni's nose wrinkled as she touched the glazed orange tiles.

"A time capsule from the seventies."

Her mouth tweaked slightly. "I guess it's not as bad as you said it would be."

Joel exhaled. As much as he loved his sister, he still couldn't figure her out at times. He'd been concerned that she would just dismiss the place out of hand, so it was good to see she could appreciate the good points of the house. *Thanks, God.*

The patter on their roof swiftly escalated into a heavy dump of rain. He hurried to close windows they'd just opened, as Toni shivered at the cooling temperature.

"I'm hungry."

Joel studied his sister; with her pigtails and fresh features, she looked absurdly young. "Me too."

He found a pizza delivery service in the welcome pack the realtor had given him, so after ordering several pizzas and drinks, he scooted through the rain to retrieve a couple of suit-cases so they could find clothes to be warm. He got some light jackets, and when Toni requested that he bring in the box with the kettle, Joel happily obliged. Her pregnancy had seen her take a liking to cups of herbal tea, and after the long day, making a cup of tea would be a nice way to be refreshed for a few moments.

Just as he finished paying off the pizza delivery man, his truck rumbled into view, with the moving van following behind. With a quick wave at Matt and Wade, Joel gestured them in.

"Hey, good to see you. Directions okay?"

"Yeah. We only got lost once, and that was only when we got to town."

Wade laughed good-naturedly. "It was getting dark. I couldn't see the sign."

"You got here in the end. Let's have some food while it's hot, then we'll get onto the unloading."

The pizza and garlic bread was surprisingly good for a small town, the talk easy, and even Toni started to relax. Ever since her older boyfriend had dumped her when he discovered she was keeping the baby, she'd been suspicious of men. It was nice to see her more at ease with his friends now.

Twenty minutes later they'd finished the meal, and then headed outside to start unloading the furniture. The rain had stopped, which made things easier. He hoped to swiftly move the furniture in, set up the beds and larger pieces, move in the boxes until the truck was empty, then Matt and Wade could drive home tonight.

Appreciation for his friends surged again. Matt and Wade were gold, taking the day off from work, helping without complaint. He'd had plenty of offers to assist but keeping the move kind of quiet meant he could savor this time for himself, with only his most trusted friends in the know. He'd figured that'd work better for Toni too.

Finally the furniture was all in, even if it wasn't all properly situated yet. There'd be plenty of time for rearranging things.

"One last coffee for the road?" Joel asked.

"That'd be great, thanks." Matt's gaze drifted to Toni, hovering in the kitchen. She seemed to notice too, turning away to focus on the kettle.

Huh. Did his friend have an interest there? Toni might not be in the market for a new man right now, but she could definitely do worse than gain an investment banker suitor. Even if the two of them seemed the ultimate of opposites, to the point that Joel wasn't even sure if Toni believed in God anymore. But then, opposites attracted and all that…

The kettle sang, coffee was made and drunk quickly, Wade eager to get home before midnight. They made their farewells, and Joel couldn't help but see how Matt's, "Take care of yourself," to Toni was met with a shrug and averted eyes. Ouch.

"Thanks again. Anytime you want to come stay, you know we have room."

"Great, thanks," Wade said, climbing into the cab.

"Maybe once you're settled in," Matt said, gripping Joel's hand. Man hugs had never been Matt's thing.

Joel lifted a hand as the truck exited, turning back inside to find Toni was halfway through finishing putting the sheets on her bed. A quick scan saw his bed was already made. Bless her.

"So they're gone?"

"Coast is clear." He eyed her, tempted to ask about the weird vibes between Matt and herself. But nearly ten at night on moving day probably wasn't the best time to ask. He tucked in the final corner and smoothed out the duvet. "You want to see if the hot water's working?"

Toni's face wore fatigue. "I'm so tired, I just want to go to bed. I'll have a shower in the morning."

"You got everything you need?"

"I'll be fine, Joel. Have a good sleep." Her lips lifted at the corner.

Not exactly a smile, but he'd take what he could get. "Thanks for being okay about moving here. I know the past few weeks haven't been easy."

She shrugged. "Who says I'm okay?"

He blinked.

Her lips pushed out and up. Yep, definitely a half smile at least. "I'll be okay. One day." She added something else he couldn't quite hear.

"What was that?" he pressed.

Another shrug. A glance away. "I said those friends weren't very good to me. Hopefully I'll make some new ones here."

"I'm sure you will." That was his prayer. For both of them. He looked at her fondly for a moment. Sometimes when she was tired, he could see in the relaxed lines of her face the little girl she used to be. The happy girl she used to be was still in there somewhere. "Goodnight, kiddo."

She wrinkled her nose at him but didn't protest when he hugged her and pressed a kiss to the crown of her head. "G'night."

CHAPTER 4

Two days later, Serena was typing up reports in her office at Muskoka Shores Resort when her phone rang. Joanne. She took a moment to brace for whatever her boss was going to say, knowing it'd likely be some sorry explanation for why she'd been a no-show yet again today. Was this what being responsible and nice got you? Working overtime to make up for the messes in other people's lives?

"Serena, I'm sorry, but I have to take a personal day, and I can't be there to oversee the energy conference. I'll need you to step in for me again."

Again? The events team had already been down a member, and now with Joanne's absence they'd be even more stretched than normal.

Serena bit back a sigh. Is this what a doormat looked like, letting people take advantage of you all the time? But something wouldn't let her say no. Joanne's mom was pretty sick, after all. "Sure. What do you need me to do?"

Joanne filled her in, adding, "Thanks. I don't know what I'd do without you."

Joanne's voice wavered, much unlike her usual no-nonsense

self, which kneaded fresh regret and new resolve. Okay, so she didn't want to feel exploited, but neither could she let someone suffer when it was in her power to help. That's what Jesus would do. "Is it your mom?"

"She's struggling," Joanne admitted. "She wants me there, but I can't keep taking time off work. I know it's not fair on you all, for you especially."

Guilt for her previous thoughts pricked her heart. "Please tell her I'm praying for her. And for you."

"Thanks." Wait, was that a sniff? "That means a lot."

"Take care of yourself," Serena added softly, waiting for Joanne to hang up before she pressed end.

Well, that was unexpected. She exhaled, remorse for her impatience needling her to wonder whether she could steal time later this week to buy Joanne's mom an Agatha Christie book. Brandi's Books & Gifts always had a great selection. But there was no time to think on this now. Not when some of Canada's top energy executives were meeting in the Grand Ball-room in less than two hours.

The rest of the day flashed past: double checking the technology booked for use, coordinating with the kitchen staff about some unexpected gluten-free guests, checking the room was presented as promised, and hurrying to the front desk in time to meet the conference arrivals. This, combined with the organizing that still needed to be arranged for a Saturday wedding, kept her at work until late, snatching what meals she could at the staff restaurant. Like this delicious chocolate pudding.

She propped her head on her hand and trailed a spoon through the dessert, blending the last of the sauce with the remaining traces of ice-cream. A big day deserved rewards like this. She pushed the empty bowl away, easing back in her chair as she undid the buttons on her jacket. Okay, maybe she'd enjoyed that a little too much.

She bit back a groan as she slowly rose from her seat, as her knees resumed their aching. Wasn't twenty-eight too young for knee problems? Or was it the fact she'd been comfort eating a lot lately, and had still not taken up Anna's birthday gift from last year of a gym membership? She'd been tempted to take offense at the time, but maybe it wouldn't hurt to visit. Just once.

"Ah, Serena, I see you're still here." Adrian Jennings, Muskoka Shores' General Manager paused, eyeing her in that way she was never sure boded well or not.

She straightened, quickly buttoning up her jacket, hoping she looked professional and that the garlic bread aroma wasn't too obvious on her breath. "Hello, sir."

"How is the conference going?"

She filled him in on what had been happening, which met his nod. "It's good to see our staff are committed to excellence."

"Of course, sir."

He eyed her. "But don't you have a family or someone to get home to?"

Her heart wavered. Not anymore. "I want to keep busy, sir."

"I appreciate that." He glanced at his phone. Sighed. "My wife is expecting me. I'm running late. See you tomorrow. And keep up the good work."

"Yes, sir. I will."

He said goodnight to several other staff members as he exited, drawing her to wonder how he managed to balance his work and personal life. But then he'd climbed to the top, being general manager of one of Muskoka's top resorts by his mid-thirties. Maybe this was a season for her to focus on work, instead of her pathetic dreams for a personal life she clearly wasn't meant to have. And if she did, maybe, just maybe, she could prove to them all here that she was deserving of a pay raise, and one day get bumped up the ladder. Then Hope's words about Serena having no direction would be proved wrong, and everyone would know she had something to offer after all. Her fingers clenched. She'd show them. She'd do all she could to prove Hope wrong.

∾

COFFEE DRIFTED on the early morning air, the scent of The Coffee Blend a siren call as potent as any mermaid song. Joel slowed his pace, peering in at the golden light suffusing the café filled with rustic décor. Definitely a place to visit once they were more settled in. The past two days of sifting through boxes had finally convinced him to stretch those muscles by finally returning to his regular morning routine. And really, was there any better way to get to know a new town than by jogging?

He jogged past the small stretch of shops that constituted the town's central business district which said this town catered to tourists. He didn't figure too many of the locals would be repeat purchasers enough to sustain a vintage toy store. But hey, it helped add to the charm of the place, something aided by the trees and landscaped parks, and the gleam of the lake, and the rush of the waterfalls. He smiled to himself. He hoped Toni would see the small town appeal too.

He passed a doctor's clinic that was advertising for staff—he bet some summer tourists would see that position filled in no time—then veered across to Poplar Drive. The houses here fit more of the vibe suggested by cottage country, rather than the huge estates consisting of triple storied houses and recreational facilities some of the rich and famous preferred. Not for him, though.

He drew closer to number twelve's front door then paused, stretching his arms now to avoid his sister's certain complaint about his sweaty, stinky smell. He eyed the garden. Was it too soon to think about revamping? Maybe add some flowers to brighten the place up? Maybe he should see what Toni thought.

He pushed open the front door with a, "Hey honey, I'm home," and bit back a laugh at the groan from behind his sister's closed door.

He tapped on her door. "Hey sleepyhead, you getting up anytime soon?"

The door sprung open, revealing his sister dressed and looking more alive than he'd seen her in months. "Who's the sleepyhead? I'll let you know I've already had my morning walk, breakfast and a shower. What's your excuse?"

"Couldn't sleep again?"

"Not much," she admitted. "So I've put my morning to good use. My walk took me downtown and I found a cool looking coffee shop and a great bookstore."

"The Coffee Blend?"

Toni nodded. "And Brandi's Books & Gifts."

"We'll have to visit. Maybe try out the coffee."

"As long as they have hot chocolate, I'll be happy."

"That's all it takes for you to be happy? Wow. I never knew."

She rolled her eyes at him and moved to close the door, but he shoved his foot in the way. "Hey, we should probably get you seen by a doctor soon."

She sighed. "I really didn't want to have to think about it yet."

"I know, but once it's done, you can focus on other things."

"Like what?" she said, with a return to the petulance of previous days.

"Like maybe painting some of the amazingness that surrounds us. Honestly, you could sit on the back porch and just paint the lake. That'd never get old."

"Using what? The doctor told me to avoid using oils and acrylics, and I hate charcoal."

"I've heard this person I know and love talk about water-colors before. Maybe you could give that a go."

She made another face but judging from the shrug wasn't

dismissing the idea completely. "What about you? Have you set up the office yet?"

"Just about. I've got a ton of emails waiting to be downloaded as soon as we get the internet sorted."

Her groan said something of the frustration she'd found since learning their home internet would take a few more days to get connected. Honestly, she was almost as bad as some of the teenagers he'd had to deal with. But it would be good to get it fixed and feel connected with the wider world again.

The day passed with the last of the kitchen stuff sorted, and Joel's promise to take her to the local hardware store that afternoon to pick paint colors for their bedrooms and the room they'd use as a nursery. He'd spend the next two days prepping and painting the rooms, and if he had time, give the office that would double as a guest room a lick of paint too.

Lunch saw them eating on the back porch, where the lake sparkled under the mid-July sun. After Monday night's gloomy welcome, it was like the town was trying to compensate, showing off its best features. The warm weather meant there were plenty of people out on the lake, using their boats for fishing, water skiing or just lazing about. And here, with their yard giving onto the lake, there was even the opportunity for Toni to have a swim if she wanted, without feeling as self-conscious as she might if they visited the public beach.

"This is such a lovely place."

"Glad we came then?"

"Yes."

Joel studied her thoughtfully. So far neither of them had made much progress in the way of making friends. They'd met some of the neighbors, elderly people who'd been kind enough to drop off homemade bread, or homegrown tomatoes, but people their own age didn't seem to live around here. But hey, if they were in this for the long haul, they would need to take their time in this friend-making business. They both knew from experience that the quicker they came, the harder they fell.

JOEL SPENT the next few days painting, which saw him depositing his sister away from harmful paint fumes in the small bookstore next to The Coffee Blend. "I know, I feel bad that I have to leave you here, doing your favorite things, but I hope you'll manage."

"I'll do my best," she said meekly.

He'd worked as fast as he could, the warmer weather helped, and drove back to collect her. She was sitting on a park bench out the front, under a tree, scrolling on her phone. "Hey you."

She jerked, as if he'd broken her concentration. "Wow. Way to go sneaking up on a pregnant lady."

His, "You're welcome," was met with a roll of eyes. "I thought you'd still be reading." He nodded to the small store whose sign proclaimed it as Brandi's Books & Gifts.

"I read. I found the latest Staci Everton book I wanted." She patted a brown paper bag beside her. "I bet you didn't know she grew up around here."

"You got that right."

Her smirk suggested her sarcasm detector was working well. Her head tilted. "Hey, did you know you have paint on your cheek?"

"Do I?" He scraped at his jaw.

"So you're finished already?"

"I've got skills, baby."

"You got something all right," she muttered, his defensiveness at her mockery yielding in delight at the return of her sass.

"Well, I guess that's what happens when you have a very loving and committed brother, you know, the type who paints your room for you, leaving you to be a lady of leisure to read and drink coffee."

"Hot chocolate," she corrected, amusement lurking around her mouth.

"My mistake. But really, in this weather?"

"I don't care what the temperature is like. I like hot chocolate. Anyway, I'm always hot."

Her sweaty strands of hair suggested that was so. "Did you have fun?"

Her features lit some more. "You know, I actually did."

Was that the first time she'd actually acknowledged having had fun this year? *Thank You, God*. He shoved his hands in his pockets, aiming for nonchalance. He didn't want to put her on her guard by getting more excited than she was. "Yeah?"

"Yeah." She glanced away. "I think I may have met someone."

His eyebrows shot up. Uh oh. "Toni," he began, "don't you think it's a bit early for a guy—?"

Wry laughter cut him off. "What do you take me for? No, I met her in the bookstore."

He'd learned a lot about not showing a judgy face in years of youth ministry, but from the flinch she showed maybe he hadn't been quick enough.

"Wow."

"What? Sorry. Put it down to the late nights or something."

Toni raised her eyebrows. "Are you ready to pay attention now?"

"Yes," he replied meekly. Was this the same Toni he'd dropped off several hours ago?

"I was in the bookstore when I met a woman who was looking in the same section as I was. Yes, it was the murder mystery section, if you must know."

He jerked a nod. They'd had 'discussions' about this before. Joel had always wondered how his gentle, sweet-natured sister he'd grown up with could tolerate the gruesome descriptions and storylines of crime novels. Ensuing arguments meant they'd since agreed to disagree.

"Anyway, it turns out she has the missing book from the last series, you know the one I've been searching for for ages? She lives here in town and said I could borrow it. Turns out we have a similar interest in other books too. So I'm going to meet her and get it."

"Aww, you have a friend."

She slapped his arm. "You're a doofus."

"That I am."

She laughed, as he'd intended, and slowly rose. "So are you taking me home or what?"

"You got it, babe. Come see – your palace awaits."

Toni's broad smile when she saw his hard work was the best thing since young Chris's salvation. "Wow." She pivoted on her heel. "It's like a different house."

"It doesn't quite have that depressed vibe anymore, does it?"

She sniffed. "It has a different smell, that's for sure."

"Yeah, I figured if we keep the windows open for the next few days it should clear out pretty soon."

"Thank you," she murmured, hugging him, the swell of her belly poking into his side.

"You're welcome." He pressed a kiss to her hair, gladness filling his heart. Maybe here in Muskoka they'd finally get things back on track.

SATURDAY THEY WERE REPLENISHING their grocery supply at the small supermarket when Toni disappeared up an aisle. Joel looked at his list again and was just reaching down for a couple of boxes of granola when his sister reappeared, this time with a woman behind her.

"Joel, this is my friend I told you about. You know, the one who's going to lend me the book? Joel, this is Serena Williamson."

"Do you play tennis?" he joked. The woman's brow wrinkled,

and he heard the echo of Toni's introduction. Oh. Right. "Williamson, not Williams. I get it."

"Oh my gosh," Toni muttered, turning to the woman. "Please excuse him. Sometimes he acts like he has a brain injury."

"Wow." Joel stuck out his hand. "Please excuse her. It's hard to believe we share the same last name sometimes. Joel Wakefield."

Her hand met his in a tentative clasp. "Hi."

He shot a querying look at his sister then back at the non-tennis player again. This Serena woman wasn't exactly what he'd expected. Toni's friends in Toronto had been an eclectic mix of attractive, sophisticated, arty types, who took great care with their appearance. While Toni herself wasn't dressed or made up like she used to, she still was a startling contrast to the woman wearing sweats who stood before him now. She was a few years older, with messy mousy graying blonde hair, glasses over sad green eyes, and she wasn't skinny by any means. In fact, plump was being charitable.

"So, uh, you and Toni really are friends?"

Serena blinked, but not before he caught a flash of hurt that twisted remorse deep in his gut. Her head lowered, her tentative smile dropping away, then she muttered something to Toni before turning on her heel and walking away, wiping her hand on her hip like she couldn't bear his touch.

"Joel!" His sister hit him on the arm, stealing focus from a sudden inclination to chase after Serena and apologize. "You were really rude," she hissed.

Guilt streaked through his insides. "I was just taken aback. I'd pictured another one of your city type friends, and she just seemed so...plain and ordinary."

She gasped. "Do you even hear yourself? What happened to being a pastor and Mr. Sensitive?" she whispered. "And do you really think I'm so shallow that I only make friends with people who wear nice clothes?"

Best he didn't answer the question.

"She's nice, the first person I've met here, and I hoped that maybe we could be friends."

"You still can," he protested lamely.

She shook her head. "She won't want anything to do with me now."

Remorse cut deeper at his failure. An agent of God's grace? Hardly. Way to go to make a good first impression as the new pastor in town. "She's probably way more forgiving than that."

"You *hope* she is, you mean," she said, eyes narrowing. "She probably thinks you don't like her."

"That's not true. I don't even know her." And judging from her reaction, it looked like he probably never would now. He knew another impulse to chase after her. He ignored it, anchoring his feet to the floor. Best thing they could do was finish their grocery hunt and get out of here.

"Well, you'll need to apologize or something next time you see her."

"I will," he promised, conscious there were people wanting to move past them. "Next time I see her."

CHAPTER 5

Serena shakily moved to the supermarket cashier. What had that man said? Had he really called her plain? Hope's words rose again in all their ugliness. *Fat. Boring. Nothing to offer anyone.* Add to that now *plain*, which everyone knew was just another word for ugly.

Tears blurred, bile rose, and she quickly paid and exited the supermarket to her car. She stowed her bags and sat in the front seat, breathing deep to calm her rushing pulse. She'd never really known what fragile felt like until this week, and between the giant shock of a week ago and the lack of sleep, she still felt brittle, like her emotions might break at any moment, like she had 'rejected' written across her forehead for everyone to see.

At least she'd had a week-long conference and several elaborate weddings to prepare for to help distract her from the shambles of her own life. But that still didn't explain that man's strange reaction to her. She'd only met Toni yesterday, when they'd gotten into a discussion about Agatha Christie while perusing the same shelf at Brandi's. Toni seemed to possess a wry amusement that escaped in sarcasm that Serena appreciated. And maybe she'd also felt a little sorry for the young soon-to-be mother. It must be hard to move to a new town for her husband's work and be so pregnant, knowing only her husband. But Joel seemed the total opposite of what Toni had implied. Instead of nice he'd been rude, dismissive, and condescending, as quick to judge as anyone else. Good luck to whoever he'd be working with in his new job.

As she drove home, she thought over the strange interaction again. As much as she'd wanted to just run and leave, she knew she had to get an item that was down the next aisle to where Toni and Joel were standing. She hadn't wanted to be spotted, so she'd scurried down, plucking the box from the shelf, but not before overhearing that last comment of his.

Plain? Tears pricked her eyes again. So she shouldn't be so overly sensitive about what a stranger thought of her. But it still hurt. Why did looks have to matter so much, anyway? Why couldn't people dig a little deeper to discover someone's personality or talents, and focus on that rather than facial features or height or things a person couldn't do anything about?

She slowed for a car to turn, stretching out a hand to stop her groceries from sliding off the front passenger seat. Somehow, her hand found the family-sized chocolate bar and, as oncoming traffic made them wait, she quickly unwrapped it and sank in her teeth, savoring the delectable taste melting on her tongue. Another bite, another, and the sugar high chased more of her hurt away. She might be a failure in lots of ways, but she could still eat chocolate like a boss.

Back at home, Serena unpacked her groceries. She had a couple of hours before she had to be at the resort for tonight's wedding. She still needed to check if her clothes fitted her— they'd been getting a little more snug lately—and set out her dress for church tomorrow so there'd be one less thing to do.

She put away the bag of potatoes and noticed she'd somehow opened a pack of cheese-flavored chips. How—? Oh, whatever. But somehow, she'd started eating without even noticing. Maybe she did have some sort of problem. She frowned, as the chips taunted her with their promise of comfort. Should she? Hope would say not to. Heat flared, and she stuffed the remaining chips in defiantly.

A scatter of bright yellow crumbs now littered her top. She winced at the old T-shirt—why had she thought wearing her schlumpiest, yard work-worthy clothes to go grocery shopping was a good idea? She brushed off the crumbs to join those littering the counter. Ugh. More cleaning to do now.

Her phone rang, and she stared at the name. Miranda. Her heart fell. But knowing her sister would only question why Serena hadn't answered the phone, she pressed answer. "Hi."

"What's this I hear about you and Dwight breaking up?"

Serena closed her eyes. "What did Mom say?"

"Mom? No, I heard this from someone else. Apparently, this Hope friend of yours has been having an affair with him for months."

She needed another pack of chips. Or to open that new pack of chocolate cookies. Stat. She moved to the dining table and sank into a seat, propping her head in her hands. This phone call had every sign of being long and requiring sustenance.

As Miranda assured Serena that she'd never really trusted Dwight, that Hope had always taken advantage of Serena's niceness, that Serena constantly played it safe and didn't aim high enough, etc., etc., Serena thought on the many times when Miranda had said similar things. Like when she'd chosen to study hospitality instead of business. Like when she stayed home and baked instead of going out dancing. Miranda had never been a warm or sympathetic person. Serena had often thought her sister's middle name should have been 'I-told-you-so'. Miranda was one of those people who always knew something wasn't right, and always felt it necessary to share this information—after the fact.

Despite Miranda's constant criticism of her life, Serena hadn't had energy to argue, and history had grooved inaction into habit.

"You need to find yourself a new man."

Like that was easy.

"Dwight doesn't deserve you—"

Well, that was more like the sisterly support she needed to hear.

"—and you sure as anything don't need to let another man use you up again. I can't believe you put up with it for so long."

Ah. That was more like the sisterly support she was used to. "I didn't know anything until last weekend."

"Mmm. But you've always been a little naïve, haven't you?"

Naïve? Tears threatened again, and she managed to say, without too much wobble in her voice, "I have to get back to the resort. Thanks for calling. And for your encouragement. It's always *such* a pleasure to talk to you."

"Wait—"

Serena jabbed end call and swiped at fresh tears. Was she so pathetic? Had she always been this way? She shouldn't let her sister's words needle her but trying to let it go proved a lot harder than merely saying it. Maybe some of Toni's sarcasm had settled on Serena. Her heart panged at the memory of the earlier debacle.

Her phone flashed with her sister's name again, but she ignored it, pleasure stealing through her at the knowledge her refusal to answer would drive her sister nuts. She pushed herself to her feet and groaned. The twinge in her knee seemed to have gotten worse. Ugh. Maybe she should do something about exercise. But not when she was so busy. And speaking of, if she didn't start tackling those chores that she just didn't get time to do during the week, then life would be even busier later.

As she gathered the trash for this week's collection, she realized just how many empty bags of junk food were filling up her trash. She frowned. Okay, so maybe her need for junk food wasn't exactly a need. She'd deal with it. Eventually. Probably. Maybe.

But the unease returned after her shower as she stood struggling to get into her work clothes. The full length, timber-framed mirror hadn't been her friend for a while now, and as she caught sight of herself, she stopped. Sucked in her stomach. It barely made a dent in her appearance. Who *was* that person with the double chin?

"I don't look like me anymore."

She looked like a pregnant lady. And not a cool pregnant lady like Toni, someone whom it was obvious by the slenderness everywhere else that the chunky belly was there for a reason. No, instead Serena looked like someone who'd had nineteen children already and her body had forgotten what a waist was. How had this happened?

Stupid question. The trash can held the answer.

She slumped onto her bed as nausea rumbled. Was it any wonder that people overlooked her? That people called her fat and plain? It was true. It was fact. And denying it was stupid. Comfort eating was making her uncomfortable, affecting her wardrobe choices, and how she felt about herself.

Another stolen glance at the beckoning mirror saw her cringe. Who *was* that? She'd become someone she didn't recognize; someone she didn't want to be. And someone rejected by others because she basically couldn't be bothered to change.

She angled the mirror away, unwilling to see her reflection anymore.

A glance at the clock saw her grimace then scoot back to her car, noticing for the first time just how much heavier she felt. Heavy in her heart, sure, but heavy in her body too. As she drove to the resort her mind refused to focus on the upcoming wedding, toying instead with what she could do. She flicked off the radio.

"Come on, it's not hard. Everyone knows what to do. You have to eat healthier. Exercise." She grimaced. "Limit how much you eat. Don't eat your feelings."

How many times had Hope said similar things? But then, Serena had never really paid much attention. Who wanted to eat cottage cheese when real cheese tasted so much better? Who wanted to eat vegetables when chocolate was a gift from heaven? But maybe there was something in it. And yes, this afternoon's inhalation of food she'd not even noticed meant she had to find a different way of dealing with her pain.

She pulled into her parking space and went straight to the Ballroom. The staff had effected a quick turnaround, changing the configuration from a conference to a wedding venue again, and the tables looked as they ought, apart from the flowers.

She frowned. Annette wasn't usually so late in delivering the floral centerpieces. Where was she?

She drew out her phone to call her, but it vibrated with a message from an unknown number. DO YOU KNOW WHERE ARABELLA'S FLOWERS ARE? SHE'S FREAKING OUT!

Serena winced. Okay, this wasn't good.

She dialed the number as she hurried to the bridal suite. "Hello, this is Serena Williamson, and—"

"You're the bridal consultant, right?" a nasal voice asked. "I remember meeting you at one of Arabella's appointments."

Ah. She recognized that voice now as belonging to Macy. The sister of the bride and chief bridesmaid—she'd refused the term 'matron of honor' on account she said it made her sound frumpy. Macy was a lawyer from Toronto with a penchant for nitpicking. Sometimes the worst Bridezillas weren't the brides. "Yes, we met."

"Well? What are you going to do about this? Arabella is beside herself—"

Faint protest in the background suggested that wasn't perhaps entirely true.

"You recommended this Annette person," Macy steamrolled on. "And—"

Serena placed a hand on the wall as she caught her breath.

"Are you puffing?" Macy asked suspiciously. "Are you on a treadmill or something?"

Serena held the phone away as she dragged in a deep breath. "Excuse me while I check with her." She ended the call, and tried Annette's number, only to meet with her voicemail. "Hello, Annette? This is Serena from Muskoka Shores, just wondering if you have an estimated delivery time for the flowers. Some of the Woodrow bridal party are getting a little concerned."

Her phone buzzed again. Another message from Macy. Awesome. Following up on flowers wasn't in her job description, but Macy was right. Serena had recommended Annette, so it did reflect poorly on the resort if the flowers weren't delivered soon. She tried Annette again. Still no answer. Sweat trickled down her spine.

Yet another message from Macy chased Serena up the grand staircase to the floor of suites that catered to important guests requiring more space. Including the bridal suite the Woodrows had reserved for their younger daughter Arabella. She knocked on the door and straightened her jacket. Wiped her brow. The pulse of music she could hear through the door expanded into hip-hop boom as the door was finally opened by a blush taffeta-draped bridesmaid.

Serena pasted a smile on her face. "Hi. I'm Serena, the assistant events coordinator and I just wanted to check—"

"Who is it, Macy?" a voice called from down the hall.

"Hi, it's Serena from the resort. I just wanted—"

"Where are the flowers?" Macy, a Kim Kardashian wannabe, scowled at her, almost certainly creasing the heavy makeup Linda, their 'aesthetic artist' had applied.

"I'm sure they will be here soon," Serena soothed.

"We have photos happening, and my sister needs her flowers!" she snapped.

"And she will have them as soon as they arrive," Serena promised, working to keep her voice low and controlled like when dealing with the Minimites. Her phone buzzed again. "Excuse me. I need to check this."

She turned, blocking the scowl, her heart easing as she recognized the number. Thank goodness.

"I think it's extremely unprofessional—"

"That's the florist," Serena interrupted Macy. "She's just pulled up now. We'll be back in just a moment with your flowers."

"You better."

Serena faked her smile until the door was closed in her face, then hurried away and back down the stairs. Macy was a delight. Not.

Outside the front reception area she found Annette struggling to balance two large buckets filled with roses as she drew them from her van.

"Hey, Annette," she called, hurrying to assist the plump lady in her fifties, who had been responsible for many floral arrangements at the resort over the years. "Let me help you."

"Oh my goodness, what a day." Annette wiped her shiny forehead. "First my assistant called in sick, then the van got a flat tire on the way. Do you know how long it's been since I've changed a tire? If it wasn't for a nice young man who changed it for me, I might never have gotten here."

"God bless the nice young men of this world."

"God will bless Joel, I'm sure."

Joel? She stilled. Then relaxed. No. It couldn't be. She didn't have any further time to wonder as Annette handed her two buckets filled with bunches of pink and red roses, before placing a heavy tub atop a cooler on a wheeled trolley.

"These look amazing," she said, burying her nose in the blooms. Even if the scent was very faint.

"Not quite as striking as last week, but then, nobody from Australia is here getting married this weekend, right?"

"Right."

Serena led the way to the bridal suite, carrying the buckets, hoping giant sweat patches hadn't formed under her aching arms. Who knew flowers could weigh so much? Maybe she should see this as a workout for her arms. Besides, it probably didn't hurt to look for excuses to do more exercise, especially when most of her job entailed sitting down.

They reached the top of the stairs—add a leg workout to that list—and knocked on the door. It was flung open by Macy. "I was just about to call you! It's about time."

Serena bit her tongue as Annette offered her excuses, none of which were met with understanding from the bride's sister. She snuck a look at Arabella, whose slender form was encased in ivory. "You look beautiful."

Arabella's worried expression eased. "Thanks," she murmured, her teeth gritted as the photographer—not kind local Alexa—barked at her not to move.

"Here we are," Annette said, lifting the lid on the white cooler and drawing out the teardrop bridal bouquet. Macy's complaints ceased, as the room filled with a joint sigh.

Serena smiled. "This is why we always recommend Annette."

Arabella shifted closer; her face alight. "Oh, it's perfect!"

"Here is the comb," Annette said, drawing out a clear plastic comb decorated with tiny pink and cream rosebuds. "And the boutonnieres."

"Who's delivering them to the guys?" Macy demanded.

"Oh." Annette shot Serena a pleading look. Normally it would be Annette's job, but with the table decorations to be completed...

"I will," Serena said. She didn't mind going the extra mile. Especially if she could help save the day.

"And for the mother of the bride, we have this corsage." Annette placed a delicate arrangement of roses and tiny ferns on the dining table, which met with more expressions of delight and claims of perfection, before the photographer barked at people to resume their places.

"Now quick, hand me that bouquet."

"Right, well, I guess my work here is done," Annette murmured. "Now to get those centerpieces on the tables."

Serena exited also, this time to deliver the men's buttonhole floral artistry to the four-bedroom suite that the groomsmen often used when staying on site.

Five minutes later, she was again breathless at her fast walk, and had to pause outside the room to steady her breathing before knocking. "Delivery," she called.

"Hey—oh." The groomsman's face fell, then, as someone asked who it was, he yelled back, "I thought it'd be the cute chick with more beer, but it's some middle-aged woman instead."

Middle-aged? She must've shown her shock for he added, "No offence."

"None taken." The man had obviously imbibed a little too much, she'd put his rudeness down to that. And maybe the weekend's hot weather. And maybe her gray hairs. "I have your boutonnieres."

"My what?" His gaze traveled down her, his expression holding mockery. "Hey lady, I don't think I really want anything you can offer."

"Maybe not." Her smile was stiff. "But the bride wants these delivered." She shoved the tray of tiny floral arrangements at the man.

"Huh? What are we supposed to do with these?" he asked, crossing his arms, his wedding ring flashing.

What was the bet he was married to—?

"Macy never said anything about wearing dumb flowers."

Bingo. "You wear them on your jacket's lapel to signify you are part of the bridal party," she said, fighting for patience. Had he been raised in a barn?

"How do you put it on?"

She spent the next five minutes showing them how to attach the flowers, tweaking ties, and doing her best to bring some peace into a situation that suggested the speeches would be interesting, at the very least. Alcohol-infused addresses usually were. At least the groom seemed to be treating the day with the seriousness it deserved, thanking her quietly, before his best man tried to slip her a twenty like he thought she was a stripper.

But later, as she drove home, reflecting on the vast differences between today's wedding and that of a week ago, the groomsman's ignorant comment slid under her defenses, huddling close to the increasing collection, tightening her chest.

Middle-aged. Nothing to offer. Plain.

And the thought that even someone like mean Macy could be married pricked her eyes with tears.

MAYBE SOME MIGHT CONSIDER it strange for an assistant minister to miss going to church, but after a week of moving, painting, and then helping a poor lady change her tire, Joel shouldn't have been too surprised that he had forgotten to set his alarm. Toni hadn't bothered to wake him—surprise, surprise—and it had been past ten by the time he woke, by which stage it was far too late to bother going. Good thing God knew his heart.

He instead read his Bible on the back porch, allowing his worship to lift on the fresh air and scent of pine. It probably didn't hurt to show Toni that a relationship with God wasn't dependent on how many times one went to church.

"It's really hot," she said, fanning herself. "Did you buy ice-cream yesterday?"

"Was it on the list?'

"No."

"Then no, I didn't."

She groaned.

"Why don't you have a swim?"

"And scare everyone with my whale-like appearance?"

"You're pregnant, Toni. Everyone can tell your beach ball isn't because you eat too much."

Her eyes narrowed, but instead of further arguing the point, she shook her head and sighed.

"Why don't you message your friend? Maybe she could meet you there."

"She might not show if she knows you're going to be there."

"So don't tell her."

"So you can take her by surprise? That'll go well."

Good point. All day his conscience had gnawed at him to make amends. He wasn't usually so tactless. Put it down to a busy week that had stripped the filter from his mouth. Or him just being the doofus Toni often called him.

"Look, I want you to make friends, and if that means me eating humble pie, then I'm totally up for that."

Her smile flickered. "Well, in that case…"

Half an hour later they were at the town's beach, the creamy sand squishing beneath their toes, Lake Muskoka gleaming just meters away. He held Toni's beach bag and two fold-up chairs as they searched for a spot in the shade. It seemed all of Ontario had come to visit this stretch of lake today.

They spotted a shaded part between two larger family groupings, and he placed the chairs in the sand. "Happy with this here?" he asked.

"Sure."

He assisted Toni into her chair, conscious his actions probably made it look like they were a couple, something confirmed when the woman in the group next to them murmured, "Is this your first?"

His first what? Her tilt of head at Toni's tummy made things clear. But how to explain things… "Uh, yes." That was the simplest explanation. And true. Neither he nor Toni had experience with babies.

"How long to go?"

"Um, a month or so?"

She nodded wisely. "Summer is never an easy time to be pregnant. She'll be glad when this ends."

"Yes, she will." Judging from the complaints that seemed to be levelling up each day.

Toni poked his side, and he excused himself to focus on his sister. "What?"

"See that ice-cream van?" She pointed to a pink van near the parking lot. "I need a chocolate ice-cream."

So did he. He slapped on his hat and sunglasses and pushed to his feet. "Be back in five." Or maybe longer, judging from the line that seemed to be increasing with every step he took.

A light breeze ruffled open his unbuttoned Hawaiian shirt. Not the usual attire for a church minister, nor something he could get away with as a youth pastor, but here, where he was anonymous, for one more week at least, he figured it was safe enough. Especially on such a hot, muggy day.

He joined the line for ice-cream, joining squawking kids, patient grandparents, and screaming toddlers. Ahead of him was a clutch of young women whose comments about "so hot" and "six pack" suggested they weren't talking about the weather. He glanced at the group of early teens behind him. Only one wasn't on his phone.

Joel nodded. "Hot enough for you?"

The teen shrugged and glanced away. Okay. Maybe talking with random strangers wasn't such a thing here as he'd been led to believe about small towns.

He followed the kid's gaze to where a group of women sat, their bikinis not exactly PG rated, then immediately swung his attention back to those trekking past licking their chocolate-cold treasures. Little kids shrieking in delight brought his smile. An old couple held hands as they enjoyed their nut-dressed chocolate-dipped cones.

A group of women strolled past, two of them eyeing his chest before smiling at him. They were followed by a more full-figured woman wearing sunglasses that had half-slipped down her nose, the position of which made eating her ice-cream somewhat hazardous and drew his smile. Her gaze met his, and he caught her widened green eyes.

Wait. He knew those eyes. Slightly almond shaped. Their pain-filled expression had haunted his dreams last night. What was the name of Toni's friend?

But before he could say anything she'd hastened away, and the man in the ice-cream van was asking what flavor he wanted, and by the time he'd paid for Toni's ice-cream the woman had disappeared.

He scanned the crowds as he slowly returned but couldn't see her anywhere. He couldn't really blame her. She probably thought he was about to offer another inanely inappropriate comment, like she thought he was always prone to bouts of word vomit.

"What's with the long face?" Toni asked as he handed her the now dripping ice-cream.

"I thought I saw your friend here."

"Serena?" she asked, propping herself up on one elbow. "She'd said she was out today."

"Maybe it wasn't her, then. Just someone who looked like her."

"Maybe." A wrinkle lined Toni's brow.

And regret wrinkled his soul. If Serena was avoiding Toni because of him, he'd better make that apology soon. For he'd do anything to help his sister find her feet and find her faith restored in people again.

CHAPTER 6

"Oh my gosh. This is the best idea ever," Anna said, licking the last remnants of ice-cream from the cone.

Serena's heart tensed. A spontaneous picnic by the lake after church had seemed the best way to catch up with her friends while dealing with the heat. That was until she'd got the message from Toni about meeting at the beach. She'd felt bad about refusing—she'd sensed Toni could do with friends—but that fragility she'd lived with all week still hadn't released her to face up to Toni's husband yet.

She glanced at her phone. Should she text again? Say she was free after all? Or was that inclination to make amends wrapped up in some twisted motive that wasn't honorable at all? For while she'd like to talk with Toni, she had no wish to see Joel. Yes, she'd forgive him some day, but his words, and those of others, kept churning around her heart in a whirlpool of pain. She would've liked to have waited until she was stronger emotionally before she could be put into a situation to speak with him. Just hadn't counted on seeing him here.

She swallowed, wincing as the overly cold ice-cream slowly traveled down her throat. Was throat freeze a thing?

"You okay there, Rena?" Jackie asked. "You've been pretty quiet."

Because she hadn't known what to say when she'd seen Joel Wakefield standing in the ice-cream line. Seeing him, seeing his tanned pecs on display, had nearly made her drop her ice-cream. No *way* did she ever want to speak to that man again.

"Did you see that guy's abs?" Rachel asked.

"Whose abs?" Jackie asked.

Joel's? Guilt washed through her. He was Toni's husband. She shouldn't be noticing him.

"His," Rachel pointed to a man nearby, who flashed her a smile.

"He's your husband," Jackie said. "So no."

"Do you never check out guys?" Anna asked, as Rachel sighed, standing up to deal with her shrieking children.

"Not if they're married," Jackie said firmly, which earned Serena's silent cheer.

Sorry, God, for being distracted by superficial things. And really, how hypocritical did that make her? She, who didn't want to be judged by others because she didn't fit society's standard-sized idea of attractiveness, had been led by her hormones to be distracted by a man's nice chest. What was wrong with her? Poor Toni. She didn't deserve a non-friend like Serena. Not someone who had basically fobbed off Toni's overtures of friendship because Serena hadn't wanted to see Joel again, then, upon seeing Joel again, had experienced quite different feelings, ones she was ashamed of. Maybe this was something like what Hope had faced, thinking Dwight was attractive, but instead of resisting she'd chased after him, like a tiger after forbidden meat.

"You're deep in thought," Jackie said.

"Yeah," Anna said, eyeing Serena. "You need to turn that frown upside down."

"You're not worried about you-know-who, are you?"

"I've got no idea who you mean," Serena said.

"We won't let them bother you."

She froze. "Are Hope and Dwight here?" she asked, glancing around.

Her friends exchanged glances, then Anna said, "I think someone said they saw Hope in the water earlier."

Her stomach tensed. Hope, in her tiny bikini, probably flaunting her meager assets while trying to prove to everyone what a coup she'd landed, stealing Dwight from under Serena's nose.

Forget trying to speak with Toni. "I need to go."

She shoved on her broad-brimmed hat and pushed to her feet, picking up the towel and shaking out the sand.

"Aw, come on. Don't go," Anna said. "You know that's just letting them win."

"I don't care." She wrapped her cover-up more tightly across her chest. No way was she giving Hope any more opportunity to criticize than possible.

"Honey," Jackie said, "you shouldn't change your plans just because they are here. Anna's right. It means they're stopping you from doing what you want to do."

"But I don't want to be here with them," she muttered. "I don't want to see them together. It makes me sick to think they're laughing at me."

"Why would they be laughing at you?" Anna said, catching Serena's hand and tugging until she reluctantly sat again.

"Because they won, and I lost, and—"

"The way I see it, Dwight's the one who lost, and you won because you now know what kind of man he is. He's the loser."

"An A-grade jerk," Jackie said with a nod.

Maybe so. But… "I'm the one sitting here alone."

"You're not alone," Jackie said.

"You know what I mean."

"I know what you're saying," Jackie said slowly, "but I think you're forgetting that you're never really alone."

"Yeah, God is with me, I know that."

"Can't He be enough?"

Jackie's soft question carved cruelly into her heart, forcing her to look away. For years she'd thought He was enough, but Dwight's attention had shown there were spaces in her heart that delighted in notice from a man. And now she didn't have that—now she knew just how poorly so many men regarded her —her heart felt too bowed and bruised to care for such questions.

Her gaze drifted over those whiling away the afternoon on the beach. Slim people, slender people, healthy people, all laughing, having fun. A savage desire to be one of those people filled her. If only she was skinny and was fit, then maybe people would be nicer to her and wouldn't think her middle-aged and frumpy. She shivered.

"I've got to go." She pushed to her feet again, ignoring her friends' pleas to stay. No. She couldn't stay here. Couldn't stay as the person she'd been for way too long. It was time to change. Time to put an end to those voices in her head that whispered she was too fat, too plain, too ugly. It was time to prove Hope wrong.

She picked her way across the hot sand, keeping her head down as she concentrated on reaching the path to the parking lot. *Please God, don't let me see—*

"Serena?"

She glanced up, and nearly fell over at the sight of the woman sitting in the beach chair. "Uh, hi Toni." She found a weak smile.

"You're here. I thought you were busy."

"I, um, was. I'd already arranged to meet up with some friends, and, um, I'm sorry."

Toni nodded, but her face held a reserve unlike the openness of before.

Serena knew a prompting to apologize, but the words trailed away as Joel lifted a hand, his shirt flapping open.

"So it is you." He smiled.

She stiffened, pressing her lips together as she glanced away. What, did he think a smile made everything okay?

"Hey, um, Serena."

Joel's deep voice drew her attention back to his direction, but she still couldn't meet his eyes. Or his chest. She settled for someplace over his left shoulder.

"I wanted to say I was sorry about my stupid comment yesterday."

"Which one?"

"Oh." A beat. "Uh, I guess all of them?"

"You guess?" Whoa. Was that sarcasm dripping from her own mouth? Way to go, non-doormat her.

"I told you it's like he's clueless," Toni said, nudging him in the side.

Her action drew focus to his open shirt, which flung Serena's gaze away again. "I gotta go."

"Hey, before you do, do you think we could meet sometime?" Toni's gaze was shy. "I, um, don't know too many people, and..."

Serena heard the plea, recognized it as loneliness. And while she might wish to avoid Joel, it shouldn't be at the expense of Toni's apparent need for friends. "Uh, sure."

"Awesome," Joel said, like maybe he thought Serena meant she'd catch up with him, too.

No way. She shot him a scowl, then refocused on Toni.

Toni's shoulders had dipped, as if she hadn't been sure she would agree, further twisting Serena's guilty heart. What kind of person was she, unwilling to befriend a stranger because she was too caught up in her own problems? "We talked about getting you a book, right?"

"That'd be great."

Toni's smile looked more authentic now, bringing further ease to Serena's heart. Maybe today wouldn't prove to have been such a fail after all.

"OMG. Seriously?"

Serena froze. No. *Please God, no.* Maybe she could pretend she hadn't heard. Maybe she could just leave—

"Serena?" Hope's voice.

"Excuse me," she muttered to Toni, avoiding Joel's gaze. "I need to go."

"Never thought I'd see you at the beach," Hope's voice taunted from behind.

Just ignore her she told herself, dropping her sandals and shoving sand-covered toes in them, even as she blinked away tears. Stupid tears. Why was she the one crying? Hope was the one who should be crying. Dwight *would* be the one crying, once he realized just what he'd signed up for in taking on Hope. How could Serena have ever believed he cared? Was she truly that gullible? Or was it just that Hope was so good at fooling people?

From somewhere behind her she heard Toni's voice call after her, but she couldn't turn around. She had to escape. She had to move on. Her earlier thought chased her to the car. It was time, way past time, to take charge of her life, once and for all.

By the time she'd reached home she'd decided two things. Eat better, exercise more. She couldn't keep going on this way. Dr. Lewisham had warned her during her last checkup that her cholesterol was getting a little high. It wasn't about to come down unless something changed.

Sunday night was trash collection night, which made today the perfect opportunity to get rid of all the garbage that tempted. Goodbye chips. Goodbye chocolates. Goodbye cookies. Goodbye soda. She didn't want to think about how much money she'd spent on stuff she was throwing away. Her cupboards were looking Mother Hubbard-like bare by the time she finished, but that was okay. "It's just allowing more room for the healthy things I'll buy."

Healthy foods: fruit, vegetables, brown rice, quinoa. She wrinkled her nose, but no, this was what she *would* do. Nobody was going to call her fat anymore.

After throwing all her junk food in the trash and firmly shoving on the lid, Serena dragged her old exercise bike from the garage, wiping off the dust before placing it in Hope's old room. There was a certain triumph in proving her fake friend wrong as she sweated and grew bright red in front of the glass-mirrored closet doors. After an hour on the bike she felt exhausted, red-faced and aching, but also better. Maybe those endorphins Hope had talked about were an actual thing. But doing this once was obviously not going to be enough. The challenge would be doing this every day. But she *would*, she told herself fiercely. Just watch this girl change.

A DAY off on Monday allowed for an emergency haircut (goodbye, gray-hairs; hello, gold foils); stocking up on healthy groceries; a quick coffee with Toni—thankfully Joel free—and more time for exercise. A walk along the lakeside path might not be everyone's idea of exercise, but yesterday's perusal of health sites suggested that for exercise to become a habit it had to be do-able, something she'd want to fit into her day, rather than find excuses not to. Maybe she should get a dog, which would mean she'd have to go walking every day.

The rest of the week was filled with meetings and a rare Sunday wedding which meant she had to miss church and Sunday school. It also meant she had to learn via the grapevine called Anna's phone call that night that the new assistant minister had been welcomed to the church. Wow. Showed how much she'd been paying attention.

"So what do you think?"

"He's good looking," Anna said.

Serena rolled her eyes, glad this was a phone call. "That is the most important criteria, isn't it?"

Anna laughed. "Come on. Don't blame a single gal for appreciating the fact we have someone more our age."

"What's his name again?"

"Joel Wakefield."

What?

Serena's ears barely retained sound as Anna prattled on saying something about sisters. No. It couldn't be. Not Mr. Insensitive, Mr. Foot-in-Mouth, Mr. Filter-free. Toni had said they'd needed to move here for Joel's new job. It couldn't mean moving here to work at the church Serena had been part of for years. How was she going to avoid him now?

Maybe there was a mistake. Maybe she was just jumping the gun. "So, um, what does he look like?"

"Says the woman mocking me for appreciating a fine-looking male."

"Don't tell me then. I don't care."

"No, it's good to see you taking an interest again in guys."

Yeah, but he was married. Why didn't people respect that? "Is he about six feet tall, with dark hair, and, um, fit?"

"Yes! Have you met him?"

Serena grimaced. "I think I have."

Great. Now she'd be expected to play nice, especially as Anna's comments suggested that the Sunday school team would likely fall under his jurisdiction. At least Toni would hopefully be in church regularly. She rolled her eyes at herself—how could Toni not be if her husband was a pastor there? But Monday's coffee catch up had further reinforced a liking for the girl, even if Toni obviously had poor taste in men.

"So anyway," Anna continued, "I needed to let you know that

there's a Sunday school leaders' meeting on Wednesday night to meet Joel and talk about new directions."

"New directions? What, he's here five minutes and wants to change everything already?"

"I don't think it's that bad," Anna cautioned. "I think he just wants to get a feel for the different ministry areas. Apparently, he's worked in youth ministry before, and he's wanting to see how things can go forward."

"I can't believe it."

"Hey, you know John has been talking about taking some time off—"

He had?

"—and reducing his workload to free them up for ministry elsewhere occasionally. I think this will be a good thing."

"Right." Ooh, this sarcasm thing was getting easier.

"Come on, Serena. We both know you don't like change."

Yeah, but she was trying to embrace it. She loved her new hair. Walking was fun. And she was trying to enjoy green smoothies, even if they tasted kind of gross.

"This could be a good thing," Anna persisted. "I think you'll like him."

"The jury's out."

"Aw, come on. What's he ever done to you?"

Telling Anna what she'd heard now seemed rather petty. And everyone was entitled to a bad day, she supposed. And it probably wouldn't do to color someone else's perceptions before he had a chance to prove himself. Her lips flicked up. Judging from her previous encounters with him, it wouldn't take long before he proved his true colors anyway.

"Sorry, it's been a big week." Exercising each day was making her tired and cutting out sugar and cutting down on carbs was making her cranky, to use a word her grandmother used to say.

"I'll see you Wednesday night, okay?"

"Can't wait."

Anna laughed. "It's going to be fine. Good things are coming your way, you'll see."

"Sure."

She ended the call and wrinkled her nose. She was up for good things. As long as Joel Wakefield didn't get in her way.

~

TUESDAY AND WEDNESDAY filled with a myriad of tasks that kept her busy. She glanced at the clock. Already she'd edged past into usual overtime. But staying busy at work meant she wouldn't be worrying at home, wondering just what would happen at tonight's meeting.

Her phone rang. "Serena? Oh good, you're still here. Can I see you in my office?"

Her mouth dried at Mr. Jennings' request. She had to swallow twice to find enough moisture to reply. "Yes, sir."

She placed the phone down, glad she'd decided to wear her power suit today in preparation for tonight's meeting at church. Nothing gave confidence like looking like she was dressed for success, and after ten days of healthier choices she found the skirt and jacket fitted better than it had in months. And now her navy power outfit could do double duty, giving her courage as she obeyed Mr. Jennings' summons.

She smoothed down her skirt as she sat down opposite him in his luxuriously appointed office. What would he wish to speak about? Had someone complained about her? Had Macy?

"Serena, as you know, you've been filling in quite a lot for Joanne, in her role as Resort Event Coordinator."

Even as she nodded, a knot of fear coiled in her stomach. She really did love her job; she wasn't ready to hear she'd been fired. What had she missed? Had she left something undone? Was Joanne upset?

"We've heard so many reports from guests who have interacted with you and been very impressed with their experiences here due to your hard work. Sarah and Dan Walton sent us a lovely email, singling you out as someone who truly went above and beyond for their special day."

They had? Oh, God bless them.

"For some time now we've been watching you, and all of us in management agree you're someone with a golden touch at making people feel special. We're so glad to have you on our team."

Wow. Serena eased back in her seat, letting out her breath with an inaudible sigh of relief. It didn't sound like she was going to be fired. "I'm so pleased to hear that, Mr. Jennings."

The general manager continued, "I've just received Joanne's letter of resignation. As you know she's been spending a lot of time caring for her mother and with the time and energy that demands, she just doesn't feel like she can commit to the hours we ask of her here. We would like to offer you the opportunity to step up to become the resort's Event Coordinator."

Breath suspended. "Really?"

"Yes." Mr. Jennings leaned forward and smiled. "We believe you'd do an excellent job. Now, you don't have to give an answer straight away, but if you can let us know by the end of the week if you're interested, that would be good. Otherwise, we'll need to begin advertising for someone else. But," his eyes twinkled at her, "we'd much rather fill the position from in-house."

"Oh, thank you, sir. That's wonderful."

After discussing further details, then shaking his hand and promising she'd think about it and let him know soon, Serena floated from the room. She didn't really need time to think about it. Her answer was going to be a big yes. For months now she'd been doing Joanne's job, so to continue it, only with the extra money, office, and prestige was a no-brainer.

After a quick collection of her bag and a healthy power bar, she got in her car. She turned the music up, dancing in her seat as she drove to the church for the meeting with Joel about the Sunday school. It almost didn't matter what he'd say, her good news the perfect shield. Not bad for someone who'd been accused of lacking ambition, she thought. Her lip curled. *Take that, Hope.* Finally, things were falling into place, and people were appreciating what she could do.

She parked, then took a moment to quickly reapply her lipstick, smooth her hair back into its ponytail, and blink in some eye drops so her contact lenses stayed moist. She exhaled, scrutinizing her appearance. About as good as she could get.

Two minutes later she entered the church's conference room, waving a hand at Anna, who gave her a thumbs up. She took a chair next to Anna at the far end of the long table, settling into her seat. Looked like she was the last to arrive. Oh well. It didn't matter what anyone thought of her. She was going to be the resort's Event Coordinator! Maybe she should organize another soiree—a healthy one this time—because this news was definitely worth celebrating.

Joy rippled through her, spilling out in a broad smile, until she glanced at the man seated next to John McPherson at the opposite end.

JOEL STARED at the woman seated at the other end of the room. Dressed in a navy business suit with heels, hair sleek and slicked back in a low ponytail, he'd thought she looked very professional and attractive, with those unusual cat-like eyes.

And then she'd smiled. It was as if she were lit from within, as she glowed with happiness. His chest tensed. If she was one of the Sunday school teachers it could prove interesting, a heart for ministry more appealing than the prettiest face. He'd long avoided relationships with women in the churches he worked in, as nobody needed the difficulties of negotiating awkward relationships should things not work out. This self-imposed policy had provided a handy excuse for when women batted their eyelashes, and he'd wonder whether it was himself or the glamor of ministry that drew their notice. But—he glanced again down the table to where the latecomer sat—maybe it was time for a change.

"Welcome everyone, thanks for joining us tonight," John McPherson said.

Joel refocused, breathing past his earlier agitation as he was reminded why he was here. John McPherson was amongst the most genuine ministers Joel had been blessed to work with, his easygoing nature and genuine commitment to connect and encourage believers making the invitation to work here an easy yes. He and his wife's understanding and acceptance when Joel had explained Toni's situation just showed the man's grace.

"What's the point in talking about God's grace if we can't show it?" John had said, a far cry from some of the people in their previous church. "Bring her here, and we'll love her back into the kingdom. And as for people wondering if this will affect your ministry, well, I think it just makes you more approachable. Who has a perfect family, after all? Anyway, who among us is perfect? God loves your sister, and God loves that little innocent baby too, so we look forward to both of you joining us here."

"I know some of you are very busy," John said now, glancing at the woman who'd come in late, "so we'll get straight to it. For those of you who haven't met him already, this is Joel Wakefield, our new assistant pastor. He'll be employed four days a week and taking the reins in a more full-time capacity in a few months while Angela and I take some long-service leave."

Joel nodded, offering a smile to those seated around the table. When he glanced at the woman seated opposite, her smile dimmed, her gaze veering away. His heart twinged.

"Before we go any further, I'm going to pray, then I'm going to let Joel explain a little about his experience and what he hopes to bring here."

Joel closed his eyes as John prayed, refocusing his attention heavenward. Excitement bubbled up as he joined in with the "Amen," then, when invited, he stood.

"Good evening, thank you for coming out tonight. I appreciate the chance to get to know you all some more." His gaze flicked to the woman at the end. She was now studying her phone. Huh. Okay. "It's wonderful to be in a church like this, where people from all walks of life are involved in ministry. From what I've seen so far, the people here seem a very friendly, hospitable family of believers, which is exactly what I believe church should be."

His words were met with nods, a few smiles, but the professional-looking blonde's gaze remained averted. Oh well.

"I've never really understood those who treat church as a once-a-week duty or obligation. To me, that just misses the heart of what I think church should be, which is love, community, and family."

He went on to share about his experiences in the city, working with young people in schools and community groups, working with elderly people in group homes. "I was also involved in helping to set up TASK, the Toronto Area Soup Kitchen, which has been blessed with the recent support of Dan Walton and some other high-profile Christians."

This drew some more nods, as he'd figured. Dan attended this church in the summer, and now he'd married John's niece, it wasn't surprising that people would know about that too.

He continued to share about his life, treading carefully about the details concerning his sister, then noticed the woman at the opposite end look up from her phone and lean close to whisper to the woman next to her. Um, okay. That didn't quite vibe with the professionalism her clothes shouted at her as being. He moved onto speaking about some of the practicalities he'd assist with, then finally invited each of them to introduce themselves and share about their role in the Sunday School ministry.

One by one the various workers went round the table, giving their name and sharing a little bit about themselves. Anticipation built as it came time for the woman at the end to speak. Who *was* she?

"My name is Serena Williamson."

He blinked.

"I teach the Minimites Sunday school group. I enjoy reading." Her voice was flat, her green eyes held no smile.

Joel stared at her, his stomach twisting. She was Toni's friend? The last time he'd seen her she'd looked nothing like this. Granted, that had been at the beach, but even so, she'd possessed an air about her, something that looked like defeat, which had only grown when that skinny girl had called to her.

But now, she looked the polar opposite. Cool, collected, everything about her, from her professional attire to her demeanor, so different from the frumpy woman he'd first met in the supermarket. And didn't she wear glasses?

As the next person introduced herself Joel kept sneaking glances back at Serena, but she avoided his gaze. Regret knotted within. Was she still upset with him? He'd thought he'd cleared the ice during their beachside encounter, but maybe that'd just been wishful thinking.

The introductions continued, and he knew he'd have to ask John about the last few teachers as he was unable to remember their names, let alone anything else about them.

Later, after the official introductions were finished, coffee and cookies were served and Joel got the chance to chat more informally with the Sunday school team. But each time he drew near to Serena she moved off in the opposite direction. Finally, after chatting with everyone else in the room, he realized she'd gone.

Anna, Serena's co-worker with the junior girls, was still hovering nearby. "Where's Serena?"

"She had to go home. She's just received some great news about work and has to call her parents."

"Okay, thanks." Disappointment warred with curiosity. What was her great news that meant she'd had to hurry away?

The evening continued with more questions and conversations, until others had to leave, and John clapped him on the back. "It's great to have you here, Joel. I can tell you'll be making the right kind of impact with our church. You and Toni will have to come for lunch on Sunday."

"Sounds great, thanks." Toni mightn't like it, but she'd have to get used to socializing. There was only so much interpersonal distance the ministry allowed.

And, a thought niggled, maybe one day he could figure out whether Serena might ever be willing to forgive him, and overcome this distance between them, and be interested in socializing, too.

THE NEXT DAY Joel mentioned John's lunch invitation to Toni as they ate breakfast together, which met with her wrinkled nose and sigh. "Do I have to?"

Technically, no. But this was for her own good. "Yep."

A louder sigh, and a shake of her head.

"I saw your friend Serena there."

"Where?"

"Last night, at the church meeting."

His sister spooned in her granola. "How is she?" she asked, over loud crunching.

"Don't know. By the time I finished chatting with everyone, she'd gone."

Toni shrugged. "She works long hours. She probably had to get home."

"That's what Anna said."

"Anna?" Toni's eyebrows lifted, her head tilting slightly.

"Serena's friend." And someone whose smiles and fixed attention put him into full alarm mode.

"What does Anna look like?" Was that a tiny smile hovering around her mouth?

He shrugged. He couldn't remember what Anna looked like. And why was his sister looking at him like that? "I don't know. Brunette, late twenties, pretty, maybe? Anyway, I'm asking about Serena."

Toni held up her hands. "Whoa. You don't need to get upset with me."

"I'm not upset. I just want to know about Serena," he said, hearing—and not liking—the trace of impatience in his voice.

"Why?"

"Is she okay? Or is she avoiding me? You meet with her on Mondays, don't you?"

Toni's look could cut glass. "Believe it or not, when we talk, we don't spend our entire conversations talking about you."

"I didn't mean—"

"Did you ever apologize to her?"

"Yeah. You heard me."

She rolled her eyes at him. "Joel, you're such a man sometimes. If you mean that time at the beach, that was hardly an apology."

Wasn't it? He'd said sorry. Hadn't he?

Toni collected her bowl and mug and headed back to the kitchen, leaving Joel sitting alone, wondering what to do. Remembering back to how Serena had looked yesterday he realized just how much he'd misjudged her, and he rubbed his forehead, wishing he could ease the tension his thoughtless words had caused.

Toni's words floated in from the kitchen. "If it's any comfort, she's invited me to her place for dinner on Friday night." She came in and looked pityingly at him. "I could find out for you."

Why did this feel like grade school? Still, beggars couldn't be too choosy, could they? "I'd appreciate it." Her raised eyebrows drew further defense. "It's just that I don't want to get off on the wrong foot with anyone from church."

"You're sure?"

"Yes!"

"Hmm. Sounds like it may be too late for that."

A knot in his stomach suggested he'd better make sure that wasn't so.

CHAPTER 7

The floaty feeling accompanied Serena to work on Thursday, where she told Mr. Jennings she'd accept the role, all the way through to her celebratory soiree on Friday night.

And now, with the candles lit, and delicious scents drifting from the kitchen, the space looked ready for some fun. She hoped Rachel, Anna, and Jackie would accept Toni. During their Monday get-togethers and from what she'd gathered from others it seemed that Toni wasn't exactly the most talkative of creatures with groups of people—something Serena put down to her newness, and maybe the discomfort of advanced pregnancy—so she'd invited Toni to come early to help her feel more at ease.

The doorbell rang, and she opened it. "You're here!"

"And you're here." Toni grinned. "It's good to finally know where you live."

Serena invited her inside. "I thought I could show you my book collection before the others get here."

Toni tensed. "Others?"

"Just some friends from church. You've probably seen them

if not met them already. Anna, Rachel, and Jackie. We've all been friends for ages. Don't worry, they're nice."

The meal continued baking as Serena drew Toni to the tall bookshelves anchored next to the fire. Agatha Christie, Georgette Heyer, John Grisham, other names she loved. The tension lining Toni's face eased as they shared about book love, and a tall stack of books was placed near the door for when she left.

"There's just something about a real book, isn't there?" Toni said.

Serena nodded. "I love the convenience of an e-book, but it's just not quite the same."

"Right? I love to smell the pages, which Joel says makes me some kind of freak, but I don't care."

How could a man—a pastor, no less—say that about his wife? "What would he know, anyway?"

"Right?" Toni chuckled. "Hey, I don't suppose you have any books by Staci Everton? I heard she was from around here."

"Staci?" Serena's brow wrinkled. "She lived with her grandmother for a time—Rose goes to our church, too—but Staci hasn't lived in Muskoka Shores for years. Last I heard she lives in Chicago." She shrugged. "Her books haven't really been my cup of tea, though." Her chest tightened, as she remembered her former housemate's preference for trashy historical novels of the Staci Everton kind.

The doorbell rang, and Anna's entrance was soon followed by Jackie, and Rachel, who couldn't stop exclaiming at the chance to leave her rug-rats at home.

"Oh, it's so good to feel like a human, to be myself and not just Mommy." Rachel slumped in the leather lounge, accepting Serena's offer of a Friday night beverage, taking a sip, proclaiming it delicious and very necessary, before turning to Toni. "Don't get me wrong. Being a mother is amazing. But it's also exhausting. And it never stops. You think it might turn off when they go to bed at night, but no. They're up five times wanting this or that, so you never really feel like you get real sleep. I don't think I've had a solid night's sleep in five years."

"Yeah, I think you're really convincing Toni that motherhood is good, Rachel," Serena said, having caught Toni's look of dismay.

"Oh, but it *is* good," Rachel tried to assure Toni. "Like, such a blessing. You must feel that, mustn't you?"

Toni lifted her mocktail—her condition meant no alcohol tonight—dipping her chin before taking a sip.

Yeah. That response didn't say Rachel had made things better.

But Toni soon relaxed again as Serena brought out the snacks—she'd tried for healthy, so the cheeses and dips were lower fat, and she'd made sure to include more vegetables and fruit—and the conversation continued.

Anna shared about her work as the receptionist for the medical clinic run by Dr. Lewisham and Dr. Strauss. "I think they're wanting to get someone in part-time."

"Ooh, maybe they'll get a young hot single doctor," Rachel teased.

"That'd be the day," Jackie scoffed. "Can you imagine a hot doctor in town?"

"I can." Anna sighed. "And I bet I'd not be the only one who'd be on time for appointments if that was the case."

Jackie and Rachel laughed, which drew Serena and Toni's smiles.

"You're all single?" Toni asked, her gaze switching back to Serena.

Serena swallowed, the question sounding raw in the dimness. Not when this was a place where she and Dwight had cuddled. Not when this room was where she and Hope had shared their hearts. Shared one particular heart, it seemed, before that heart and Hope had broken hers.

"I'm married," Rachel said, "but these ladies are all footloose and fancy free."

Fancy free? Serena would like to think so, but sometimes her heart whispered foolish things. She glanced at Anna, who seemed to understand her inability to speak, judging from her nod.

"Serena recently broke up with her boyfriend," Anna murmured.

"That's right," Jackie said. "She just needs some time to heal before she starts thinking about anyone new."

"Like a hot doctor," Rachel added, which met with more laughter.

"But whoever he is, he has to be faithful, trustworthy, and kind," Anna said, ticking off her fingers. "And it goes without saying that he has to be a Christian."

Toni nodded and took another sip of her juice. "I might know someone like that."

Rachel chuckled. "No offense, but he's got to be willing to live in a small town, right Rena?"

"And that's not everyone, as we all know."

Anna sighed. "I wonder if we would've had more of a chance with Dan if he lived here full time instead of living in the city."

"You'll never know now," Jackie said. "So be happy for him."

"They made the sweetest couple. Sarah is a real sweetheart," Serena said.

This prompted demands to see some photos Serena had snapped of the venue before the wedding ceremony, and the others oohed and ahhed over the flowers and cake.

"Lifestyles of the rich and fabulous, eh?" Anna exhaled. "If only miracles happened for all, huh, Serena?" Her eyes widened. "Wait. I didn't mean to remind you of Dwong and Dope."

"What?"

Anna snickered. "Dwight was definitely not your Mr. Right,

so he was Mr. Wrong. So Dwight becomes Dwong, and Hope becomes Dope. Get it?"

Serena's heart grew tight even as she nodded. Except she still felt like the main dope around here.

"Let's not spoil this evening with talk about them," Jackie said.

Bless her.

"That's right." Rachel nodded. "Your Mr. Right will come one day."

Serena shrugged. "It's okay. I know miracles aren't there for everybody. I'm happy being me for a while," she lied, her neck tingling.

"And so you should be, especially with your new promotion." Anna held up her glass and tapped the edge of Serena's. "Congrats, again. Well deserved."

"What promotion?" Toni asked.

Oh. Hadn't Serena mentioned it? The general clink of glasses paused as she explained about her step up into being the resort's Event Coordinator.

"That's awesome," Toni said.

"It's about time," Rachel said. "You've basically been doing Joanne's job for months now, so it's good you'll finally get the pay and recognition you deserve."

"Amen," said Jackie.

"Who's the boss? You're the boss," Anna said, lifting her Virgin Mojito.

Cheers and laughter met this proclamation. "I'm not exactly the boss," Serena clarified. "But I do get to sit in on some of the important meetings with the real boss now."

"Here's to being bossier, then," Rachel said, to more laughter.

"And can I say that this new role is working for you?" Anna said. "You're looking good, girl."

Others had noticed? "Thanks."

"The other night she came strutting into the Sunday school

meeting like a supermodel," Anna said to the others. "You should've seen her."

"A supermodel? Please." That'd be the day. "And I didn't strut," she protested.

"You looked good, and you still do," Anna continued, pointing at Serena from head to toe. "Tell us your secrets, Great One. What are you doing differently?"

So it was working. People were noticing. "I just decided to make an effort. I've felt a little schlumpy lately—"

"Not surprising after what happened with They-who-shan't-be-named," interrupted Rachel.

"Boo, hiss," Anna murmured, her eyes narrowing.

God bless her friends. "So I got my hair done—"

"Revenge haircut," Rachel said, nodding. "Love it."

"And decided to eat better and exercise more."

"What are you doing to exercise?" Toni asked.

"I'm trying to take a good walk each day or get on my exercise bike when the weather's not great. I find it a good opportunity to listen to podcasts or worship music or pray. And when I'm at work I look for excuses to walk instead of phoning people, and I think it's working. I'm not puffing as much as I was, and I've lost four pounds already."

"You go, girl." Rachel clinked her glass.

"And it's funny, I think I'm feeling better in my head too. Happier, even."

"That's those endorphins working," Jackie said.

Toni nodded. "Joel always says that. He goes for a run each morning and says it's great for clearing his mind." She smiled suddenly. "Maybe you and him could go running sometime."

Yeah, no thanks.

"I've heard running helps you lose more weight more quickly," Anna said.

"But I don't want to run," Serena protested. "It hurts your knees, doesn't it?"

"Are you a grandma?" Rachel asked. "Come on. The time to do it is now, and not when you've had two babies. Things down there are never *quite* the same, if you know what I mean." She shot Toni a quick glance. "But having a baby is awesome, okay?"

"Uh huh," Toni murmured. But her smile said she was relaxing into Friday night ease.

The evening continued with food, more stories, jokes and laughs. Serena's new pasta bake recipe was met with the appropriate manner of appreciation, which was a relief, as it wasn't as laden with fat and carbs as she'd usually done in the past. But she'd always loved to try new dishes out on her friends, inviting them over frequently to taste her latest creations, even sometimes dressing the house with appropriately themed decorations. Maybe it was her natural gifting that her workplace further cultivated. Or maybe it was that cooking a meal, preparing food, relaxed her. Cooking for one just wasn't the same. Opening her home regularly to her friends and church family was like a gift of love to them. Hope might have avoided the gatherings, saying they were boring, but John and Angela had said she had a gift of hospitality. She'd always shrugged that off because she'd just found it fun.

She glanced at Toni, meeting her smile with one of her own. It was good to see Toni coming out of her shell more. Although she remained a little shy at times, refusing to share much about her past, they gleaned enough to learn she was a talented artist. Toni even showed some pictures of some of her work on Instagram.

"You're really talented," Anna said, scrolling through Toni's phone.

"Do you sell your work?" Jackie asked.

"I try." Toni shrugged. "I have an Etsy account, but I don't do much with it."

"I do freelance web design and can set you up with a website if you like," Jackie offered.

Rachel nodded. "She's awesome. She set one up for my husband's construction business and it's doubled our leads."

"Thanks. I'll need to think about it." Toni patted her stomach. "I don't want to get too carried away, not until I know how things will go in upcoming months."

"Is Joel going to be your birth partner?" Rachel asked. "Damian was mine, and I gotta admit it was fun to see him squirm. Like, hello, this is all your fault mister, so you might as well be there for the gory parts, too."

Toni's nose wrinkled amid the laughter. "I, um, haven't really thought about it."

"Well, you might want to sign up for classes soon," Anna advised. "How much longer until you're due?"

"Four weeks, maybe?"

"Then I'd do it straightaway. Like, see if you can get in next week," Anna said. "I can ask for you if you like."

"Um, sure."

The night concluded with the swapping of emails and phone numbers, and Serena's heart bloomed to see her friends adopting Toni into their group.

Maybe spending time focused on others was good for her soul.

And, like a cactus blossoming in the desert, maybe the joy of catching up with her friends was proof that joy could still be found after tears of rain.

IT WAS NUDGING ten by the time Joel completed the men's breakfast, something which ensured he'd need to double the length of his run later in an attempt to work off the croissants and bacon. But the house was silent, something which knotted concern, as he tapped gently on his sister's door.

"You in there?"

The door swung open, and Toni emerged, still rubbing sleep grit from her eyes.

"Good morning."

"Morning." She yawned then stumbled across to the bathroom.

He moved to the kitchen to boil the kettle and had just finished making her a cup of tea when she returned. Her movements were slow and renewed that strange mix of compassion for her and anger at the man who'd left her this way. Joel might be a Christian, and even shared about forgiveness this morning, but sometimes forgiveness felt miles away.

"Is that for me?" she asked, pointing at the cup of tea, then, at his nod, pounced on it. "Best brother ever."

"You know it." He studied her as she sipped her tea. With her oversized t-shirt, her hair loose and that sleepy look on her face she could be the same Antonia of ten years ago, grateful for small gifts like hair elastics, a new book, or the chance to go out with friends.

"Good time last night?" He'd heard the car late last night, but when she hadn't come in to his study, he'd thought it best to treat her as the adult she was. So, rather than make her feel like she needed to give him an explanation for the late hour arrival home, he'd stayed in the study finishing off his message for this morning.

"Yeah." She took another sip, then looked over at him. "I met some of Serena's friends from church at her place, and she cooked us some Italian food. It was fun."

"Nice food?"

"Delicious. She's a really good cook, but I couldn't fit much in, unfortunately." She patted her belly. "I might've drunk a bit too much, which is why I had to get up to the bathroom so many times last night and didn't sleep too well."

Drunk? Okay, so he didn't want to do the judgy thing, or go

all over-protective big brother, but Serena had got his pregnant sister drunk?

"Wait, you don't think I was drinking alcohol?"

It wouldn't be the first time.

Apparently he hadn't blanked his face in time, for her expression twisted into hurt. "I don't know what you take me for. I'm pregnant, and I haven't had a drop to drink since I found out. Anyway, I'm not like that anymore. How long until you believe me?"

"I'm sorry." There went his brownie points from earlier.

She shook her head. "Serena's not like that, anyway. I can't believe—"

"Forgive me. As you've pointed out more than once I can be a doofus."

"That's for sure," she muttered.

"So, uh, anything else to say about last night?" Redirect, redirect.

"The girls were really nice, although Rachel might've over-shared a little about what to expect as a new mom." Her nose wrinkled. "But she's pretty funny. I haven't laughed like that for —" She paused. "Not for years."

Gladness filled his heart. Toni really needed some good friends, and it looked like maybe this prayer was being answered. "So how is everyone?"

Toni's earlier offense faded as she smirked at him. "By everyone you really mean how is Serena."

"No." Yes. Joel's neck heated. "Not necessarily," he amended.

"Ha." Toni eyed him, her sardonic expression softening to thoughtfulness. "Did you know her parents live in India?"

"No." How could he know? He'd barely exchanged more than a dozen words with Serena.

"They're missionaries there, teaching."

"Really?" Huh. As much as he loved his job, one of his dreams was to one day work overseas.

"She mentioned she might see them, but with her new job, who knows?" She put her cup on the counter. "Her house is so cute, just two bedrooms, but so sweet, just perfect for her, with old-fashioned pane windows, a cute flower garden out the front and a fancy birdfeeder. She said the house used to be her grandmother's."

"So she's got roots here."

"Mmm." Toni studied him. "She just got a big promotion at work this week. She's now the resort's event coordinator, and she'll have an assistant, rather than be one."

"Good for her." That must have been why she looked so excited on Wednesday night. It certainly hadn't been because of him. He shifted to the sink and rinsed out the empty cups, rolling his eyes at himself. Seriously? Since when had he gotten so self-interested?

"Do…do you think we could have her come over for a meal sometime?"

"Uh, sure." He could do that. He could pretend this woman didn't disconcert him. Couldn't he?

"Okay. I'll invite her for lunch."

"Not tomorrow," he reminded her. "We've been invited to John and Angela's, remember?"

"Fine. I'll invite her here next week."

"You can, but I won't be here. I'm running a service at the Golden Elms retirement community in the afternoon. I'm going straight there after church."

"That's perfect. If you're not here, then she'll be sure to come."

Toni's laugh filled the room, but somehow weighed down Joel's heart. He didn't like being someone others avoided. Maybe he should try harder to fix things.

"Oh, and I told her you'd be available to take her running sometime," she said, switching on the kettle.

"You what?"

She shrugged. "She's on a fitness kick, and I said you'd be happy enough to take her running." Her eyes rounded. "You would like to spend time with her, wouldn't you?"

Maybe. "You know I don't date women in the church I minister in."

"Remind me why again?"

"Because it never works out. You saw what happened with Mel."

"That was years ago," she said, pouring boiling water over her green tea bag. "And you were dumb then."

"Excuse me?"

"You were younger, thought you knew everything. You're lucky your friends still talk to you," she said, eyeing him over her teacup.

"Wow."

"I know! Wow." Her laughter contained mockery. "But then, as someone we both know and love likes to say, you shouldn't let decisions made when you're young and dumb stop you from making good choices now."

He studied her, not sure if she was mocking him for what he'd said in the past to her. She stared back, and he figured it wasn't some dig at his over-zealous self. "Good choices like—"

"Like going after Serena. Did you know she's just broken up with her boyfriend? So now is the perfect time to start proving you're not the Dumbo she might've thought you were, so by the time she's ready to date you're looking pretty good."

"You sound like you've really thought this through."

She shrugged, taking another sip of her tea. "I'm not just a pretty face."

"Obviously." He leaned against the kitchen counter, arms crossed. "I'm still not sure why you care so much."

"About you and Serena?"

He dipped his chin.

Toni placed her teacup on the counter and stuck her hand

on her hip. "She's about the only person I've heard you mention since we've arrived."

"That's not true." Her arched brow drew further protest. "I've talked about others."

"Not the kind of others who are attractive available women. You've never mentioned Anna except in relation to Serena. And I've never once heard you mention Jackie."

"Who?"

She chuckled. "But you do seem to care about what Serena thinks, which makes me think you might even like her. And if that's the case, then this might help her see you in a better light."

"You really think running will help with that?"

At her nod, he blew out a breath.

"She doesn't strike me as a runner."

"But she wants to get fit. Look, I'm just saying, you need to make a better impression than what you have so far. And your job is to help people, right?"

"Yes, but—"

"And if you want to help her, then why not start there?"

"I don't think you understand. She doesn't seem to like me."

"So get her to like you. I thought you were supposed to be a man of faith."

"Wow. Look who's on fire today."

"Somebody needs to tell it to you straight."

He chuckled and drew her into a hug. "Love you."

"Get off me, you big doofus."

But the way she laughed filled his heart with ease. Maybe coming here was an answer to prayer after all.

Toni's words about Serena chased him through the rest of the day, as he did laundry, as he prepared for his message at Golden Elms, even as he took a late afternoon run and kept his eyes peeled for a certain Sunday school teacher who might also be taking advantage of this awesome weather. When he returned, without sighting her once, the little thread of disappointment suggested he might've taken his sister's words a little too close to heart.

Would it be a problem if he spent time with Serena? She was hardly likely to reciprocate, so it was probably safe enough to see if there might be any interest there. Maybe he should see how things went at church tomorrow.

"Now, do you think you'll remember that address?"

"Absolutely. Maple Street. Number ten." Joel smiled at the sweet elderly lady, his appreciation for her invitation to dinner threaded with relief. He'd received a few invitations from congregation members wishing to welcome him with meals and finding excuses for avoiding those invitations from single ladies was growing more difficult. Maybe he should just be open about his no-dating congregation members policy after all. Still, Rose was harmless enough. "Thank you. I'm looking forward to it."

"Oh, you're very welcome." Rose smiled her pink-lipsticked smile. "I'll have to see if I can get that granddaughter of mine to come and visit. I think you'd like her."

Oh. He forced a smile as she patted her arm and moved to talk to someone else, his attention falling on Serena. His entire body tensed, then tensed some more as her gaze lifted to connect with his.

He tried for a smile which fell as she glanced away, her own expression pleating into anxiety as she glanced at a middle-aged couple.

"You okay here?" Angela asked, moving beside him.

He nodded. "Just wondering who that couple is." He motioned to the graying pair.

"Ah." Angela followed his gaze and winced. "That is unfortunate. I thought they were away a little longer."

"Okay…"

"Oh! I didn't mean it to sound like that. No, Eric and Dawn are nice, but they're the parents of Serena's ex, and if history is anything to go by, I'm going to bet Dwight hasn't told them about the breakup."

"Dwight was Serena's boyfriend?"

"You know Serena, then?" she asked, glancing up at him.

"I've met her a few times." Without leaving her with one good impression yet. "Toni is a fan."

"We're all fans of Serena," Angela said softly. "She wouldn't want to hear this yet, but it was a good thing for her when she broke things off with Dwight. He proved to be a liar and a cheat. But I don't know if she's quite ready to explain things to Dawn yet."

She moved as if to go and interrupt them, when an elderly woman blocked her path. Angela glanced at him. "Joel, would you—?"

"Sure."

He threaded his way through knots of conversation and drew near Serena. The older man crossed his arms as the woman hugged Serena, then brushed non-existent dust from Serena's jacket.

"Welcome back," Serena's voice was soft. "I'm glad you had a good trip."

"Tampa Bay is awful in July. I don't know why people like it there. So hot and humid. But never mind that. How are you, Serena? Our boy hasn't mentioned you much in recent months, Serena. How are things between you two?"

Serena took a deep breath. "He hasn't told you?"

"Told us what?"

"We...we've broken up."

"What?" His mother looked shocked. "I can't believe it!"

"Yes, well, I've had some trouble believing a few things myself."

As the congregation filtered around them, Serena was

pummeled with questions from the couple, drawing Joel's compassion, forcing him to step in. "Excuse me, I'm sorry to interrupt." He flashed them a smile. "I'm Joel Wakefield, the new assistant pastor. It's a pleasure to meet you."

Eric and Dawn introduced themselves, and Joel shook their hands, noticing from his peripheral vision that Serena had inched away. Was it because of him or because she was relieved at his intervention? "I'm sorry to have to steal Miss Williamson away for a moment. She's needed downstairs."

"Really?" Serena asked.

He nodded. Well, she would be, as soon as he figured out what he needed her for.

They made their excuses and he escorted her downstairs, catching Toni's widened eyes as she talked with Anna. He tilted his head to Serena and his sister smiled. Maybe she'd get the silent memo and come join them.

He found an empty classroom and opened the door, but church protocol meant he didn't close it. "Are you okay?"

She crossed her arms. "Why would you ask that?"

"Because Angela thought you might not be."

She stared at him, then bit her lip. "Did you hear all that?"

"I heard enough. So," his voice softened, "are you okay?"

"I will be, but I just wasn't expecting to see them. They were supposed to be gone all summer." Her shoulders hitched. "And surprise, surprise, Dwight hadn't told them we'd broken up, leaving it to me, as usual. So you can imagine how much fun that was to break that news to them."

"I'm sorry."

Her gaze met his for a second then slid away. Regret at what he'd once said kneaded his soul. What could he do to make it up to her?

"Hey," he waited until she looked at him. "For what it's worth, a man who can't man up to tell his parents the truth isn't someone who you should want in your life."

Her eyes shimmered, and she bit her lip.

Aww. He didn't want to make her cry. Why was he so bad at talking to her? "And on a completely different note, I wanted to say thanks for inviting Toni to your place the other day. She had a ball."

She nodded stiffly, but her shoulders crept down, losing that rigidity from before. "It was fun."

"She mentioned you got a promotion at work."

Now her features eased too. "Yeah, that was unexpected."

"Congratulations."

"Thank you." Her smile was sweetly shy, uncertain.

The room filled with something almost tangible, something he sure wasn't used to feeling, especially with someone in his congregation. Maybe she felt it too, for her gaze dropped, and she inched back.

"So you mentioned something about me being needed down here?"

Oh. Right. That. "Yeah, um, I didn't really want to get you here under false pretenses—"

Her eyebrows rose.

"No, I didn't mean it to sound like that." He rubbed his forehead. Doofus was right. "Anyway, I wanted to talk to you, because, uh, Toni mentioned something about how you've taken up running."

Her forehead wrinkled. "Oh, no. I'm just trying to get fitter, that's all. I'm pretty sure that I'm only a walker, not a runner."

"Well, if you decide that needs to change, I'm happy to give you some tips." He shrugged. "I'm no expert, but I've found running to be a great way to stay sane. It's good for my mental health."

She nodded. "I've found that too. There's something so calming when I go walking, breathing in the fresh air, enjoying the lake and trees. It's great for dealing with my worries."

"Yeah, but you'll find there's even less time to worry over things when running." He winked.

Whoa. Winking wasn't exactly him. Especially with pretty girls in church. He'd done that precisely…never.

And judging from the way she stepped away with a startled expression, maybe she wasn't used to it either.

Man. Was he now supposed to apologize for winking? "So, um, maybe let me know if you want to go sometime."

"Go where?" Toni's voice intruded.

He swiveled to the door where his sister stood, with Anna and another woman he thought might be called Rachel standing behind her. Great. How long had he had an audience for?

"We were just talking about running," he explained.

Serena took another step away from him. "That's all."

Anna pushed past his sister and moved to Serena. "I'm glad we found you," Anna said. "We tried to distract them as long as possible, and you know Aunty Dawn. Once she starts, she never seems to stop."

Her friend nodded. "She kept asking questions. It felt like the Spanish Inquisition."

"Are you okay?" Anna asked, rubbing Serena on the shoulder.

Serena nodded, pushing her hair behind her ear. "I didn't really know what to say."

"Good thing Joel swooped in when he did," Toni said, giving him a wink.

Serena nodded, her gaze tentative with him still, before she refocused on her friends. "I just hated having to tell them about Dwight."

"I'm sorry, but he's always been a dweeb," the woman-possibly-named-Rachel said. "I didn't mind telling them exactly what had gone down."

Serena gasped, while Toni covered her smile with her hand. "Rachel, you didn't!"

"Come on, we all know he's always been their golden-haired boy and thinks the sun shines out of his," she shot Joel a look then said, "you-know-what, so I'm happy to report that now the illusion has been shattered," she said smugly.

"You told them everything?" Serena asked.

"Honey, you weren't the one who messed up. Dwight did that all by himself."

Serena winced. "I still feel like such a fool," she whispered. "I don't know if I can ever trust a man again, let alone trust my own judgment."

Rachel squeezed her shoulders affectionately. "You'll be fine. Just give yourself time." She turned to him. "Hey, thanks for helping out before."

"No problem." He studied Serena. "You'll be okay?"

She nodded. "Thank you."

He caught his sister's running arms movement. "Oh, and if you're interested in running sometime, let me know."

"Thanks." Her gaze didn't meet his, seeming to fall on his shoulder. "I, um, I'm still adjusting to new work responsibilities, so I'll keep that in mind."

He nodded, willing his disappointment not to show in his face. He knew a blow-off when he heard one.

"Well, I'll leave you ladies to it. Have a nice lunch." He motioned to Toni who nodded, then gave the other women a quick smile before departing.

"Good for you," Toni murmured, punching him on the arm, before pausing to stretch her back.

"He's *so* nice," Anna's voice traveled from inside the room.

"Such a honey," agreed Rachel, drawing Toni's muffled laughter.

"Aww, come on, don't look like that, Serena." Anna's voice again.

Look like what? Why didn't she like him? He moved to leave

—obviously eavesdropping wasn't doing him any favors—but Toni refused to budge. She was clearly enjoying this too much.

"Not all men are evil, Rena. Besides, I'm allowed to appreciate a finely crafted specimen, aren't I?" Rachel laughed.

"But not him. He's taken, Rachel," Serena finally said.

"Taken?" Rachel scoffed. "By the church maybe."

Taken? Toni mouthed, her brows raised. "Are you taken?" she asked, when they reached fresh air, a teasing smile on her face.

He ignored her and gestured to where John and Angela waited. "Let's go to lunch."

CHAPTER 8

"Are you serious? This is amazing."

For the first time since stepping into Toni and Joel's place Serena felt at ease. Sure, she'd been relieved to know he wasn't going to be here, but there was still something unsettling about the man, something that had stirred in that moment in the Sunday school room a week ago that set her on edge. Yes, she'd appreciated his help in extracting her from an awkward situation, but she couldn't help feeling there was something wrong about a married man who gave her long looks, then had the nerve to wink at her. If he wasn't a church minister, she'd think he was flirting. So the fact he *was* a church minister—and married!—made her back away, unsure.

Although she was sure about one thing. Okay, make that two. One: she never wanted to stir up feelings and put a relationship at risk from too-long looks. And two: she liked Toni, and wanted to be her friend, even though Toni's connection with Joel made her wary. Which was why it was safe to be here today when he wasn't, enjoying a simple lunch of sandwiches, and looking at Toni's paintings that lined the halls and living room, paintings that held a wondrous sense of peace. "These are truly beautiful, Toni."

"I'm glad you like them."

Serena studied one of Toni's pictures, the way the path through gold-lit trees begged her to journey on, the calmness that begged her to pause and be still. Maybe her mental health wouldn't require exercise if she could stare at this picture all day.

"It's Joel's favorite too," Toni said, sliding her another of those looks Serena couldn't quite interpret.

"It's really striking, Toni. You're really talented. Have you ever sold your work to art galleries?"

Toni's laughter held an edge. "That'd be nice, but no. I used to sell at the occasional weekend markets in the city, but I haven't done anything recently." She traced a frame. "I haven't painted much recently. Not since…"

Serena waited, but when Toni didn't say anything more, moved to stand in front of a deceptively simple picture of a maple tree. "I love this. It's so vibrant. It looks like it's alive."

"It's yours, then." Toni shrugged carelessly at Serena's protest. "I love to paint and have so many canvases just taking up room. I'd be happy for you to have it somewhere you'll enjoy it."

"Oh, but—"

"Here." She unhooked it from the wall and placed it next to Serena's bag. "It's yours. No arguments."

Serena thanked her and Toni motioned toward the back room where they could watch the lake sparkle in the afternoon sunshine. As they sipped tall glasses of peach iced tea, she noticed for the first time that Toni didn't wear a wedding ring. Maybe her hands had swollen during pregnancy, like Miranda's had during her pregnancy with the twins. But then, she'd never seen Joel wearing a ring, either, which seemed kind of strange for a church minister whose looks and age meant he probably was used to fending off lots of ladies. Maybe he'd lost it or something.

"So, um, last week, it didn't sound like you were wanting to take up Joel's offer about running."

Serena shrugged. "I appreciate the offer, but I don't want to take up his time."

"Hmm." Toni eyed her.

"My job is super busy at the moment," she hedged.

"Uh huh." Toni shot her another look. "Or you don't want to spend time with him. You know he's sorry about what he said that first day."

"That's got nothing to do with it." Okay, maybe it still rankled that he thought she was plain, but his opinion really shouldn't matter. And the fact that it *did* still secretly sting was something she knew would not improve by constantly thinking about it. It was like the situation with Dwight and Hope. If she stayed busy then she wouldn't notice the bruise in her heart. Ostriches with their heads in the sand had long been the birds she could most understand.

Toni put her glass on the patio table. "So, last weekend at your place, Anna mentioned something about going to birthing classes."

"That's right." Phew. A change of subject. "Have you booked in yet?"

"I want to. But there's just one thing." Toni winced. "I actually have a huge favor to ask you."

"Sure. What is it?"

"Um, see, I don't know too many people here, and I…I want to know if you would maybe consider being my support person for the birth."

What? Serena swirled the last ice cube of her iced tea. "That's such an honor, but I don't know anything about having a baby."

"You don't need to," Toni assured. "I don't know anything about having a baby either—well," her smile was tense, "obviously I know more things *now* than what they told us in high school."

And that was a topic she had little wish to pursue. "But, uh, shouldn't Joel be?"

"Joel?" Toni laughed. "We might be close, but I think that's a step too far, even for him."

But he was Toni's husband, wasn't he? Didn't he have a husbandly obligation to attend the birth of his first child? The small measure of respect she'd recently found for him dwindled as Toni kept apologizing for him.

"...doesn't really do blood and guts. He may look tough and strong, but really, he's a marshmallow on the inside."

"Oh." That was generous of Toni. Serena could just imagine what Rachel would have to say about that, so it probably wasn't any wonder that Toni hadn't asked for Rachel's help. "What about Angela?"

"She's nice, but I, um, don't feel as close with her as I do you." Her cheeks pinked. "I kinda think that you're my closest friend."

Her heart pricked. How could she refuse? "What would it involve?"

"When I called, they told me that the support person only needs to come to my birthing classes with me, and then try and remind me of that stuff when I'm in labor." Toni's bent lips held more grit than joy. "I'm told women have a tendency to forget some of the information when they're in massive pain."

Serena hesitated. "And there's no-one else, no other family member you'd rather have?"

Toni shook her head. "Nope, no-one. My parents are gone. I have an aunt and some cousins in Alberta, but no other family. But if you don't want to do it, that's okay. It's just that the doctor said I should get to classes soon."

"When are the classes?"

"Tuesday nights, for the next three weeks, at the local hospital. Joel's got some youth Bible study or something that night, so he can't take me anyway."

Bible study over helping his wife? It didn't make sense. But Toni's look of rejection was something Serena understood. She nodded. "I'm free on Tuesday evenings. You'll have to forgive me if I seem reluctant. I've just never had any experience with childbirth so I don't know what to do."

Toni's smile tweaked into wryness. "That makes two of us."

Serena drew in a breath. "Okay, then. Count me in."

"Really? Oh, thanks, Serena. You're the best." Toni's face grew more animated than Serena remembered seeing before.

Maybe this was what God wanted her to do. Good things. New things. Helping others. Focusing on them, rather than the insidious words that still circled her days and nights. *Fat. Plain. Without ambition.* She shivered. "Let me know what time it starts Tuesday. I'll come pick you up, okay?"

MONDAY PASSED IN HOUSEWORK, groceries and a four kilometer walk. Tuesday was equally non-eventful, consisting of dealing with meetings and emails. She chewed her lip as she drove to Toni's on Tuesday night. She hoped she wouldn't encounter Joel. It still seemed unreasonable for him not to attend Toni's birthing classes, but maybe he was trying to impress John and show he was doing all he could to fit into his job. He'd be at the birth, surely.

Besides, it felt like an honor for Toni to ask Serena to assist her. Even if she felt like she'd be as useful as a wickless candle. Apart from Rachel and Miranda she'd never really known anyone who had given birth, and even Miranda's experience had been far away in Vancouver, and Serena had only met the boys when they were a few days old. She and Miranda had never been close, and had never discussed personal matters like periods, let alone childbirth, in any detail.

The door opened as soon as she stepped on the porch. "Hi!" Toni sang out, before commencing a slow waddle toward Serena's car. Serena opened the passenger door to Toni's protest of, "I'm not an invalid," and she was relieved to see no sign of Joel as she pulled away.

They chatted lightly on the way before pulling up outside the small community hospital.

The evening proved illuminating. After Dr. Strauss and the midwives gave a brief overview of the birthing process, they learned about and then practiced some of the exercises helpful for engaging the baby's head and body into the best position for birth. There was opportunity to ask questions at the end, all of which really seemed to make time fly.

As they drove home Toni gave a long sigh. "Already I'm feeling far more confident. Thanks so much for coming with me."

"It was interesting." Although a little alarming. Even if she didn't already have Godly standards, watching birthing videos was a great deterrent for the consequences of the kinds of activities Dwight and Hope had apparently engaged in.

Nausea churned. Thank God Hope wasn't pregnant. Imagine if she was…

"Hey, um, I was wondering, do you think we could maybe go walking together some time?" Toni asked. "The nurse said that's a great way to get the baby's head to engage, and it's been so hot I don't want to be pregnant a second longer than necessary."

"Sure. But I have three weddings to run this weekend, so I won't be free until next Monday." Serena pulled onto Toni's street.

"That'd be great."

What wasn't so great was seeing Joel's truck parked in front of Toni's house.

"Looks like Joel's mentoring thing finished early," Toni said, undoing her seatbelt. "Want to come in?"

And try not to show her frustration with the man who should've been at the clinic with his wife? "No thanks. I have a big day tomorrow and need to get home."

The door opened, and Joel's jean-clad self strolled down to the car, helping Toni from the front seat. He ducked down to look inside. "Thanks, Serena."

She nodded, tamping down the traitorous desire to return his smile.

"Hey, I really appreciate you helping Toni this way. I owe you."

He sure did.

"Will I, uh, we see you on Sunday?"

Suddenly she was very glad to have a full weekend. "Nope." She revved the engine and peered over her shoulder as if to reverse.

"Oh. Okay." He closed the passenger door with a gentle thud, and she flashed a tight smile at Toni before driving away.

Next Monday she slept in, the challenges of three large weddings having drained her of energy, and something she definitely wouldn't be putting the staff at Muskoka Shores through again. But when one of the weddings had needed to be moved, and Joanne's original arrangements had seen a double booking that they'd managed to switch to Friday instead, it felt a blessing that they'd managed to get out of this weekend alive.

She ignored her house-cleaning—it barely mattered, not when she was the only one who saw the dust anyway—and donned her athletic gear, appreciating the fact her stomach wasn't looking nearly as rotund as three weeks ago. Maybe people wouldn't mistake her and Toni for two pregnant ladies out for a stroll today.

Two hours later, she and Toni stumbled to Toni's door, Toni insisting Serena come inside for some water.

"It's only right, having insisted we take that short cut that wasn't short at all," Toni managed between panted breaths.

"Are you sure you're okay?" Serena checked, as Toni unlocked the door and gestured for Serena to come inside. "I don't want you having the baby today."

"I'll be fine."

"Just as well. We still have two more classes—oh."

Joel eased around a corner, towel around his neck, dressed in shorts and a tee that showed off a sculpted chest, his skin glowing like he'd just stepped from the shower. "Hey, Serena."

She managed a smile but didn't quite meet his eyes as she mumbled a hello.

"Good walk?" He lifted the towel to dry his hair, his biceps bulging.

Okay, she really didn't need to be here. "I better go."

"What about your drink?" Toni said, a glass in hand that she held out to Serena.

Great. She drained it in one long swallow.

Joel glanced at Toni. "You look tired."

"Thanks." Toni wrinkled her nose at him.

"The shower is free if you like."

Toni nodded, which seemed to be Serena's cue to place her glass near the sink, mutter a farewell and leave.

She was moving down the path when her name was called. No. She did not want to talk to him. What kind of man couldn't be bothered taking his wife to birthing class? And call her petty but his plain comment still rankled inside. There were a million things she'd rather do than talk to him. Like ironing. Or cleaning out her chimney. Or having root canal therapy.

"Serena," he called again, jogging barefoot to her side. "Hey, thanks again for helping Toni."

"No problem," she muttered, still not looking at him. Yes, okay, she was meant to be a Christian, but some people made it very hard.

"Hey, can I speak to you a moment, please?"

She sighed. What was it with the Wakefields and their constant need for help?

Maybe he heard her sigh, for he bit his lip.

"What is it?" she finally asked.

"Look, I just wanted to thank you for taking Toni to the birthing class last week and doing this today. I know she's getting a little concerned with her due date coming up so soon, so it's great to see her more confident with what's going to happen."

Serena shrugged. "I don't mind."

"Are you sure? Sometimes I get the impression you can't wait to get away."

Because that was true. "I like spending time with Toni."

"Just not with me."

Like that was something she could just come out and admit. "I guess I'm just a little confused."

"About what?" He shoved his hands in his pockets.

"I just don't understand why you can't be there," she finally said, looking up at him.

"I'm not very good with…some things." His cheeks reddened slightly.

Serena's hands found her hips. "Neither am I, but I try not to let that stop me, especially when someone asks for my help." She lifted her chin. "Was there something else you wanted?"

He studied her, his eyes dark blue and searching.

No. She would *not* notice the color of his eyes, that they held dark depths and silver glints that rivaled the lake she could see sparkling beyond the property. She took a step back.

"Yes."

"What?" She nearly winced. She'd never speak to John or Angela like this. She'd rarely spoken so tersely to anyone in her life. But this man seemed to step on her toes all the time and never apologize.

He ran a hand through his hair. "I, uh, want to know why you don't seem to like me much."

Really? Wow. "Well, I'd like to know the same."

"What do you mean?"

"What have I done to make you dislike me?"

"I don't understand."

"Yeah, well I don't understand how someone who's all about caring for others can be so rude as to call a person plain."

HE SHOULD HAVE KNOWN this would come back to bite him. Apparently it wouldn't matter how many times he apologized, she was not going to let those words go.

"I'm really sorry, Serena. I never meant to hurt you."

From the crossed arms and ice-green glare it was obvious he had.

"It's just when we were in the city Toni had all sorts of strange and exotic friends, people like her in the art world, fake friends and sophisticated types. We moved here and the first friend she made was so different, so normal and unpretentious, it was a surprise. So I'm sorry if I gave you some snooty impression."

"If?" Her eyebrows rose.

"That," he quickly amended, "I gave you the wrong impression. I didn't mean it. I can be a doofus sometimes. Please forgive me."

Serena studied him, her green eyes seeming to probe his sincerity before she slowly nodded. "Okay, fine. I forgive you."

Some of the snags in his heart unfurled. "Thank you. I hate that I've gotten off on the wrong foot with you, especially as you're someone Toni cares about. You need to know how much she values your friendship."

She shrugged. "I like her too."

"I...I love Toni very much. We don't have much family, so our friends become very important to us. Some of her friends have proved less than faithful in the past. I don't want to do anything that might cause a problem between you and her."

"Neither do I," Serena admitted.

"So, truce? Please, can we start over and be friends?" He held out his hand.

She looked at it doubtfully, and his stomach grew tense at her delay. She had that many reservations?

She sighed, and finally clasped his hand.

Spark-filled sensation rippled across his skin. But judging from the way she quickly slid her palm from his, maybe she didn't feel the same way.

She might've agreed to be friends, but he sensed it would take more for her to fully trust him. And who could blame her, especially now he knew just how hurt she'd been?

Conscious now of neighbors who had observed their long conversation—welcome to the goldfish bowl of church ministry life—he lifted a hand and said goodbye. Maybe trying to make amends with Serena wasn't going to be easy as he'd hoped. Still, a promise was a promise...

HIS WEEK PASSED IN MEETINGS, people, and coffees. He'd never known just how caffeinated church ministry could be until he'd realized how much time was spent talking with people. And while teens might be happier sharing by doing activities like (literally) climbing the walls, older people who weren't so fond of rock-climbing usually found it easier to talk over cups of tea and coffee. Of course, it usually wasn't just coffee, but all the little extra calories that added up along the way: cookies, slices, Timbits, cakes. Even the older men at the Men's Shed with whom he started connecting over carpentry and restored engines weren't averse to carb-rich treats. It all made his need for exercise very real.

He'd briefly seen Serena on his lakeside run on Tuesday morning, but she'd looked focused as she walked, so he hadn't interrupted her. He'd seen her again that night after she'd dropped Toni home following the birthing class. The mentoring with the boys meant he'd pulled into the driveway at the same time as Serena had, and while she didn't stay, the fact she at least made eye contact and offered a smile that looked half genuine felt like a win.

On Friday night he'd been left rattling around the house, wondering why his antisocial sister seemed to have more friends than he, a question he wondered about again when Matt video-called.

"Dude! Long time no see."

"You know how it is," Matt said. "Busy, busy, busy."

Matt's job often took him on business trips around the world. "Where have you been lately?"

Matt filled him in: discussions with investors in Vancouver, Seattle, and San Francisco, before swinging across to Dallas and Atlanta.

Joel nodded. He'd seen some of Matt's pics on Facebook. "How's church?"

"Not quite the same without you."

"Good to know people miss me."

"How is Toni getting on?" Matt asked.

"She's out. Again."

"Really?"

"I know, right? I'm as surprised as you." Matt was almost as antisocial as his sister.

But judging from Matt's frown he might have the wrong idea. He'd better clarify. "She's out with some friends. A woman called Serena."

Matt's brow cleared. "That's good."

Huh. Matt had never been very forthcoming about his feelings concerning Toni, but that response suggested his feelings ran deeper than Joel realized.

"So tell me more about Serena. Is she one of Toni's usual crowd?"

"No, you couldn't find somebody more different. She's a Sunday school teacher at our church, the events coordinator at Muskoka Shores Resort—"

"That's the fancy one where Dan Walton got married, right?"

Joel nodded. "Everyone keeps wondering if he'll be back in church here before the season begins again, but I'm guessing a honeymoon might take priority."

"Maybe." Matt smiled.

"Anyway, it'll be good if he does make it to a service. I've been told his wife—she's part of that Heartsong group whose music we've used—might even sing."

"Cool."

But as cool as that was, he kinda wanted to keep talking about a certain Sunday School teacher. "Anyway, Serena is genuine, and seems to have really taken Toni under her wing. Toni really likes her."

"Uh huh." Matt smiled.

"What?"

"Is Toni the only one who really likes her?"

Joel leaned back in his chair. "It wouldn't matter if I did, you know that I have a policy about these kinds of things, and I don't date women in the church I'm part of."

"So that's a yes, then."

"Dude, don't go putting words in my mouth. Even if I did like her, she isn't too fond of me, so there you go."

"Why?"

"Just something dumb I did."

"This sounds like a good story."

"Not one I'm proud of." He admitted his stupid initial judgement and how Serena had overheard.

Matt's grin widened. "Good to see the boot on the other foot for a change."

"What do you mean?"

"That you have to make the effort for a change, instead of having all the women chasing you."

"I'm not chasing her," Joel scoffed.

"Maybe you should."

Joel crossed his arms. "Explain."

Matt's brow raised. "It's been a long time since I've seen you interested in a girl. Not since Mel."

Joel's jaw tensed.

"She did a number on you," Matt continued. "You need to move on."

"She's exactly the reason why I don't date now."

"Yeah. And that's exactly the reason why you should. You shouldn't let someone else's actions color the way you see all women. Maybe this Serena woman is girlfriend material—and hey, if she's involved in Sunday school and is looking after your sister, then it could be a good fit. But even if she's not, the longer you let Mel's actions influence you, the longer you're stuck in the past. Anyway, what better way to know if a person is a genuine believer than what you see them do in church?"

Huh. Maybe Matt had a point.

The sound of the door opening suggested Toni was home. "Hey, I'd better go. I think Toni's back."

"Say hi to her for me."

"Will do." He ended the call and found his sister in the kitchen, holding a plastic-covered plate.

"How was it?" he asked.

"We watched a movie," she said, offering him the plate. "Look, leftovers."

He unwrapped the plastic, picked up a square of the dessert

she'd brought and ate it. The caramel and shortbread with milk chocolate topping practically melted in his mouth. "That's really good."

"Serena said Angela told her it's an Aussie treat called caramel slice." She eyed him.

"What?"

"You should ask Serena out."

He coughed, releasing a spray of crumbs. "Excuse me?"

"I'm serious. I see you two together, and it's like there's this connection between you."

Please. "I don't know what you're seeing but it isn't reality."

"Mm, I wouldn't be so sure." She put the plate in the fridge.

He shook his head. "I don't date women in my church."

"Maybe you should."

Twice in one night? "Have you been talking to Matt?"

"Matt?" Her face softened. "No. How is he?"

"He's fine, says hello."

"So, has he been saying the same thing?" She grinned and drew out her phone.

"What are you doing?"

"I'm going to message Serena and—"

"And what?"

"Ooh, wouldn't you like to know?"

And with that, she disappeared to her room.

CHAPTER 9

Joel had nice legs. Serena's cheeks heated just thinking that. What a hypocrite she was. As she walked swiftly along the lake path several yards behind him, she shook her head to clear her thoughts. She really shouldn't be thinking things like this. He was Toni's husband for goodness' sake—and a church minister. She should be concentrating on the beautiful scenery this gorgeous August morning.

But it was hard to concentrate on the scenery when the man in question kept turning around to ask how she was doing, checking up on her like he thought she might faint or collapse or something.

He slowed, flashing another concerned look over his shoulder, and she motioned for him to keep going.

How exactly had things come to this?

She knew exactly how things had come to this. It had started yesterday at church when she found him and, following Toni's Friday night prompting, offered him a container of the remaining caramel and chocolate tray bake.

"Toni said you liked it, and I didn't want to eat it all,"—she'd been so good at eating healthy, and already there was less in the container than when Toni had messaged Friday night to ask if she could spare any—"so really you're doing me a favor by eating the rest."

He'd looked surprised, like Toni hadn't mentioned this to him, but accepted the plastic container with a simple thanks. She'd been prepared to leave it at that, but Toni had found her and insisted Serena come for lunch, during which Toni had somehow finally inveigled Serena into agreeing to exercise with Joel on Monday, saying she felt too tired these days to do anything much more than walk from her bedroom to the front door.

Serena's protests had been quashed, and she'd decided it was better to agree than to cause Toni any more distress. She'd been more relaxed these past weeks, maybe because the pre-natal classes had given some idea of what to expect in upcoming days, but still, Serena hadn't wanted to worry her. And she hadn't been fast enough to come up with an excuse when Toni commented about Serena and Joel both liking to exercise, and both of them having Mondays off...

The summer air held heat, and the humidity made her lungs work hard, but still, she was enjoying being out and making the most of this stretch near the shimmer of Lake Muskoka. Boats were out, birds chirped, the trees fanned above the path like a garland. Leaves glistened with stubborn dew drops, and she paused to take a photo.

Laughter drew her attention to the man on the path. "Is that the third photo you've taken?"

"It's pretty."

"Haven't you lived here all your life?" Joel asked.

Most of it. How did he know that, anyway? "Just because you live somewhere a long time doesn't mean you always notice things."

"True." His gaze deepened into that look she wasn't sure what to do with.

She pulled the brim of her baseball cap lower, cutting her view of him in half. "Are you planning on standing around all day?"

"Wow. Someone's eager."

She shrugged and moved past him. But even though she still felt some awkwardness being in his company—and wondered how Toni could possibly think this a good idea when surely there'd be questions raised over Serena spending so much time with Toni's husband—another part of her was simply glad to be outdoors.

The air was fresh, the view stunning, and the chance to breathe deeply after spending most of her time at her desk was liberating. She was getting fitter. Over the last month her healthier food choices as well as these regular lakeside walks were slowly paying off. She'd already dropped a dress size, and the combination of daily exercise and healthier meals meant she had so much more energy. Even some of her friends at work had commented on her improved looks.

She took another gulp from her water bottle. Now if she could only swallow these stupid feelings. Over the past week or so she'd realized he actually was the helpful, friendly guy Toni had always painted him to be, someone who wielded encouragement like others carried scowls. The rudeness she associated with her first meeting with him had faded—maybe she had been a little over-sensitive, after all. And while the loss of her double chin and the return of her cheekbones meant she felt prettier and less plain, she was conscious that the very thing that had caused the issue in the first place—his comment about looks—was what she still struggled with now.

It wasn't his fault he was good-looking. Good looks were such a superficial way to judge a person. She *knew* that. But when coupled with his niceness she found herself battling this stupid, stubborn attraction. Ugh. How ironic, that she, who had always despised women who were attracted to married men, was now finding herself in the very same bind. If only he wasn't so nice. Serena took a breath. *Lord, help me not to have feelings I shouldn't.*

Joel turned back to study her. "You okay?"

"Yep." Not really. But as soon as they finished here, she'd give herself a good tongue lashing, and a cold shower, and—

"You know I've been thinking."

She raised an eyebrow. "Good to know you can."

"Sassy. I like it."

He did? No. She pushed down her smile. She didn't want to encourage him. "What?"

"Maybe you should start running."

"Running? Are you serious?" She shook her head. "I barely do walking, let alone running."

"Maybe it's time you started."

"I don't think so." She swung her arms faster for emphasis.

"You know," he glanced over again, "power-walking really is something older women do."

Her jaw dropped. "You sound so sexist! And ageist."

His lips curved. "Come on. Running is going to help you get fitter much quicker than anything else."

She stared at him. Should she be offended?

"What? Toni said you were wanting to get fitter, and hey, like I said, I'm trying to stay fit too."

His mention of Toni drew her back to her resolve. No, she would not wonder about why he cared.

"Or are you happy to plateau?" He shook his head. "You seem like a have-a-go kind of woman to me."

She blinked. He thought that? Why did her silly heart insist on sweeping his words inside? Everything he said was throwing her off-kilter. She hurried on, as they passed another grandly proportioned 'cottage' that made up Cottage Country.

"You know there's a Muskoka marathon event coming up in October." Joel's words chased her. "I thought we could enter it."

"We?" She choked out the word.

"Why not?"

"I can think of a dozen reasons why, starting with I don't run."

"But you can."

"But I don't want to. Especially not a marathon." She glanced across at him. "Are you kidding?"

"Hey, there are half marathon, five kilometer and ten k options, too. You could easily manage the five."

"Are you crazy?"

"Come on. You won't know unless you try."

"I know I don't want to try," she grumbled, even as she chided herself for enjoying this easy banter.

She shouldn't do this. This was what Dwight and Hope used to do, banter that obviously had led to flirtation, then led to other things…

"What's wrong?"

"Nothing."

"You're frowning. That's not nothing."

"I, um, just remembered some stuff I need to do." Like guard her heart.

"Oh, okay. Well, want to jog back?"

"No."

He grinned, and her heart spasmed. "How about trying for me? You could do a jog-walk."

"A jog-walk?"

"Like this." He demonstrated: running slowly for ten meters, then walking, then jogging again. "You'll find it builds your stamina and makes it easier to adjust when you start to run."

"What makes you think I'm going to start running?"

He shrugged. "Like I said, you seem open to new things."

Really? What happened to people thinking she was boring, and that she'd never change? And why did something within insist on knowing why he thought about her at all? "Why do you care whether I run or not?"

She winced. That had come out more snappily than she'd wanted.

He shrugged. "Because Toni thought it was a good idea. But hey, nobody's pressuring you to do something you don't want." He jerked his chin. "I'll see you at the end."

Serena gritted her teeth. Why was she so rude? But attraction was a dangerous game, and it seemed the only way to curb it was to dampen its pull with bluntness and snark.

She waited until he'd disappeared from view before trying his stupid jog-walk idea on her return journey. *Please God, let nobody see me.* She puffed, and her knees twinged, but it wasn't as bad as she'd thought it might be.

But spending time with him was. Because she had no wish to hurt Toni the way she once had been.

THE WEEK PASSED in a blur of conferences, August weddings, and early morning walks—interspersed with occasional bouts of jogging when she thought no-one was looking. She spent time with Joel again on the next Monday, making the most of the Muskoka sunshine as she fought against Joel-appeal while she followed his instructions on finding a rhythm and learning to steady her breathing as she jogged. This wasn't about him anyway. This was about getting fitter and making the most of Muskoka in this beautiful weather.

Sunlight filtered through the golden leaves as her sneakers slapped the pavement. A smile peeked out. Look at her, trying new things, making changes. If only Hope could see her now. Her nose wrinkled. Actually, scrap that. It probably was a good thing Hope couldn't see her now. There was no need to provide a target for more of her special brand of criticism. But hey, at least she was improving. She still thought Joel's idea of registering for the Muskoka running event was dumb, but maybe he was right, and she might possibly manage the five k.

She heaved out a breath, laboring to match his pace. How unfit was she? She might die if she had to keep this up! Air sawed through her nose and lungs, her mouth tasted of blood and metal, black spots danced—

"Hey, it's not a race," he said, slowing.

She wheezed to a stop, forced herself to stand upright, wishing her puffing didn't make her sound like a steam train—how red was her face?—before muscles spasms ripping along her side drew her gasp. "Ow!"

"Do you have a stitch?"

She grimaced and nodded. "Hurts."

"Stretch it out, lean over one side then the other."

She obeyed, and the cramping slowly eased. "I need water," she managed to say between puffs.

He drew out a small bottle of water from the back of his short's waistband and handed it to her. "I haven't touched it," he promised.

Yeah, but the bottle had touched him. She shuddered, hating how her thoughts betrayed her loyalty to Toni. But surely a sip from his water bottle wouldn't hurt?

"So, are you going to register? You know you don't have to race," he said, after she handed the bottle back. "It's supposed to be a fun run."

"Fun?"

He grinned. "Hey, it's good to have challenges that motivate us, right?"

His words sparked memories of other words: *Never going to change. Never will amount to anything.* Yeah, maybe this was the motivation she needed to prove a certain someone wrong.

She gritted her teeth. "Okay, fine. But only if I can get the day off work. It's a Saturday, so there's probably a wedding scheduled, but I'll see."

"Awesome." He lifted a hand to high-five her and after a second—or five—she reluctantly slapped his hand.

No, this wasn't awesome. The challenge wasn't just about whether she could prove things to Hope or run for five kilometers or even finish. The challenge was whether she could do so with an intact heart.

THE NEXT MORNING Serena had just settled at her desk when an email pinged. Cherry, her new assistant, had requested extra shifts, Saturdays included, as she was saving for a trip to England in the new year. Guess that solved the question of whether Serena could be free to participate in the non-fun run.

A quick phone call confirmed that fact, which led to a request about whether Cherry would be willing to work on the Cranberry Festival weekend (she was), and the extent of her availability in upcoming months. Serena had just hung up when a tap came on her open door. She glanced up. Smiled. "Good morning, sir."

Mr. Jennings nodded. "Good to see you here bright and early."

"The medical conference started today, and everything seems to be going well so far."

"Good, good. I'm pleased you seem to have settled into the new role well."

The new role which wasn't actually that different from what she did before. Except for the title, pay, and acknowledgement like this. "Thank you, sir."

"I'll be keen to hear more about your ideas for future events. That's one of the benefits of hiring someone with a fresh perspective."

"I do have some ideas, sir." She briefly mentioned the marathon, the fact it would be happening nearby, bringing an influx of visitors to the area. "I'm participating in it this year, actually."

"You are? Good for you." He nodded. "Maybe we could look at having a team go in it next year, raise the profile, show we're supporting the community."

"That'd be great! Perhaps we could even see about raising money for a local charity, which might help gain more interest." His nod encouraged her to continue. "Next year I also hoped we might investigate ways of raising our support of the Cranberry Festival, especially as that closely aligns with our values concerning supporting local food and wine producers."

"Send me an email with your thoughts and we'll see what we can do."

"Yes, sir."

He nodded, his gaze drifting behind her. "Serena, I have to say that painting of yours is most remarkable."

Serena pushed back from her desk, above which hung Toni's maple tree painting. "It's gorgeous, isn't it?"

"Very striking." He studied it some more. "Do you know anything about the artist?"

Her pulse increased. Maybe this was a way to showcase Toni's work. In one of the recent heads of department meetings she'd heard about a potential rebrand, and that Muskoka Shores was keen to focus on more local suppliers and talent, as part of a sustainability push. She tapped open her phone and quickly scrolled through to Toni's Instagram feed.

"Her name is Toni Wakefield. She lives in town and has sold her work in Toronto." At markets, but hey, she'd sold. "Look, here are some of her paintings."

He glanced through. "I think you should bring this up at the meeting next week." The meeting for the resort's department heads. "It'd be good to know if she'd be willing to consider doing other artwork. Something that really says Muskoka Shores."

"I'm sure she'd be very excited at the opportunity." Toni would be, anyway, once Serena had explained the financial benefits this could possibly entail. From the canvases that she'd seen lining Toni's house it seemed there were enough paintings to line half the halls of the resort.

Mr. Jennings spoke about other matters then left, but she kept thinking about what this could mean. Surely once resort guests saw Toni's work, they'd want to buy it. But maybe it could be bigger than that. Perhaps Toni could host art week-ends. Perhaps she could be the artist in residence! That was a thing, wasn't it?

Her phone rang, and, as if she knew Serena had been thinking of her, she saw it was Toni.

"Hi! I was just thinking about you. You know Mr. Jennings was here and—"

"Rena? Oh, Rena, I really need you to come. My water's broken and I need to get to the hospital and Joel isn't here and his phone is switched off. Could you come?"

"Of course! How far apart are your contractions?"

"I don't know. I haven't been—ohh, ow!"

Sounded like she was having one now.

"Okay, you've got this. Now remember to breathe. Get your bag near the door, and take it easy, and if you can, count how many minutes between contractions, like they told us at the classes. I'll be there as soon as I can. Okay?"

"Okay." Toni whimpered.

Lord, be with her. Serena rang Cherry and issued instructions, glad today's conference was straightforward. She made her excuses then drove to Toni's house, praying for Toni, for the baby, for herself, that all would go well. She pulled up outside Toni's, racing in to find her friend loading a suitcase.

"I thought you had this all packed weeks ago," Serena said, taking over.

Toni braced against the wall as another wave of pain rippled through her. Once it was over, she gasped and replied, "I've been so busy trying to make sure everything is ready I thought I'd better rewash the baby clothes again. They'd been sitting in the bag too long, and I wanted them to smell fresh and pretty."

Serena zipped the bag closed. "How many minutes between contractions?"

"I don't know. Six minutes? Maybe five?"

What had they said at the clinic? That's right. The five-one-one rule. Five minutes apart, one minute long, occurring for one hour. "How long are they lasting?"

"I don't know. Thirty seconds? Fifty?"

Not one minute, then. "And it's only been going for the past half hour?"

"Yes. Ow."

Okay, so it wasn't quite at the one hour mark like the nurses had suggested. "Have you called the hospital yet?"

"Yes. They said I could come in as it was pretty quiet."

Thank you, Lord. That was something at least.

Serena eased an arm around Toni, gently steering her to the car. Once Toni was safely inside, Serena gathered up the bag, locked the door, then raced to the driver's seat. "Did you call Joel?"

Toni's face paled as another contraction gripped more fully. She grabbed hold of the dash. Soon she gasped, "I had to leave another message."

Serena gritted her teeth. How irresponsible was he? Surely, he should be around for this moment. He'd known—they'd all known—that Toni had hit her due date. He shouldn't have anything scheduled. What sort of minister would be too busy for his own wife and child? Irritation rose, but Serena tried to tamp it down as she reminded Toni to focus on her breathing, while doing her best to avoid traveling over any bumps.

Fifteen minutes later, Toni was being wheeled to an examination room. Thank goodness they'd gotten here in time, and

Toni was now in the hands of the professionals. Birthing classes were good, but it wasn't the same as reality, when adrenaline and pain and tears were very real.

"Serena, right?" one of the midwives asked. "I remember you from the classes. You're the birth partner, right? The father isn't in the picture?"

"I'm the one here today."

And Joel *should* be. Her fingers clenched. Just wait until she saw him. She'd give him a piece of her mind, and—

"Well, birth partner," the midwife continued, "I want you to keep your friend calm. We want her to concentrate on what she needs to do, not worry about anything else. Okay?"

She nodded. The next hours passed in a surreal state as information they'd been given at birthing classes played out in stark reality. In between contractions Serena mentioned the interest Mr. Jennings had shown about Toni's art, fetched bottles of water, rubbed Toni's back, and encouraged her to maintain an upright posture to help gravity do its work. She took a moment to move out into the hall and call Joel. No answer. She left a message.

The warmth in the room fogged her glasses, and she took them off, wiping them on her shirt.

Toni looked up at her, with pain filled eyes. "Joel?"

Serena shook her head. "I tried, but he's still not responding, so I left another message."

"I can't believe him!" Toni cried. "Today of all days."

"I'll try again," Serena promised. But it was just the same.

After what seemed like hours, Toni's groans of pain had escalated to a deeper guttural cry, and with a quick check, the nurse announced that Toni had dilated and was in transition and would be having the baby really soon.

Sweat poured off Toni's brow. "Please, please, just give me something for the pain!" she said, between gasps.

"Sorry, Toni. You'll need to push soon, so it's too late to give you anything, because you'll need to be ready." The nurse's admonition had Toni whimpering, and it was all Serena could do to encourage her friend.

It didn't take too much longer before the midwife and Dr. Strauss were both there, guiding Toni through the cycles as her body worked to bring the baby down the birth canal.

"Come on, Toni, let's have a big push, now."

Serena braced for another huge squeeze of the hand as Toni concentrated on pushing. Gasping with the effort, Toni relaxed, and Serena took a quick moment to ease back in the squeaky chair and stretch out her squashed fingers and massage her hand.

"Toni, let's have another one. Now!"

At the doctor's instruction, Toni pushed again, resulting in his cry, "The baby's crowning. Come on, Toni. You're doing really well."

Adrenaline rushed, and Serena shifted to peer into Toni's pale face. "Did you hear that, Toni? Your baby's almost here. You're going to be a mom really soon."

Toni looked up from under half-closed eyelids. "I feel so tired and shaky. I can't do this anymore."

"Yes, you can." Serena rubbed Toni's shoulder and prayed aloud. "Thank you, God, for giving Toni strength right now." She gently squeezed. "Come on, Toni. Let's meet your baby."

With renewed energy and focus, Toni pushed once more, and the baby's head appeared. Another few pushes and a slippery vernix-covered tiny body appeared. The nurse quickly scooped the baby up, gently cleaning and checking before handing the baby over to Toni.

Awe filled Serena as she watched the new mother with her child. What a miracle. What a privilege to be with Toni, to be asked to help guide a new life into the world. Her eyes pricked, her throat closing with emotion. And to think, she'd almost said no. Joel would never know what he'd missed out on. Well, he would, because she'd tell him.

Toni's earlier pain seemed to have been forgotten as she stared at her tiny son, tracing his cheek, his tiny fingers and toes. After a few minutes, Dr. Strauss and the nurses completed a further round of checks before departing, leaving the new mother and baby in peace, with a promise to return soon.

"Oh, Toni, congratulations." Serena kissed the top of Toni's head. "You and Joel must be so proud."

"Thanks." Toni glanced up at her, her brow knit, as if puzzled.

Serena reached out and touched the little wrinkly face. "He's so beautiful. Look at his ears. He's got Joel's ears."

"Nice ears seem to run in the family."

"How do you feel?"

Toni exhaled. "It's amazing how one minute you can be in such immense pain and the next it really is almost forgotten," she said, cradling her son.

Tears pricked again. Serena blinked back fresh emotion. Why was she so weepy? "It's a good thing he's so cute, eh?"

"Good thing he doesn't look like his father." Toni smiled again, kissing her newborn son. "You're so handsome."

What? She wasn't the only one who thought Joel was very nice looking. Rachel and Anna had made many comments in past months. Why would Toni say such a thing? "Have you thought of any names yet? Or will you wait until Joel gets here?"

Toni was wearing a look of confusion. "Why would I wait for Joel? No, I've liked the name Ethan for ages. That was my dad's name, so it's the obvious choice." Toni's expression softened. "Thanks so much for being here. I couldn't have done it without you."

"Thanks for letting me be part of it. This truly was one of the most special moments of my life." Now the drama was over, a surge of anger at Joel renewed. How dare he miss out on this most special of times? "It's such a shame his father couldn't be here."

Toni's face held a trace of contempt which she quickly masked. "I'd rather not ruin this special moment by thinking about him."

Serena felt more confused than ever. "What on earth has Joel done to make you feel this way?"

Toni looked up from cradling her son, her brow pleated. "Joel? Why do you keep going on about him? What's Joel got to do with any of this?"

Serena just stared at her. "But isn't Joel—?"

"Ah, Toni, how are you doing?" A nurse bustled back in. "Are you ready for your shower now?"

"That sounds amazing." Toni glanced at Serena. "You'll stay a little longer, won't you?"

"Absolutely." Serena stroked little Ethan's hand. "I'll look after Ethan."

The next minute saw a rush of efficient activity as the nurses stripped the bed and finished clearing up before checking on Toni and with Serena about whether she was happy to be left with the baby for a few minutes. After picking up a few items of clothing Toni had hastily discarded, Serena settled in the squeaky chair to watch the sleeping infant in his plastic portable hospital crib, his red face still wrinkled, his thumb in his mouth. Her breath caught. Oh, how sweet. What a miracle. What a privilege to be here for this special moment.

A huge wave of tiredness suddenly hit her and she leaned forward in her chair, head against the bed frame, glasses off as she rubbed her eyes. Supporting Toni had been exhilarating, but now the adrenaline was wearing off she was so exhausted, the emotions of the past hours leaving her utterly drained. Serena closed her eyes as she listened to the shower run and the snuffly sounds of the baby, the room filling with a sense of weary exhilaration that felt a lot like…peace.

At the soft whoosh of the door, Serena lifted fatigued eyes to see a huge bunch of roses, closely followed by Joel's excited face.

"Is everything all right?" he asked, placing the flowers on the bed. "Where's Toni?"

"She's in the shower."

"Is she okay?"

Anger pushed past her exhaustion. Unbelievable. "You'd know if you'd been here, wouldn't you? Where were you?" She grasped hold of the cold metal of the bedrail and pulled herself upright. Ugh. So tired. "I've been trying to call you for hours. What on earth was so important that you'd miss your own son's birth?"

"What?"

How dare he look surprised? "Did you honestly think a bunch of flowers would make up for missing this?"

"Serena," his eyes were wide, "I don't know what—"

The squeak of the ensuite door stole her words. As did the sight of a freshly showered and changed Toni, who'd already transformed into a more svelte version of herself. "Joel! You're here at last!"

Serena stared in amazement as Joel swiftly stepped forward and gave her a hug which she accepted with a smile. "Hey, sis. Congratulations! How d'you feel?"

Sis?

"Much better after a shower." She saw the flowers. "Are these for me? They're beautiful. Thank you."

"I'm so sorry I couldn't get here earlier. My phone died. But anyway, where's my nephew?"

Nephew?

"Serena hasn't shown you?"

At Toni's questioning look Serena just shook her head. No. Oh no. How had she not known? She blinked, feeling dizzy, and sat down with a thump. *No.* Had she really misunderstood? Nothing was making sense anymore.

Joel moved to give baby Ethan a cuddle, and Serena watched as if seeing him for the first time. If he wasn't the father, then who was? Where was Ethan's dad? Why hadn't anyone said something? Or had they said, and she'd simply not heard? Had she really been so distracted by her own personal dramas and assumptions that she'd not paid attention to an essential piece of information like this?

"Serena?" Toni asked. "Are you okay?"

No. But she nodded. How could she explain? She kneaded her forehead, trying to clear the whirling thoughts. It had happened again. Just when she'd grown comfortable with people, her assumptions had been proven wrong. Again. "I thought—I know it sounds dumb—but I thought you and Joel were married."

Joel laughed. "We're close, but not *that* close."

Serena studied him, still feeling woozy. All those comments, all those long looks—she'd misunderstood everything. She drew in a shaky breath and pushed to her feet. Dwight and Hope were right. She *was* naïve.

Toni looked at her in concern. "Are you sure you're okay?"

"No." She didn't know what she felt right now, but knew she needed some privacy to try and sort out her thoughts. "I'm sorry. I'm really tired and it's been a big day. Now Joel's here, I might go."

She quickly kissed Toni's cheek, gently touched baby Ethan's ginger-fuzzed head, but couldn't meet Joel's eyes. Had she ever felt like such a fool? Dwight and Hope had hidden their relationship, and taken everyone by surprise, but this misunderstanding was one she'd managed all by herself. *You're so stupid. So naïve. Fat. Ugly. Such a fool. You're such a fool!*

Embarrassment radiated from her skin, and she stumbled from the room. Ignoring a nurse's call of "Miss, are you okay?" Serena staggered outside, her thoughts heaving to and fro. She *was* so stupid. They must think the same. Everyone would know how much of an imbecile she'd been. Oh, she could never face them again.

She found a wooden bench under a tree and huddled on the cold timber. The sunset was spilling the last of its golden rays but soon it would be dark, and nobody would see her, so she'd be safe.

Except she'd never really be safe. She'd cracked open her heart and let Toni in, and now something intangible tethered her to that tiny boy inside. Anyway, she couldn't leave, they would find her, they knew where she lived. Oh, why, why, *why* hadn't she known?

Because you're stupid, you're so naïve. You'll never amount to anything.

She dragged in a shaky breath. Were Toni and Joel laughing at her? Were they mocking her naivete? Oh, why hadn't she known?

Fragments of memories from the past weeks collided with what she knew now. The fact they didn't wear wedding rings. The separate bedrooms. She gritted her teeth—honestly! The fact she'd never seen Joel kiss Toni—the thought made her shiver. The fact that, now she'd thought about it, she'd never actually heard Joel refer to Toni as his wife. Because, of course, why would he? "I'm such an idiot."

More questions begged for answers: so who was Ethan's father? Why hadn't they announced it, or at least made things more clear? How could John and Angela bring someone on staff who had so much baggage?

But then, why did it matter? It didn't matter, not really. God loved Toni and Ethan, and it probably was good for the congregation to practice what got preached and show grace and love to others.

If only she could be sure that Toni and Joel would be so understanding...

"They probably hate me. They must think I'm stupid. I need to get out of here."

Her words fell into the night air. She should leave. She *would* leave. Except, where was her bag? "In the room," she groaned. Emotion pricked. She swiped at the dampness on her cheeks.

See? Such an idiot. She couldn't even manage her escape from humiliation without further shame. Maybe she should call a cab. Except—of course!—she didn't have her phone. It was in her bag. In the room. Back with the brother and sister who must think her the world's biggest fool. "You're so stupid."

Escaped tears turned into sobs, sobs she tried to muffle in case someone came to investigate, or thought she'd escaped from a mental facility. But really, maybe that's where she belonged. She obviously couldn't think straight. Maybe she really was as gullible as Dwight and Hope had believed, too dumb to notice the obvious, hopeless at love, easy to deceive.

Another breath shuddered in, released. It was getting cool, and insects were buzzing near her face. She should leave, but where? And how? Somehow she'd have to retrieve her bag, and she couldn't face Toni and Joel. Not yet.

For they wouldn't want to see her. They must think Serena was the world's biggest fool. And they'd be right. All this time she'd been fighting this attraction to Joel only to learn he wasn't married? "I'm such a fool."

CHAPTER 10

Joel turned to see his sister holding tiny Ethan, staring at him, her eyebrows aloft. "She thought we were married?"

"I don't know how."

"Did you ever tell her about Bryant?"

Toni shook her head. "You didn't either?"

"No."

Huh. So in that case, maybe he could understand why she might think that. Joel knew he was openly affectionate, more so than most brothers. And now he thought about it, when he'd been making his explanations about his relationship with his sister he remembered now that Serena had been focused on other things, like a bad breakup. Still, the fact that she'd not had things made plain to her in all this time amazed him. "I can't believe it."

"I can't either."

Ethan made more snuffling noises near Toni's chest, like he was trying to feed. Yeah, that was something Joel *really* didn't need to see. "Uh, you want me to find a nurse or something?"

She pointed to the bell beside the bed. "Just press that."

He did, and as they waited for the nurse to appear, Toni continued. "Serena has been so wonderful today. I wanted to give up so many times and she just kept encouraging me." Toni's eyes filled with tears. "I hate to see her run off like that. She must feel so embarrassed. No wonder she made all those strange comments. Oh, poor thing. It's starting to make sense now."

It still wasn't making much sense to him. "You're sure you never told her about Bryant?"

She shook her head. "She never asked, and I didn't want to talk about it. Anyway, why would she when she obviously thought…"

He downed a spare bottle of water, his feelings teetering between horror and amusement. But whatever Serena's misconceptions, he hoped she'd understand it was innocent, even if it was for Toni's sake. For as Toni learned to adjust to being a mom, she'd need all the friends she could get. Even if they were sometimes a little complicated, like Serena.

"Oh, look, she left her bag."

Toni's voice broke into his reverie, and he noticed a brown leather bag tucked in the corner of the room. "I'll see if I can find her. I'll be back in a minute."

Joel raced out the door, passing a nurse.

"Are you the husband?" the nurse asked.

He winced. How many others might've thought that too? "I'm the brother. But Toni wants some help."

The nurse frowned. "What happened to the other girl?"

"She, uh, had to leave. I'm just going to go find her."

"It's getting dark out there. You'd better hurry."

He nodded, but when he reached outside, he didn't see her anywhere. Maybe…the parking lot.

He hurried to where he'd parked his car but her silver Mazda remained where he'd seen it earlier. Of course. He glanced at her bag. Her keys were probably still inside. And her phone. And her wallet. Should he look inside?

He refrained. So, if she had no money, no way of contacting people, where would she be? "God, please give me a clue."

As he started walking back to the hospital entrance, a faint sound met his ear. It sounded like…sobbing.

No. His heart softened. No, it couldn't be.

He followed the sound to several large trees, and through the dimness found a woman huddled on a seat. A woman wearing the same clothes as he remembered Serena wearing earlier, with her hands covering her face.

"Serena?"

She stiffened, peeking through her fingers before giving a faint "No."

No?

He drew nearer. "Serena—"

"Please go away." With a heavy sigh, she straightened, although her hair covered her face. "I don't want to talk to you."

The space between them grew thick with hurt. Why didn't she want to speak to him? She wasn't that embarrassed, surely? "Before I go, you may want this." He held up her bag.

She rubbed her face. "Thanks."

He placed the bag on the seat beside her, then followed suit. *Lord, what do I say?* He had some idea about what might have caused her embarrassment, but nothing that should make her as volatile as this.

"Toni keeps saying how amazing you were," he said softly.

Her hair swung as she shook her head. "She was the amazing one, pushing that tiny boy into the world."

"It's pretty awesome, isn't it?"

"Such a miracle." She sighed.

He wrapped his fingers around the cool wooden edge of the seat, still not looking at her. "His name is Bryant."

"Who?"

"Ethan's father." He clenched his hands, then released them. "He was one of her work colleagues, an art professor, married, of course, but he told her they were separated."

He glanced across. Saw her wince.

"Some men can't be trusted."

She nodded, lips pressed together. Yeah, given her experience with Dwight, he didn't think she'd argue.

"I'm sorry you don't feel like you can trust me," he said gently.

Her breath shuddered in. "I didn't know—I got it wrong, I'm so ashamed—"

"Hey." He dared to place his hand on hers. "You have nothing to be ashamed of."

"I can't trust myself with anything anymore. I don't even know what's right, or who can be trusted. I feel like such a fool."

"You're not a fool. I'm the one who should've explained things better, but I didn't want to expose Toni too much. She's been afraid of being judged, because it's happened before, so maybe I was a little too careful in what I said and didn't quite say enough."

Another sigh. "You probably did, but I might not have been listening."

"Hey, it's okay."

"No, it's not. Not really."

He gently squeezed her hand. "Toni feels so bad that you were upset. Please come back inside."

"I...I don't want her to see me like this."

"You look fine to me."

"You say that because it's dark."

He smiled. "I say that because it doesn't matter what you look like. Toni wants your company; she doesn't care about whether you're wearing makeup or if it's all washed away. She cares about you, your sweet heart, your generous nature, your kindness."

She slid her hand away. "I can't see her," she whispered.

"Hey, you don't need to be embarrassed."

"That's always easy for someone else to say."

"It's still true."

They sat in the darkness, his fingers now next to hers so he could feel the heat from her skin. All he'd need to do was move an inch and he could hold her soft hand again.

He didn't. "Are you cold?"

"No."

He wondered if that was a lie but figured it didn't matter. He'd wait out here a little longer, until he was sure Toni would be finished with the nurse. There were certain things no brother should ever have to see.

A yawn escaped her, and he realized that perhaps some of Serena's overreaction was due to tiredness. "It's been a big day."

"Huge."

She gave another shuddery breath, and he was sorely tempted to wrap her in a hug like he'd do for his sister. But the feelings he had weren't like any he'd ever have for Toni. Which reminded him. "Do you want to come inside?"

"No."

"Please?"

She shifted, and a shaft of streetlight streaked across her face. "I look like a mess."

Yeah, she'd had better days. "You look like you've had a big day supporting your friend, who I'm pretty sure sees you as the big sister she never had."

Her sigh was shaky. "I still feel like such a fool."

"But you're not." When she shook her head he said, "Serena, you're not. Don't let the enemy get into your head and tell you lies. You're not a fool."

"I misunderstood."

"That doesn't make you a fool," he said gently. "It makes you human. Who of us hasn't messed up and misunderstood things?"

Her gaze lifted and met his through the darkness, and in that place of quietness he knew a sudden urge to tell her about Mel. "I messed up. I fell for a woman who I thought wanted the same things, only to find out she was playing me all along."

"Like Dwight."

He nodded. "I decided after that to never date women in my church, it just gets too messy and complicated."

"And nobody wants complicated," she murmured.

There was something about the way she said that that threaded concern, but he couldn't chase it now. "Relationships are tough, but we can't let someone else's actions feed into our self-talk. God doesn't want you speaking negative things over your life. That's the devil, who is a liar, who comes to steal, kill, and destroy. If he can make us believe false things, or separate us from believers, or make us mistrust God and His promises, then he wins. And as God's followers we can't allow that."

Her lips pressed together.

"We *can't* allow that," he repeated.

"No," she whispered.

"So please, come inside, say goodnight to Toni so she knows you're okay. I can drive you home if you like."

"You don't need to do that."

"I want to make sure you're safe."

"Why do you care?"

But her words held none of the truculence of before. They seemed to hold a genuine question. But the rawness in her whisper was not something he could give an easy explanation. Not yet anyway. Not until he'd sorted out some more of just what had happened tonight and figured out how that might affect his future.

She pulled back. "Don't bother answering that," she

murmured, shifting away, taking away the tentative peace between them also.

And as she stood, it seemed the space between them grew even more distant, because he hadn't had the courage to finally admit what was in his heart.

~

OKAY. She sucked in a breath. She could do this. Just because a girl had a near breakdown the night before didn't mean she couldn't fake it and maybe make it through today. Serena plastered on a smile, juggling the large blue teddy bear and flowers and her bag as she entered the hospital's main doors.

"Want some help, miss?" an elderly man asked her.

"No thanks. I've got this." She hitched her smile higher. "I'm carefully balanced, see?"

Yeah, right. Maybe she wasn't quite as unbalanced as last night, but a good sleep after a big day had helped. Somewhat. Even if she knew she'd never be quite the balanced person some people believed she should be. Of course, she'd possibly feel more balanced if Joel wasn't in Toni's room today. That'd give her time to recalibrate from her stupid emotions that had led to crazy dreams, when she'd rewritten his silence into something that said he actually might care. Which was extra dumb. Hadn't he said just last night he didn't date women from his congregation?

So hopefully he wouldn't be there. And maybe Toni would be asleep, and she could just leave the bear, flowers and card, and—

"Serena!" Angela called from the open door of Toni's room. "You're here too."

Too? Her heart sank. Okay, change of plan. If others were here maybe she could do the quick "hi" and "bye" she'd originally thought she could manage while on her walk this morning. She did have to get to work soon, anyway.

Angela stayed at the door, her eyes rounding as she saw the flowers. "Oh, how beautiful." She touched a rose. "Annette's?"

"Of course." She'd owed Serena a favor.

Bracing, Serena entered the room, willing her smile to look genuine, as she hoped Toni would forget the tear-stained mess she'd seen last night when Joel had virtually dragged her upstairs to say goodnight.

"Serena!" Toni exclaimed, pushing higher against the pillows, little Ethan covered by a muslin wrap draped over her front.

"Good morning," Serena said, offering the flowers and bear.

"Oh, they're so lovely." Toni leaned forward, cradling her baby, and took a sniff. "They even smell pretty."

"Only the best for you," Serena said, wondering if she'd see them for what they were: a mix of apology flowers and congratulations.

"Here, I'll put them in a vase," Angela said, scooping them away and heading to the door. "Give you a chance to talk."

"I can't stay long," Serena said, moving to prop the bear up next to several cards. "I'll need to get to work soon, but I just wanted to pop in and see how you're getting on."

"Yeah, feeling better. It's amazing how not having this squirming creature inside makes for a better night's sleep."

"You make it sound like you had an alien inside."

"It all feels pretty alien to me, but hey, I'm coping." Toni eyed her. "How about you?"

Okay, fake smile time. "I'm good. Got a busy few days with some conference—"

"No, I mean about the Joel thing."

She shook her head. "I don't really want to talk about it anymore—"

"I know he feels bad."

He did? She hesitated, wondering whether to share. But it

was only fair Toni got a fuller explanation. She moved to sit on the visitor's seat. It emitted the same squeak she was familiar with from yesterday. "I feel like such an idiot, I'm so sorry. But ever since Dwight deceived me, I've second-guessed things, not trusting myself. It's made me extra cautious with guys, not knowing if what they say is real."

Toni nodded. "I know what you mean."

Serena chewed her bottom lip. Yeah, from what Joel had said last night, it seemed Toni knew that better than anyone. "I made dumb assumptions, and," she shrugged, "I've always hated it when people go on about how hot a married person is."

Toni gave a raspy chuckle. "Really? People think Joel is hot?"

"Some do, apparently."

"Do you?"

She shook her head. Did that count as a lie? "He's attractive, I know that, but that's why I didn't want to have too much to do with him. And then when you talked about a shared last name, and I knew you were pregnant, I just assumed. I swear, no-one ever said anything about you being brother and sister."

"They mentioned it in church in the beginning."

"Summer is a busy time for weddings, I must've been away. But still, I feel like such an idiot."

"You can, you know," Toni said, as she readjusted the muslin draping the baby at her chest.

"Can what?"

"I'm giving you official permission to think that Joel is hot."

Serena's mouth sagged.

A cleared throat swung their attention to the door.

Lord, have mercy. Angela stood, all twinkling-eyed, right next to Joel. Serena's cheeks flamed, and she ducked her eyes. That alien thing? She could really do with being abducted, or maybe even vaporized, right about now.

"Are we interrupting?" Angela asked, moving inside, as Toni drew Ethan out from the modesty screen.

"Nope." Serena rose. "I've got to get to work." She had to leave before her skin's shimmering waves of embarrassment made her self-combust.

"Don't leave on my account," Joel said.

She wouldn't look at him. She couldn't, anyway, especially with all these avid spectators to her heart. "I'm not." She could high-five herself for sounding so calm. "I've got work so I'd better go." She stroked Ethan's downy head then hitched up her bag.

"Oh, before you do," Toni grasped her hand, "I wanted to ask, would you consider being Ethan's godparent?"

Her heart grew soft. "Really?"

"There's no-one better." Toni's eyes assured.

"Thank you." No one had ever asked her to do such a thing before. "I'd be honored."

"Good." Toni's smile held appreciation and something else. "Because Joel will be Ethan's godfather."

Serena's gaze shot to him, to a grinning Angela, then back to Toni. "You're evil," she whispered.

The sound of Toni's laughter mitigated some of Serena's confusion. But she still couldn't look at him. "Now I really need to leave, otherwise I'll be late. I'll message you later, Toni."

She flashed Angela a smile, forced herself to almost meet Joel's eyes, and with a blown kiss for Toni exited the room. Okay, maybe now was a good time to try out that jog-walk thing again. Then she could get out of here before someone else exited the room and called—

"Serena? Have you got a minute?"

She grimaced and closed her eyes, her steps slowing, even as everything within her begged to run away. "Sorry, I'm going to be late for work. You'll need to walk and talk."

"Hey." Joel hurried closer, drawing to her side without a puff. Clearly he had the jogging thing down. "I just wanted to check. Are you really okay?"

"Don't I seem okay?" She paused and dared meet his eyes.

He smiled, and her heart skittered like a kitten after a ball of wool. "You seem great."

Great? When was the last time a man had said that to her and she actually thought he might mean it? But no. He probably didn't. A familiar refrain whispered: *You're fat, you're plain, you're ug—*

No! She shook her head, willing the stupid negativity to leave.

"No, really," he said, obviously mistaking her head shake for what he'd said. "You look great, Serena."

His words stole inside, chasing away the remnants of the former terms like golden butterflies might chase away brown moths. Talk about evil. Why *did* she pay attention to such nasty words? It was time to make a change. Her smile stretched into genuine. "Well, maybe that's because I am great."

And with a flourish worthy of a Kardashian, she swung her bag on her shoulder and strutted—yes, strutted—out the door.

CHAPTER 11

Okay, he was officially amazed. How come nobody had ever explained to him the inverse effect of one's size compared to influence? Take little Ethan, for example. How could one tiny newborn, no bigger than the length of Joel's forearm, have turned their world so completely upside down?

Joel had known having a baby in the house would make a difference. Just hadn't fully anticipated the chaos one tiny bundle of joy could cause. Ethan's clothes were now strewn through the house, his lusty cries filled the night, and dozens of casseroles filled the freezer from people he barely knew who kept turning up at all hours of the day. Several of the church ladies had helped get his house sparkling clean while Toni was in the hospital, but now she was back home it was almost like it hadn't happened. Even getting in the car to go to church had proven a monumental feat. Eventually, after safely strapping everyone and everything in, they'd made it to church, to be surrounded by well-wishers.

But it was more than Ethan who had turned his world inside out. Three little words had opened his eyes to something else. Not the 'Joel is hot' comment—he hadn't dared prove the depths of his self-interest by asking his sister to explain *that* conversation—but those last three words Serena had said before sashaying away like a movie star, all curves and sass and smile that had woven beneath the tumult of emotions from past days.

Serena *was* great. There was something about the woman that demanded his attention, even during Sunday services when he should be paying attention to all the congregation members. Her kindness, her generosity, and support of Toni had long impressed him, and those sparks of humor and determination left him wanting to know more. Who knew training for a five k run with a self-confessed non-athlete could be so much fun? But more than this, she owned a courage, something he'd not seen at first, but the way she'd picked herself up after nearly falling apart the night of Ethan's birth, rocking up the next morning to the hospital like a boss—she'd impressed him. Still impressed him.

He stole another look at her as they stood at the front of the church while John spoke the words of Ethan's christening service.

Serena stood, her head bowed as she smiled at little Ethan, sleeping in Toni's arms. Her hair shone in the light falling through the stained glass, and she wore a pretty ruffled dress that hinted of her shape, something that made her seem light years from the woman he'd first encountered all those weeks ago. Her gaze lifted, and he met those green eyes that intrigued him.

His heart rippled, releasing his small smile which was echoed by her lips. Lips he wondered about at night, when Ethan's cries stole his sleep, leaving Joel to lie in bed wondering whether his averred commitment to not dating women in his church was of God, or just of him. Because he'd really like to know more about those lips of Serena's, and about her kiss—

"Joel and Serena—"

Joel straightened, refocusing. *Sorry, God.*

"—do you intend to pray for Ethan, and help draw him by your example into the community of faith and walk with him in the way of Christ?"

"I do," he said.

"I do," Serena's voice echoed.

His skin tingled. These promises sounded awfully similar to other vows of commitment.

The service continued, prayers were prayed, and then they were released to resume their seats at the front of the church. Again, sitting next to Serena, it felt like something bigger than simply being two godparents, almost like the two of them being a couple was ordained by God.

Another shiver rippled through him, drawing Toni's questioning glance, to which he shook his head. No. He needed to stay focused, needed to keep the main thing the main thing. Serena might be great, but could he really forgo his declaration to keep congregation members off-limits?

But later, over at Serena's house which she'd offered for Toni as a venue for a special lunch, he caught another insight into the capacity and talents of this woman. Everything from the under-stated elegance of her home to the gracious way she welcomed in people like Matt, Wade, and others of his and Toni's city friends spoke of dignity and grace. She had a flair for putting people at ease, making them feel comfortable, and he was glad to see Toni finally relax as she sat with Anna, Rachel, and Jackie, and spoke with her arty friends, their heavily styled hair, makeup and clothes contrasting with the more down-to-earth people who called Muskoka home.

"You know, I never would've expected to see your sister so at ease with being a mom," Wade said, downing another pastry-encased meat savory Serena called a party pie.

"Why not?" Matt asked, frowning.

"She's always seemed more artsy than family-minded."

"What are you saying? You don't think she can be both? I

think she's doing an amazing job," Matt said, his eyes shifting to where Toni sat on a floral sofa, surrounded by women.

"Hey, didn't mean to upset you, big guy," Wade said, shooting an upraised look at Joel as if to say, 'did you know he had a thing for Toni?'

Joel shrugged but wondered again at Matt's interest. As far as he knew Matt barely communicated with Toni, but maybe they messaged or something. Or maybe they should. In fact, maybe he should invite Matt to stay for a weekend soon, under the guise of fishing or something. Maybe.

"Hey, these are really good," Wade said, polishing off another of the savories. "Did you say Serena is single?"

"I don't know that I did," Joel said, a tight stomach accompanying his own frown.

"Well, if she is, maybe I should introduce her to my brother. Don't tell my wife, but we could do with a good cook in our family."

"Dude." Matt's attention swiveled back to Wade. "This isn't last century. You can't define a woman by her kitchen skills."

"Hey, I'm sure she's got other skills. I mean, she obviously likes to clean," Wade said, glancing around.

"Wow. No words," Joel said. "Excuse me."

He left as Matt murmured something about Joel and Serena which he didn't really want to hear. Let people speculate. It didn't mean he had to pay attention.

He joined a knot of conversation with John and Damian, and Jenny Wells and her husband Mitch.

"…should be coming home very soon, I'm so excited." Jenny turned to him. "Oh, you might not have heard. I was just saying that our eldest son, Jem, is coming home at long last."

He vaguely recalled John once saying something about Mitch and Jenny's sons. "Is he the doctor?"

"Yes. We're so proud of him, he's been working so hard in Africa, but it's taken a toll, so he's taking time off and will be here for a while. He'll be working at the hospital and part time with Dr. Lewisham."

Joel smiled. "Working two jobs is considered taking time off?"

"It is compared to what he does now," Jenny murmured, as Mitch wrapped an arm around her.

Clearly there were things not being said today, but maybe he'd find out down the track. He noted Jenny's empty plate and offered to clear it away for her.

"You're a sweetie, aren't you?"

"Yes, I am," he said to their shared laughter.

He moved to the small kitchen where he found Serena wiping down the counter. "So are you being Cinderella as well as the Fairy Godmother?"

She paused. "Fairy Godmother?"

"Making Toni's dream come true with all this." He gestured to the blue bunting, the blue-dusted cupcakes waiting for dessert. "This is amazing."

"She's worth it," she said, wiping the crumbs into her hand before depositing it into a lidded cream container labeled 'Birds.'

His heart expanded. Sure there were a lot of people here who wanted to be part of Toni's life, but to hear this woman recognize his sister's value seemed extra good. "You've been really generous."

"I enjoy doing this," she said. "Angela says that hospitality is one of my gifts, so I find this fun to do."

"Work hasn't got in the way?"

She shrugged. "You make time for what's important, don't you? And this is important."

Yes, it was. "How has the training been going?"

"Good." Her smile flashed. "I managed to jog a whole kilometer the other morning before having to slow to walk."

"Nice one. We'll have you in the Boston marathon before

you know it." He smiled at her snort of disbelief and leaned against the counter. "So work isn't too busy?"

Her pretty hair swished as she shook her head. "The weddings will soon wind down, so we're entering a more quiet season at the resort. We'll do something for Thanksgiving next month but after there's only a few conferences booked in."

"So does that mean you'll finally get a chance to get away?"

Joel swiveled to see Anna who'd asked that question, who winked at him like they were part of a conspiracy. But what conspiracy he didn't know. He shifted his attention back to Serena. "Are you going away?"

"My parents are always at me to come visit them. I wondered about going sometime after the Cranberry Festival."

"Which is October, right?"

She nodded. "The weekend after Thanksgiving, which is the weekend after our 'Fun' run." Her lips lifted. "You might want to remember that, considering the church is involved in running a couple of stalls."

"Yep," Anna said. "Every year we do a carwash and help run Chili at the Church."

"I kinda forgot," he admitted. "There's been a bit going on."

"That there has," Anna agreed. Her gaze flicked to Serena then back to him. "Well, let me know if there's anything I can do."

Serena pointed to the plate of cupcakes. "Could you take that out for me, please?"

"I certainly can." Anna lifted the plate and sent him another wink.

Okay, he wasn't sure if that was flirting or some subtle way of saying *do something about Serena*. Whatever. "Hey, is there anything I can do?"

"Um, not really, no."

He motioned to the pile of dirty plates. "I've been told I've got skills in the washing up department. I'm happy to do that for you." Maybe he'd get the chance to talk to her some more. Find out about this trip she was threatening to take.

"Really?"

He nodded.

"Well, in that case." She backed away from the sink, sending him a smile he felt all the way to the soles of his feet. "I'm a big believer in the emancipation of men to do housework."

He chuckled.

"What?"

"Oh, just something I heard Wade say. I knew it wasn't going to fly with you."

"What was that?"

"I think he wanted to set you up with his brother."

"What?" Her cheeks pinked. "He doesn't even know me."

"But Wade likes your cooking. And your neat and tidy house." He shifted to the sink, started filling it with hot water.

"Are you joking?"

"Nope."

"I hope you told him no."

"Sorry." He squirted in lemon detergent, then dipped the first glass. "I didn't really know what kind of guy you might be interested in."

He looked up, his gaze fusing with hers. Saw how her cheeks pinked. Saw how she bit her bottom lip.

"Hey, Rena—oh!" Rachel halted at the breakfast bar, then plunked down two more glasses. "Well, I can see you two are busy here."

Serena blinked, then pivoted. "Nope. Joel's offered to wash up, and I thought it must be my turn to hold the baby. Where is that cute little godson of mine?"

Rachel's smile widened as she joined Joel in watching Serena leave. Then she turned back to him. "Hey, sorry about that."

He shrugged. "I don't know what you mean."

"Oh, I think you do." She nodded to the sink. "Nice try, anyway."

Heat filled his neck and he resumed cleaning, wondering if all of Serena's friends thought the same, and whether he could ever get a chance to speak with her alone.

An hour or two later, after coffee and cake (that was delicious, and he'd learned Serena had also made), there were yet more photos, stories and laughter, and he noticed Matt and Toni talking quietly in a corner, Ethan asleep in Matt's arms.

"Who is he?" Serena asked Joel, Anna behind her, listening in.

"Matt's a friend of mine from Toronto. Good guy, we knew him from church."

"He seems quite smitten," Anna observed.

Smitten? So others thought that too? "I don't know how something would work. His work means he's always hyper busy."

"Yet he's here today," Serena said.

"Hmm. I guess it's true then. People make time for what's important."

Serena glanced at him, her lips pulling to one side as if recognizing he'd quoted her, before Jackie requested refills for coffee.

He mingled more, and as people started to leave, he assisted Anna and Jackie in completing the second round of washing up and straightening the house once more.

"Thanks for that, guys," Serena said, as he joined the others waiting at the door.

"Serena, today has been amazing." Toni hugged her tight.

His chest squeezed. Toni and Ethan did deserve to feel as special and loved as any much-wanted baby born to a loved up young family. Serena was right, and today she'd pulled off something that he'd never be able to do, with all the sweetness and grace that wasn't native to him but seemed part of God's character.

"I'm just so glad it's worked out." Serena pulled back with a smile.

"You must be exhausted." Joel lifted the baby car-seat carrier, little Ethan already fast asleep, his tiny thumb in his mouth.

"Like I said, I enjoy this. But I'll sleep well tonight."

"You deserve to," he said warmly.

Her smile flickered, then she turned and hugged Anna and Jackie goodbye, then bent to kiss Ethan on the top of the head before turning to him. "See you, Joel."

He stood, wondering for a moment if he'd be the lucky recipient of a hug, too, but when none came, pushed past the disquiet and said, "Bye, Serena."

He caught Toni's bemused glance. "What?"

Toni chuckled. "For a moment there I thought you looked like you wanted a hug or kiss, too."

Serena blushed even as he felt his own cheeks redden. "I don't think Joel really wants a hug or a kiss from me," she murmured, refusing to look him in the eye.

Joel placed the baby carrier down and gave her a swift hug, catching the scent of her perfume, enjoying the press of her curves against his frame. His pulse quickened, and he was sorely tempted to linger. He stepped back instead. "Um, thanks again."

Her eyes were wide. "You're welcome."

"See you tomorrow?"

She shook her head. "I'll have to skip training in the morning as I'll need to catch up with my parents."

Disappointment creased his chest, but he wouldn't advertise it. "Catch you Sunday, then."

She nodded, her smile squeezing his chest. "Bye."

And as he drove home, he did his best to ignore Toni's teasing comments and Ethan's just-woken-up tears and wondered about the name of Serena's perfume.

~

"...AND yesterday was little Ethan Wakefield's christening. I'm his godmother, and we had the lunch here."

"Wakefield? Who is that? I feel like I should recognize the name," her mother's brow furrowed.

"John and Angela's new assistant minister, remember? His sister, Toni, just had the baby."

"Oh, the assistant minister, that's right. I remember Trudy emailing us a church newsletter concerning that." Her mother nodded. "What's his name again?"

"Joel." She felt her cheeks heat. Why had he hugged her yesterday? Just because his sister goaded him? He couldn't like her—he'd made it very plain that he didn't date women in his church—but in that moment, his look of uncertainty before he'd wrapped her in his arms and she'd inhaled his musky scent, she could've sworn he cared. A little bit, at least. That's what Anna and Jackie seemed to think, anyway.

"Is he nice?"

She didn't trust herself to speak, only managing a non-committal "Mmm," before quickly adding, "Toni is great, and her son Ethan is so sweet."

"Well, I'm glad you had a nice time."

Serena nodded. She *had* enjoyed the time. Even meeting Toni and Joel's friends had helped her understand a little more about Joel's initial assessment. Toni's city friends were nice, even if a little more coolly stylish and more artistically attired than most of those who lived in Muskoka Shores.

"Now, Serena, I wanted to ask you if you had plans for your birthday."

"To be honest I haven't really thought about it yet. I've been training for a fun run—"

"A what?"

Hadn't she told her mother this in previous conversations? "I'm going in a fun run, Mom. It's a five kilometer run."

Her mother blinked. "Are you sure you should be doing such a thing?"

No. But, "I'm getting fitter, Mom. I thought you'd be pleased."

"Well, I'll agree you are looking like you've lost weight."

"I have. Over ten pounds."

"Well! That's good."

Her chin lifted. Yes, it was. "So anyway, that's in a few weeks, then I've got some important Thanksgiving things at the resort the following weekend, then it's the Cranberry Festival in Bala after that, so those things have taken up my time."

"Right. Well, it won't be too long after that, then it's your birthday, and, well, your father and I were wondering if you'd like to come and visit us here."

"In November? I don't know if I could arrange that so soon."

"Well, you won't know unless you ask, will you?" her mother asked. "It would be nice to see you, especially after all that's occurred with Dwight and that Hope character."

Oh. She hadn't had much time to think on them in recent days. "I'm doing better, Mom." Mostly. Even if the voices that compared her to others still sang at night. *You'll be alone. Nobody wants you.* Except to cook and clean, it seemed. Ugh.

"Of course you are, honey."

She did her best to keep from wincing. Mom couldn't help sounding patronizing at times. "I'll see if I can get some time off. But it wouldn't be for long," she warned. "Maybe a week, two tops."

"A week is barely worth coming," her mom complained.

"Mom, I do have a new job I'm committed to doing. I'm owed some time off, but it can't be too close to Christmas. Leave it with me and I'll see what I can do."

"Just think, you'll be twenty-nine! I still remember when you talked of twenty-nine as being old."

Back when she'd been a twelve-year-old, but whatever.

"We'll be sure to visit some of the old haunts. There are some people here who remember you."

"Mom, I need to first check if I can get the time off. Don't go planning anything yet, please."

"Live by faith, that's what your father always says. Don't be so negative."

Serena soon ended the call, promising, again, to do her best to get time off. But her mother's words had struck deep, especially as they echoed what Joel had said in recent weeks. How often did she let those negative thoughts dwell in her head?

Her Bible reading recently had shown the importance of taking thoughts captive, reminding her that she wasn't a passive victim of whatever evil words were sent her way. But how often did she simply sink under their weight, and pay more attention to that than to God's words? How could she be the example for Ethan she'd promised to be just yesterday? She sighed. "Lord, help me be aware so I can take those thoughts captive."

The rest of her Monday passed as most did: housework, groceries, exercise. She was jog-walking along the shoreline, hoping nobody would see her, when a familiar car passed by. Her heart stuttered. Dwight. She turned, watching as it disappeared. Was that Hope inside?

Agitation rose, along with a familiar murmur: *You're fat, so naïve, you'll never amount to anything.*

"No, I'm not fat." The mirror was kinder these days. She'd needed to buy a new dress yesterday when even those that she'd stashed in the back of the closet that used to fit didn't quite work anymore.

And maybe she'd always be more inclined to innocence, but that wasn't such a bad thing. Better that rather than being cynical, mistrusting everyone she met.

"And I am amounting to things." Her chin lifted. Hello: Muskoka Shores Resort Coordinator. Entering the marathon, even if it was only five k's. "You were wrong, Hope. Completely wrong."

But even as she spoke the words aloud, a strain of something deeper trickled uncertainty within. Self-improvement and enhanced circumstances were all well and good, but what happened next time? Would she still feel this way if she wasn't the resort coordinator?

Her phone buzzed, and she glanced at the caller ID. Trudy, from church. "Hello?"

The conversation about next month's open house Thanksgiving in the church hall took up the rest of her walk home—no more jog-walking for her—and chased her into an evening spent making apple and blueberry pies. These were desserts she could freeze, for the upcoming few weeks would be busy at the resort as families escaped to make the most of the Autumn color before the winter cold crept in. And while the pies baked, she checked her online diary for upcoming resort commitments, then found the form for leave and filled it in. Maybe such short notice could be met with a miracle after all. Mom was right. Faith wasn't just believing but sometimes required action behind it as well.

Her mind flashed to a face, to dark blue eyes, a rasp of cheek. Maybe a step of faith was needed in other areas as well.

CHAPTER 12

Race day arrived, and after the past weeks of training, it felt good to pull up outside Serena's house early Saturday morning, knowing today would prove their hard work had all been worth it. Joel moved through pre-dawn darkness and knocked on her door. It opened, spilling light and warmth.

"Morning."

"So it is." She covered her yawn, then smiled apologetically. "Give me thirty seconds and I'll be ready."

"Sure." He wasn't sure if that meant to wait inside or not, but he decided to stay, seeing it gave him another chance to see her space. She'd moved to the kitchen beyond, so he took a moment to check out the photos on the mantelpiece near the fire. An older couple in a black-and-white shot might be her grandparents. Another photo, a middle-aged couple near a temple, might be her parents, judging from the woman's eyes. A third photo, a woman, man and two boys—a sister, maybe?

A squeak of the floor announced Serena's return. "I see you've found the family photos."

"I noticed them the other day but didn't get to examine them. Your mom looks like you."

"You think?"

"You have similar shaped eyes."

She nodded. "That's about it, really."

"She's pretty, so are you."

She squinted at him. "How much sleep did you get last night?"

"Enough. Why?"

"Hmm. Maybe you're not caffeinated enough yet." She motioned to the dining table. "I made coffee for the drive, and there's some paleo chocolate slice. Don't worry, it's tasty, but should provide the energy hit just before the race."

"Fun run, remember?"

Her smile flared. "Yeah, you mention it so often it's kind of hard to forget."

Two minutes later they were dodging roadwork on the road to Bracebridge, clutching coffees as the lit houses of early risers flashed past. They soon left Muskoka Shores and traveled through the stretch of forest before the next town. They passed the spotlit sign for the resort. "No weddings today?"

"Only a very small one, less than twenty people, and Cherry has everything under control."

He wondered if Serena had ever been one of those women who had planned out their whole wedding before meeting the groom. His line of work meant he'd come across some people like that. Probably best he didn't follow through with the temptation to ask that question.

"Do you enjoy working at the resort?"

"I really do." She glanced at him. "I know my job may seem a little pointless at times, that some might call it basically pandering to rich people, but I like the fact we are there to smooth the way for people at significant moments in their lives."

"Who has called it pandering to rich people?"

A beat. "My mom and dad."

He glanced across, saw her shadowed profile. "Ouch."

"I think they sometimes forget that God loves rich people as much as beggars."

He nodded. Sometimes that was easy to forget.

"Anyway, I don't want to talk about that. I want to talk about the race. Have you done many before? What do I need to expect?"

He shared a little about his previous race experiences, answering her questions as best he could. When he'd first heard about the Muskoka marathon, he'd been tempted to up his training to see if he could reach the Boston marathon qualifying time. But then helping Serena had trumped that goal, and the past few weeks had proven fun, as he dared her to test her limits, while he danced around his own.

Was it wrong to be in this space of friends-but-wondering-about-more, especially when he was a pastor? He was tempted to talk with John and Angela about it, but they'd been visiting their niece in the city, and he hadn't wanted to intrude on family time. But the more time he spent in Serena's company the more drawn he was to her. But he still wasn't sure how she felt about him.

"I still don't understand why we needed to taper off the week before we race."

"It's so your body is rested enough so it has enough energy to push through on the day. It also gives your body enough time to heal in case training has taken a toll."

"I've hardly trained enough for that to happen."

"You'd be surprised. And even for five kilometers it can make a difference."

"You know I've never actually run all five kilometers. Not in one attempt, anyway."

"I know that you're putting yourself out there and having a go. And I dare to think you've had more fun than you thought."

He glanced across again, caught her smothered smile. "Maybe."

"Definitely. Come on, admit it."

"You'll never get me saying that I think running is fun."

"You say that now."

Thirty minutes later they were in a crowd of other runners, runner's bib (complete with GPS timing chip) now securely pinned. The marathon runners had already left, the half marathon participants were about to leave, and soon it would be their turn. He'd figured coming early would allow time for Serena to know more of what to expect, for her nerves to calm.

"Want to do some stretching?"

She glanced across to where some of the more obvious athletes were bending, others being massaged with foam rollers. "They all look so fit," she murmured.

"Fitness isn't about a body shape."

She bit her lip, tugging at the bottom of her pink tank top, as if unconvinced. "I don't think I'm dressed right."

"You look great." So she was curvier than most women here. He didn't mind her curves one bit. "Come on. Stretch with me."

He took them through a few warmups, and the cool, moist air of morning soon warmed with the rising sun. The sky was threaded with clouds, and puddles suggested there'd been overnight rain. He kept up the small talk, assuring her that the route would be beautiful, especially with the lakes they'd pass, and the ripening tree color.

"It is really pretty here." She glanced around.

"Sure is." He drew in a deep breath and looked away, sucking down some fresh air. With that glow on her cheeks and sparkle in her eyes, how could he ever have called her plain?

The crack of the starter's pistol sounded through the air, and a mass of bodies heaved along the stretch of road, closed for today's race. "Okay, they're going to call us in fifteen minutes.

Let's collect whatever stuff you don't need and lock it away and get back here."

They grabbed baseball caps, sunglasses, and phones then locked the rest in his truck along with their jackets. She rubbed her hands along her bare arms, and he was tempted to warm her in his hug, before noticing some of her friends had gathered nearby.

"Looks like someone has some fans." He pointed to where Anna stood with Jackie, Rachel, and Toni, Ethan in her arms. They saw him notice and waved. He grinned and nudged Serena's shoulder. "I think they're proud of you."

She waved back. "I think they're about to be disappointed."

"Whoa." He shifted to study her. "Don't say that, please."

"Say what? The truth? I'm not going to do well today, I'll be lucky if I make it to the finish line, and having others here will just show them how bad I am."

"Serena." He waited until she met his eyes. "They're here because they love you. They are proud of you. It doesn't matter how you do today, what matters is that you're doing it. Are any of them running? No. Have any of them competed in a race like this before?"

She shook her head.

"Then own this moment and be glad that you have put yourself out there. You have made a difference in your own life, and you feel better than you did three months ago, right?"

"Yes."

"Who knows who you'll inspire because you're doing this today? And because you're you, not some athlete who does this all the time, but you, just having a go, trying something new, that's what really counts."

She blinked, and he could see a familiar shimmer of tears. As she shook her head his heart fell. He hadn't meant to sound mean.

"Why do you have to be so nice?" she murmured, dashing at her eyes. "Now I need a tissue."

He smiled, then hurried to a nearby registration table, snatched several tissues from a box and hurried back to her side. As she wiped her eyes and blew her nose, he gave a thumbs up to her friends.

"Thank you."

"You ready? Pumped? Excited?"

She rolled her eyes. "So pumped. So excited."

He laughed. "It's gonna be okay. Just slow and steady. We're not aiming to break records, just having a go, okay?"

She nodded, her chin lifting, her shoulders straightening. "Okay."

The race marshal gathered the five k competitors near and issued instructions. "All right. You guys are next. You're pretty easy, you'll be racing to the drink station and back along the same road to finish here. Any questions?" There were none. "Well, let's go."

Joel rubbed Serena's shoulder. "You've got this. Have fun and enjoy the journey."

She smiled. "You too."

And ten seconds later, the pistol cracked and they were away.

SERENA BEGAN A SLOW JOG, weaving in and out of the crowds of runners as from one side she heard, "Go, Serena!"

She glanced across and managed a smile and a small wave as Rachel and the others waved back.

"You and your fans," Joel teased, jogging beside her, his pace a thousand times slower than normal.

"You know, I'm really going to be okay," she said, between careful breaths. "I don't need you to hold my hand."

His mouth curved. "You sure?"

Her heart pattered. She refocused on the tarmac and the yellow strip along the center of the road. They'd now left the crowd of well-wishers behind.

"Maybe I want to keep an eye on you," he murmured.

Oh goodness. Did the man know the effect his words, that tone, had on her? But she couldn't deal with this. Not when it would be all she could do to keep jogging. "Just go. Please. I'll be fine."

"You're sure?"

"Yes! Now go!" She flashed him a smile.

Finally, he nodded and threaded his way through the crowd of joggers who all seemed young and built for speed, not comfort eating. But even as she slowed her pace to her usual shuffle speed, her mind flicked back to his encouragement from before. Today wasn't about how well she did, how far she managed to jog before dropping to a walk, or even if she reached the finish line or not. Joel was right. Today was about the fact she'd counted herself worthy enough to compete. To have a go. She might not win, but this, doing this, amounted to something.

That thought strengthened her legs as she heard the cheers of spectators sitting in their driveway. That thought kept her going as she passed a silver lake, the autumn color reflected in the mirror-like water. That thought pushed her on as she was passed by many, many people. Older people. Fatter people. Fitter people.

But it didn't matter so much anymore. Now she'd committed to this, she felt the draw, the lure to press on. Even when her knees hurt, and her mouth dried, and her head ached. Even when she noticed people in the distance who were heading her direction—seriously? They were heading back already? How had they run that so fast? Were they even from her own race? A glance at her runner's bib showed the same color. Huh. Maybe they were. But it didn't matter. She wasn't competing against them anyway. Joel was right. This was about competing against herself. And she could do this. She *would* do this.

She inhaled deeply of the fresh morning air, catching the birdsong over the *slap, slap, slap* of her sneakers. The times of training might not have been long but they had conditioned her to take time to appreciate her surroundings. And this part of Muskoka expressed yet more of this region's beauty. Clear lakes. Honey-tinged trees. Nature at its finest. Pity the poor people who lived elsewhere in the world.

The people heading the other direction increased, and she nodded, smiled, and thumbs-upped those who offered encouragement. Joel passed her, his smile like a shot of adrenaline that pushed her onwards. In the distance she caught sight of the drinks station, the halfway mark. Blue shirted people had gathered under a tent, and as she neared, she could see they were handing out clear cups of water and Gatorade. She slowed but didn't stop and stammered her thanks as she collected one and gulped it down. Joel had said not to drink too much during the race, and she tossed her empty cup at the used cup table, refusing any more.

She pressed on, her mouth starting to taste of blood and metal. Her breath rasped, heaving in and out. She slowed some more—any slower and she really would be walking—and spent some time concentrating on her breathing. Deep breath in through the nose, long exhalation through the mouth. The focus on her breathing calmed her heart, and she refocused on the rhythms of her movement. Moving onwards. Pressing forward. Letting go of what had been. Reaching for the new, for what awaited.

What does await, Lord?

New things. Good things. Good people, like Toni and Joel.

Her heart fluttered. She barely trusted her own thoughts and heart's desire these days. And while nice, and encouraging, Joel had not given much indication of his feelings. Should she even dare contemplate what a relationship with him could be like?

She almost stumbled, so refocused, putting one foot ahead of the other. She might be jogging at tortoise speed, but she hadn't dropped to a walk yet—even if some of those might consider this speed slower than their usual walking pace.

By now it seemed she was the only one in the race. A glance over her shoulder revealed only a few walkers behind her. Everyone else was ahead. But that was okay. She was nearing the end. And—she barely dared admit it—this had actually been kind of fun. She passed another stretch of lake, then drew near the people sitting in their driveways who cheered again.

"Come on! Nearly there!" they called.

Her pace picked up, and she could see the blue banner of the finish line ahead. Just keep going, just keep going...

A haze of dizziness washed across her, and nearly stumbled again, but blinked hard. "Lord, help me make it," she muttered.

Her breath was loud in her ears, her lungs heaving, her throat raw. But she was almost there, almost there...

"Come on, Serena!"

Anna's voice. She glanced across and saw her friends waving. Her heart lifted. She could do this. She *would* do this. She gritted her teeth.

"You're doing awesome," Rachel called.

She nodded, unable to call out in case she lost focus. But she *was* doing awesomely well, she was going to make it.

The crowds at the blue banner signaling the finish line had swollen, and she knew a moment's embarrassment for coming in so slow. But she was finishing, she was *finishing*. It felt like a miracle, but it was true. And it was all due to the man waiting at the end, his broad grin testifying to his joy and encouragement that had seen her see this through. She grinned at him, saw him clap his hands, and her heart and pace lifted.

"Come on, girl! Just fifty meters more," Rachel's voice again.

She could do this, she *would* do this. Twenty, fifteen, ten.

Her mouth sawdust dry, her legs aching, she crossed the finish line to whoops and cheers. "You did it!"

High fives on either side. She laughed between gasps as she stumbled through to the blue-flag lane as directed by race volunteers, then she was handed a blessed bottle of water, a medal, and a bag of sponsor materials.

"Congratulations."

She pivoted, meeting Joel and his grin.

"I knew you could do it."

He opened his arms and with her last ounce of energy she rushed to hug him. He swept her up, and it didn't matter that she was sweaty (so was he), or that her face had to be a hundred shades of scarlet, or that she felt close to dying and needed a drink and a good sleep. As he twirled her in his arms, she knew he'd been right. She'd needed to do this. To break through. For herself, not for anyone else.

"I'm so proud of you," he said, easing her down, rubbing her arms. "You did amazing."

"I feel amazing," she said. "I never thought I could do that."

"I knew you could." He stared at her and the hubbub around them hushed. His hands closed gently around her upper arms. "Serena, I—"

"Oh! There you two are!" Rachel called.

Joel dropped his hands fast and stepped away as they were swarmed with her friends and Toni, their excitement bursting the moment of tenderness from before.

"Let's look at your medal!" Anna said.

Oh, right, her medal. Serena glanced at it—a generic weighted-plastic trophy of what she'd accomplished today—and handed it over. She'd have time to look at it later and think about what it meant.

"You're barely even puffing!" Jackie said after giving her a hug, before slipping off her puffer jacket, and draping it over her. "Don't get cold, okay?"

"Thanks." Her friends were so good to her.

Joel handed Serena a bottle of Gatorade, with the caution to drink it slowly.

Serena nodded, twisted open the lid, and sipped it as Rachel cheered some more. "I thought you promised that you'd be bright red afterwards. You're hardly pink!"

She wasn't? But suddenly it didn't matter what she looked like. It was what she'd done, what she'd overcome, that really made the difference.

"You were awesome," Toni said. "I'm so inspired."

"Oh, don't," Serena murmured as Toni drew her into a hug. "You'll make me cry."

"Honestly, we're all really proud of you," Anna said, rubbing her back.

"Especially Joel," Toni murmured in Serena's ear, before pulling back.

Serena's glance flicked to him, and he nodded. "You did great," he said.

"You know I actually ran the whole way. I didn't walk once."

"See? You never know what you're capable of unless you have a go."

"Exactly," Rachel said, her head tilted to Joel. "You'll never know what might happen unless you have a go, Serena."

Serena blinked, and shook her head, as her friends laughed, and Joel smiled, but she'd bet anything that he didn't get *that* joke.

Except...was it a joke? What if there was something to pursue there? What if pushing forward and living by faith meant daring to risk her heart again?

"Come on, people, please move off the track. The half marathoners are nearly here," a blue-shirted official called.

Serena shifted to the side, the crowd's movement bumping

her against Joel. He steadied her, placing a hand on her back as he guided her through the crowds. "How are you doing?" he asked, his eyes intent on hers.

"I'm okay."

He shook his head. "You're more than okay. You're amazing."

Happiness glowed within her heart, and she was about to wrap her arm around his waist when the surge of excitement suggested the first of the half marathoners were almost here.

"It's a tight race," someone called, and she pushed to her toes, but the crowd didn't let her see.

The roar of the crowd picked up, and she joined in with a smile as she clapped and cheered. She angled away and grinned at Toni. This was fun. A fun run indeed.

"So, are you going to do anything to celebrate?" Anna asked, her smile shifting between Serena and Joel.

"I, um," Serena shook her head. "I hadn't dared think I'd finish, so—"

"You should though," Toni said. "What do you think, Joel? Seeing as you're the one who made her put in all that hard work, maybe you should take her out to celebrate."

His gaze fell on Serena, his smile tentative. "What do you—?"

Rachel's gasp stole their attention.

"What?"

She pointed, and Serena swiveled, to see two faces, two dropped jaws. No. Oh no.

"Are you serious?" Hope said, her gaze trickling down Serena's attire. "Did you come here to compete?" She sidled into Dwight's sweaty side.

Judging from Dwight's heavy breathing he'd either just finished the half marathon or just finished a make-out session with Hope. Judging from the different colored runner's bib dangling from his singlet she guessed the former, but it didn't mean the other hadn't happened already. Her stomach tensed.

"I thought you didn't run," Dwight said to her.

His words stole hers. How to explain her motivation in running today?

"Maybe she's here because she knew you'd be here too," Hope crooned, her hand stroking Dwight's chest.

"No," Serena whispered. "No," she said louder. "I ran for me."

"Right." Hope's cold eyes flickered to Joel, and down his shirt. "I see."

What did she see?

"Five k, huh?" Hope's lip curled.

Why did her sneer feel like a bullet? Serena peeked at Dwight, but he was frowning at Joel, and any thought of making introductions fled.

"Looks like you've found someone more your speed," Hope said.

What?

Serena glanced at Joel, who wore his own furrowed brow as he looked at her then pivoted away.

Her breath hitched. No. Surely Joel didn't think she'd done all of this in some stupid attempt to win Dwight back?

That thought drew fresh dizziness, and she stumbled back, back into the protective arms of her friends, back into their murmurs of comfort and security.

"Watch yourself, Serena," Hope called. "You'll never get him back."

Get Dwight back, or Joel? Or—she saw his averted gaze, his tightened jaw—had she never really had a chance with him anyway?

All through the celebratory meal—which Anna and Jackie had insisted on, even though Serena's celebrations felt like they had ended—she listened to Rachel and Anna's complaints about Hope's audacity, listened to Toni and Jackie's forced cheer, while peeking at Joel to see if his tight expression would ease.

It didn't, and she wasn't too surprised when he took a phone call, and with an air of relief said he needed to leave. "Sorry, that was John. He's sick, and I need to get back to prepare for the service tomorrow."

"But we haven't had dessert yet," Toni complained, shooting Serena a look as if to say, 'Hey, help me out, I'm trying to keep the man here.'

But she couldn't insist he stay, especially not when he had work. Neither could she insist he drive her home. She couldn't bear another near-silent drive like the one from the fun run site to here.

So when he glanced her way, she bowed her head and murmured thanks for the ride this morning, wishing she had space and privacy to tell him all she was truly thankful for—his support, constant encouragement, kindness, his belief in her. She wished she could take that step of faith and be bold enough to tell him all she really thought, all she hoped, all she dreamed. But she couldn't. Not with her friends watching. Not when she remained unsure whether he still meant that comment earlier about not dating women in his congregation. What if she was misreading things again? Her heart was too fragile for more rejection.

And as she watched him leave, her friends berated her for letting him go, and she couldn't help but silently agree.

CHAPTER 13

The scents and sounds of Thanksgiving filled his nose and ears. Joel listened to the women across the pumpkin and gourd-dressed table share about their weeks, while the church hall filled with the chaos of the church's open-house lunch. But he was thankful to be here, especially after the questions concerning last weekend's triumph-turned-inner turmoil were soon swamped with greater problems: namely John's illness, which necessitated Joel taking over all his church responsibilities for the week. He'd never known just how much weight John bore until it was shoved onto his shoulders. No wonder the man needed an assistant.

It was only when Toni had complained about his abrupt departure from the post-race lunch, or he saw Serena's bowed head in church, or he was woken by Ethan's cries at night, that he dared contemplate what needed to be said to Serena. He had to say something to her. He had to know if her heart was still taken by Dwight or if she'd been making room for him. Because he sure didn't want to be somebody's leftovers, not when he'd thought he was finally ready to offer his heart to a woman again.

"This has been the best Thanksgiving meal I remember," Toni said, nudging him.

"Sure has." And not just because the day had proved his first respite in a week, or because his mom—God rest her soul—had not been the world's most patient cook.

The church hall buzzed with families, singles, old and young, the 'waifs and strays' as Toni privately called them. But for people like themselves, without near relatives, it was a great opportunity to connect with not just other church members but those in the community seeking a place to feel a sense of family.

And it was all good. Except for one thing. He sipped his sparkling cider, glancing at the door. Still not here. Was she going to come? He hadn't spoken to her since just after the race, their exchanges consisting of a single text message on Monday when he'd said he couldn't meet for their run and she'd replied with a NO WORRIES followed a second later by THANKS AGAIN FOR ALL YOUR HELP.

He hadn't known how to answer that—it sounded like a dismissal to him—and church duties hadn't allowed space or enough emotional energy to reply. He knew he had to talk with her, to find out if that look she'd given Dwight had been shock or delight—had she really run for herself, as she had claimed, or was it all to get back at two people who had done 'er wrong? But given the number of people here, even if she did show up, this place wasn't exactly conducive to open heart sharing.

Anyway, she was probably busy at the resort. That's what Toni had said.

But still, he couldn't help but look up with each new arrival, hoping it might be her, a look followed each time by a sharp twist of disappointment when he realized it wasn't.

"You okay?" his sister murmured. "You're really quiet. I think Suzy and Annette think there's something wrong with you."

He managed a weak smile for the two women seated opposite and did his best to act interested and ask about their businesses and years in town. But the amount of talking he'd done this past week wearied him, and while he'd usually found it energizing, he kinda wished when he returned from the day that he could relax and talk—or not talk—over the day with someone who wasn't just obsessed with baby news. He loved his sister, and his nephew, but he didn't like the way Toni watched him watch the door, her smile saying more than he wanted to hear.

He dug into his baked potatoes and turkey, saving his favorite for the end. Nothing beat the taste of unadulterated sweet potatoes.

"Hey." A nudge in his side drew his attention to his sister. "You can relax now."

"What do you—oh."

Serena stood at the door, holding two plates that looked like they might be pies. Something unclenched within his heart.

"You could be a gentleman and go help her," Toni murmured.

But as he pushed out his seat he saw Trudy, the church secretary, already hurrying to help her.

"Snooze you lose, Joel."

"Do you mind?" he muttered.

His sister smirked. "Not at all."

"Serena, you made it! I'm so glad. It wasn't the same without you." Trudy Peterson's warm welcome and the greetings from the other people filled the room.

He overheard Serena give a quick explanation for her late arrival—she'd needed to wait until the resort's lunch was underway—then she moved to what remained of the main course items set out buffet style on the trestle table at one end.

Joel tried to pay attention to Suzy's discussion about organic coffee beans, but over her shoulder he could see Serena pause, as if looking for something. Again his ears zeroed in to listen like they hadn't gotten his internal memo to stay away.

"Have you found everything you need?" Trudy asked her.

"I was hoping you might have more of the plain sweet potatoes."

Joel looked guiltily at his plate while Trudy replied. "It looks like we're out."

"Actually," Toni waved her hand. "Joel has some he's willing to share."

Serena's uncertain glance hurried him to push out his seat and take his plate to hers. "Sorry about that. I didn't know you liked plain sweet potatoes, otherwise I would've saved you some. A dinner like this isn't the same without them, right?"

"Oh, but—"

"I swear, I haven't touched them, so they're safe to eat." Using the tongs he plopped the orange vegetables onto her plate. "They should still be warm, at least."

"You didn't have to do that."

"Actually, I kinda did." Her eyebrows rose. "You looked so sad, and we can't have that. Not when today's supposed to be about thanksgiving, right?"

"I see." Her smile peeked out. "Well, thank you."

"That's the spirit," he said, earning a soft chuckle.

"Hey, Serena, there's a spare seat here." Toni waved from the table.

Huh? Was that his seat that his sister was declaring as spare?

Toni winked at him, then, once Serena sat in his chair, she rose. "Sorry. I think I can hear Ethan. Hey, Joel, can you keep my seat warm?"

Honestly. Sisters.

But he wouldn't argue—this might be his chance to make amends, after all—and took his chair next to Serena. She leaned forward and whispered, "Thank you for sharing your sweet potatoes. God bless Trudy, but I've never liked how she cooks these. I think they're sweet enough and don't need to be cooked with marshmallows or anything else."

"I totally agree. Great minds, eh?"

Her lips tipped up on one side, and he held her gaze a moment longer before Serena blinked and looked away. "Well, thanks. I haven't eaten since breakfast, I've been looking forward to this, so excuse me."

He watched as she dug into her meal with gusto. "You look like you need that."

"You wouldn't believe the day I had."

"Try me."

She swallowed, then took a sip of water. "I don't normally work on Mondays but I got a call early this morning that the power had gone out in the kitchen, which meant today's breakfast was cold only and lunch had to be delayed. People were panicking left, right and center—"

"And then you brought your special brand of calm, I bet."

Her gaze met his. "How did you know?"

Because there was something about Serena that lived up to her name.

He glanced across the table, saw Suzy and Annette were talking to the women either side of them. He swallowed. Looked like this was his time after all. "Hey, um, I wanted to apologize for running out last weekend. I feel like we need to talk, but life has been hectic this week."

"Yeah. It was kind of crazy after the race, then to see Hope and Dwight." She bit her lip. "I was shocked to see them. I don't even think I introduced you, did I?"

"I figured out who he was."

Maybe she caught the dry note in his voice, because her brows knit. "I'm so sorry they were so rude."

"You're not responsible for what others say."

"But I feel like they wouldn't have said that if it wasn't for me. And after all..." She blinked.

After all, what? After all she and Dwight had shared? Toni

hadn't exactly held back about sharing all she knew about the Serena and Dwight and Hope love triangle.

She sighed. "After all you did for me, all your kindness and support, I feel like you're my friend, and friends don't let other friends be talked about that way."

Friend? Was that all?

Maybe he looked his question, for she blushed, and her gaze lowered. "My good friend. I thought, anyway."

He thought that too. Had dared to wonder about more. This conversation had helped clear some of the confusion, but he needed extra answers. Still, he could agree with her about being good friends—

"Ahem." A voice was cleared from across the table. "Excuse me, pastor, could you pass the gravy?"

Joel dragged his attention back to Suzy and obliged. Judging from the way she and Annette were glancing between Serena and himself it seemed their private conversation had not gone unnoticed. He did his best to alleviate further speculation, talking to them, listening in to the chatter about the upcoming Cranberry Festival and what the church and other community groups did at this event. Muskoka held claim to one of the oldest cranberry farms in the province, and this upcoming weekend celebrated everything cranberry from wine to preserves, chocolates, juice and tea.

"So have you ever visited a cranberry farm?" Serena asked him.

"City boy here," Joel admitted. "Growing up, places like Wonderland and Wet'n'Wild were more our speed."

"Well, now you're here, you should check it out. It's fun to see the bogs—"

"Bogs?"

She smiled. "Do you know how cranberries grow?"

"I'm guessing in bogs?"

"Clever man. The farm has all kinds of activities during

harvest season, which is now. You can have wagon tours, taste wine—"

"Cranberry wine?"

"They do ciders, and juice as well. They even have maple products. We use a lot of their products at the resort because they're local, and their products involve less food miles, so it's fresher and better for the environment. The farm is a big attraction, so we'll often recommend our guests to visit, and they always enjoy the experience, no matter what time of year. There's a store there where you can try things. They do a nice cheese board too."

"Sounds like that'd make a nice date."

She nodded, glanced away, and smiled at where his sister was talking to Jackie. "Maybe your friend Matt might like to take Toni there."

"Maybe," he said slowly. "Or maybe you're right, and it's something I should see."

She sipped her water. "You could go there with Matt."

"Or maybe someone more local." He eyed her, wondering what she'd say. Was this something that her version of good friends did?

"That could be nice," she murmured.

"We do have a celebration to make up for."

"A celebration. Right." Her eyes lowered.

"Or..."

"Or what?"

"We could maybe see if we can make it a date."

She peeked up, her eyes wide. She tucked a loose chunk of hair behind her ear. "I heard someone once say that you didn't date people in your congregation," she murmured.

"I wonder if that person really knew what he was talking about."

Her breathing hitched. She glanced down at her empty plate. "I thought you didn't like to complicate things."

"I don't think you're complicated," he said.

Startled green eyes met his, and he smiled.

"What are you two talking about?" Toni asked, Ethan asleep on her shoulder, his tiny thumb in his mouth.

Serena glanced at him, and picked up her glass and drank, leaving him to explain. Nice. "Serena here was wondering if you'd be interested in seeing the cranberry farm."

"A cranberry farm?" Toni's nose wrinkled. "Thanks, but I don't think that's my scene."

"You might find it inspirational." Serena played with her glass. "Especially the colors at this time of year."

"You might need to sell it to me a little more than that," Toni said. "I might've moved to the country but I'm no farm girl."

"What about enjoying a cheese platter, and some non-alcoholic cider, with your friends."

"Like who? You?"

Serena nodded. "If you wanted."

"That might be fun." Toni glanced at Joel then back at Serena. "And I suppose my brother should come too."

"You only suppose?" he asked.

"You don't want to know all I suppose," Toni said, winking at him.

Okay, fair's fair. He'd call Matt later and find out which Monday he could be free to visit a cranberry farm. Then he could see if this non-dating a congregation member might work out after all.

SURELY THERE WERE BETTER ways to serve the community.

Serena dragged an arm across her eyes, as the stinging aroma from onions burned her eyes. She sniffed and propped her glasses back on. "You'd think these glasses would protect me from onion tears, but no."

Anna laughed and motioned for Serena's latest cutting board's worth of diced onions. "That's what you get for volunteering to do the hardest job."

"I don't recall actually volunteering to do this," she mumbled.

"Okay, maybe you were volunteered by a certain somebody"—she shot Rachel a glance—"but it's all for a good cause."

Chili at the Church was a Cranberry Festival tradition, a time when volunteers from local churches cooked and served all those who wanted a spicy bowl of deliciousness to combat the autumn chill. Saturday was always the busiest day, which meant they barely got a break once the clock struck eleven.

Rachel was this year's kitchen boss, which meant the various workstations saw a progression of ingredients passed along. As the person responsible for dicing onions and peppers, Serena was positioned next to Anna, who was frying the meat and onions, which then were passed along to Jackie, who was stirring the giant pots of chili. She and Rachel were serving, and Trudy and Jenny Wells were out the front taking orders and collecting money. Working in the kitchen was fun, a chance for each of them to catch up about their respective week.

"So, is anything more happening with your trip, Serena?" Jackie called.

"Yep. It's booked. I'll be gone that first week in November. It's not quite my birthday, but it's close enough."

"Your parents will love seeing you again."

"Yeah. It should be good."

And being away, having the chance to clear her head, would be good. Not having to wonder about what certain assistant ministers might be suggesting had to be good. But first she had to get through the remaining weeks of this month.

"Who's taking you to the airport?" asked Anna.

"I haven't figured that out yet."

"I know who you could ask."

Judging from the mischief in her friend's voice, Serena

would be better off not enquiring about whom she meant. "Do you think we'll need more onions?"

"Don't try and change the subject." Anna held up a wooden spoon. "It makes sense. He knows people in the city, so it's simple enough to ask if he could take you." She smiled. "I bet he says yes."

"Who'll say yes?" Rachel called.

"Joel," Anna and Jackie said in sing-song voices, before giggling like six-year-olds.

"Did I hear my name?" he asked, leaning through the servery window.

This heightened the others' laughter, and even Serena found a smile.

"What's so funny?" he asked.

"Hey, Serena, it must be about time for your break," Rachel said. "You go sit down and we'll bring you and Joel a bowl of the best chili in town."

"I'm really not that hungry," Serena protested.

"Rude!" Rachel teased. "Go sit down. I know Joel must be tired, doing whatever it was he was doing. Which was what, exactly?"

"I've been on the door, welcoming people, stuff like that."

"Working really hard then." Rachel's rolled eyes drew Serena's smile.

"You know it."

"Hey, is that nephew of yours anywhere nearby? I'm still waiting on Toni saying yes to letting me babysit," Jackie said, scooping generous portions of chili into two bamboo bowls.

"She's somewhere out there. I think the Town Crier saw her and bellowed a welcome that made Ethan cry."

"Two criers, huh?" Rachel said, adding sour cream and grated cheese on top, then placing a small bread roll on the side. "Hey Joel, we were just thinking maybe you could help Serena out."

His eyes flicked to her then back to Rachel. "I'm always happy to help."

"We figured that," Rachel said, throwing Serena a double shot of waggled eyebrows. "She's going to need a ride to the city and we wondered—"

"You know I'm perfectly capable of arranging this myself," Serena interrupted. "I don't need you to do my dirty work."

"Dirty work?" Joel's eyebrow hitched.

"It's not dirty—"

The room filled with her friends' laughter.

"Hey, want to go eat?" Joel asked her.

"Please." Anything to get away from her friends' pointed comments and amusement.

She picked up her bowl and followed him to a table in the far corner. Still under the gaze of everyone in the kitchen, but hopefully out of earshot.

"Sorry about that."

"It's okay." He motioned to their bowls. "We better eat while it's still hot."

The next few minutes passed with eating, comparing and contrasting other chili recipes, and Joel explaining about the earlier car-wash he'd assisted Mitch Wells and some of the teens in the mentoring group with.

He downed his juice—cranberry, of course—then waited for her to finish scooping out the last of her meal. "So all that before?"

She glanced at the kitchen servery window, and saw three smiling faces, and shook her head. "We were just talking."

"Did I hear something about you needing a ride to the city?"

"I'm going to see my parents."

"I thought they were in India?"

How did he know? Had she told him? She didn't think she had. "They work as missionaries there, in an English language school near Kolkata."

"That's where Mother Theresa worked, right?"

He knew that? She nodded.

"Ministering overseas is something I've dreamed about doing."

"It's been about ten years since I've last been there. I grew up there, and we'd come back for furlough. It was a great adventure, but," she shrugged, "I missed a lot of things too, like friends, and a consistent education. I came back when my older sister started high school and lived here with my grandma while my parents continued in India."

"And you went from that to working in a resort." He glanced at her bread roll. She handed it to him to his smiled thanks. "Do you think you'd ever want to do mission work?" he asked.

Serena shook her head. "Nope. I like things the way they are. I saw the sacrifices my parents made and I wouldn't want to do that."

"So you'd never want to work in full-time ministry?"

"You really want to know what I think?"

"Wouldn't ask if I didn't."

"Well." She finally looked him in the eye. "I really respect what people like John and Angela, you, and my parents do, but I don't really like how people differentiate between 'full-time' ministry and other types. I think there's a danger that the average Christian depends on the pastor to do all the ministering, and not trust God to use the Holy Spirit in themselves. I think that leads to complacent or unmotivated Christians, and busy, overworked leaders who get burnt out and frustrated." She shrugged. "I've seen my parents and others working with them end up like that, and I don't want it for anyone else."

"Wow." He chewed his bread roll, his brow grooved. "But don't you think Christians need more training to know what to say and do?"

"Maybe. Or maybe it's church leaders who need to trust the Holy Spirit more and their programs and plans less. Don't get me wrong, I love to help with Sunday school, but I think *all* of my life is supposed to be ministering to others. I know I don't always show that, but I think that if all Christians displayed God's grace and forgiveness and hope to all people, then your work would be so much easier."

"I can't argue with that."

Serena looked back at the kitchen. "I don't think 'the ministry,'" she denoted it with her fingers, "is all about church or even dealing with Christians doing Christian things. And I definitely don't feel called to be a one-woman band, trying to do it all myself."

He paused, his eyes studying her, like what she was saying was more important than food.

She swallowed. "I think it's important to delegate and encourage all Christians to be reaching out. I've seen too many good people burn out trying to be all things to all people." Serena studied him, noting the shadows under his eyes, knowing that the recent week or so with John's illness had doubled Joel's workload. She touched his hand. "Don't burn yourself out, Joel."

His gaze fused with hers, as if her touch, or maybe her words, seared him. Then he nodded, his brow furrowed again. "So, your trip to the city is actually about going to the airport."

"It's okay. I'll get a bus or something."

"When do you leave?"

She told him, and he put it in his phone calendar. "I've booked you in."

"I don't want to put you out."

"I want to take you."

The earnestness in his eyes, his tone, squeezed her heart. "Well, thank you."

"You're welcome. Oh, and speaking of booking things in, you're still free on Monday, aren't you?"

"Free for…"

"Visiting a cranberry farm with me. And Toni and Matt," he added, almost apologetically. "He only got back to me this morning and said he could swing things to make Monday work. I know it's short notice, but it could be fun, don't you think?"

She gulped her juice. Why did this feel bigger than a simple visit to a cranberry farm? Was he really suggesting they have that date he'd hinted at on Monday? She nodded.

"Awesome. I can't wait."

Her breath hitched at his deep look. Maybe this—whatever this was—had a chance of working, and they could see a way going forward.

He shared a few more details about Monday then excused himself, offering a smile and farewell that left her watching his departure with a smothered sigh. She so didn't want to be the hazy-eyed girl her friends obviously thought she should be, but her heart was fickle, as quick to admire his handsome Jesus-following form as any good Christian girl's would be.

And as she drew out her phone and quickly made a booking at the farm for Monday, she fought the smile threatening to spill all over her face. Maybe she'd know more about his thoughts concerning her after the visit to the cranberry farm in two days' time.

CHAPTER 14

Joel glanced at Serena, Toni, and Matt, each crouched in the pool of cranberries. This was so not what he'd expected. Serena looked at him and smiled, and something twinged in his chest.

"Okay, on the count of three, I want you to say cranberries!"

"Are you ready for this?" he asked.

"Born ready," she murmured.

He chuckled, enjoying this reversion to tease and banter.

"One, two, three!"

"Cranberries!" Joel yelled and threw two handfuls of the red stuff up into the sky.

A patter of little berries pelted his head, followed by Serena's giggle.

He turned to her. "Did you do that on purpose?"

"Me?"

He wrapped an arm around her and picked up another handful of cranberries, pretending to rub them in her hair. "You're kind of sneaky, aren't you?"

She laughed and pulled away. "Says the man who put cranberries down my back. I'll have red stains for days."

"Says the woman who only told us we'd be going on a wagon ride, then just happened to mention we'd be going wading as well."

Yep. In the cold water—the bog—as gray clouds threatened rain, the cranberry plunge requiring them to don these ugly chest high waders that had dismayed Matt and made Toni laugh and Joel to smile more today than he had for weeks. Who knew visiting cranberry farms could be so much fun?

"I did mention that you were supposed to dress appropriately for the weather."

"That you did say," he acknowledged.

"And that at the end of the tour you'll get to eat something."

"I'm always a fan of eating."

"I've noticed."

He chuckled, enjoying her relaxed mode, a far cry from the strain of a week or so ago.

"This is fun, eh?"

"Lots of fun," he said. Something he needed more of in his life.

"Hey, let's get one more shot of you two," Toni called.

Huh. Since when had she and Matt exited the berry-covered bog?

"Us two?" Serena asked, which met Toni's nod.

He posed in the cold water a little longer and obeyed his sister's smirked instructions to put his arm around Serena, something which seemed to chase the earlier tease away. "You don't mind, do you?" he asked, staring at the camera.

"If you mean standing close to you in a red sea of cranberries shaped like a heart, well, why would I mind that?"

"It's shaped like a heart?" he asked, looking around.

"Joel, you moved," his sister whined. "Now I've got to take it again."

"What a shame that I'll have to stand close to you in the cold for a little bit longer," he murmured through a gritted-teeth smile.

"Real shame," she said.

He glanced at her, and her face tilted toward him. In that moment he knew he could bend down and kiss her, and finally know—

"That's perfect!" Toni cried. "Awesome shot."

"Did you just take another picture?"

"Um, excuse me, miss, you may need to let somebody else have a turn," one of the farm volunteers said.

"Sorry."

After helping a giggling Serena from the water they had to remove their ungainly waders and boots. "I sure wasn't expecting all this when you talked about coming to the farm."

"I don't think many people do. It's pretty cool, isn't it?"

"Chilly even."

Her smile widened. "Harvest is the best time, but there are still things you can do in summer, like check out the blueberries, or see the maple trees in spring."

"In winter?"

"You can sit around the fire, enjoy some mulled wine and cheese."

"Did you say cheese?" Toni asked. "I'm getting hungry. But then wagon rides always make me hungry."

"How many wagon rides have you been on?" Matt asked her.

"I'll speak in the language you'll understand, Matt, and say that I've felt hungry one hundred percent of the times after I've been on a wagon ride."

"You've only been on one, right?"

"Yes."

A little while later they were doing their best to appease Toni's hunger as they sampled some of the other products from the cranberry farm store. Locally made cheeses, cranberry preserves, artisanal crackers and more, accompanied their glasses of warm cranberry cider.

He glanced across, noting the way Toni and Matt were quietly talking. He hadn't been sure about how his sister would feel about his friend visiting today, but she'd been cool. Maybe it was because she'd finally been persuaded to let Jackie babysit Ethan for a few hours and was enjoying the freedom. He suspected it might be more because Toni had her own match-making that she was keen to see occur.

And while Joel was definitely not opposed to exploring things with Serena, he did have his own questions about Matt and his sister. They were friends, that was clear, but how could something deeper work with Matt's serious nature and insanely busy work, and Toni and her artistic, creative mess? And would Matt really want to stay in the picture long term, and possibly commit to a future where he'd be Ethan's father? Joel wasn't sure.

Serena nudged his boot with hers. "You okay?"

"Just thinking."

"About?"

"The future."

She nodded, following his glance toward his sister and friend. "I don't know him well, but from what I've seen, he seems keen to make your sister happy."

"He's a good guy."

"Toni deserves a good guy," she murmured.

That she did. "I want to see Toni happy, and Ethan grow up secure, whether that's here or somewhere else." He shifted in his seat. "One day I'd like to take on a church of my own."

"Are you enjoying ministering here?"

He nodded. "But I never realized just what a big workload it can be. What you said the other day about burning out made me think."

"Think what?"

"It's easy to just go along with the flow, to put up with things, and not take action, or make changes that might prove beneficial. That's something I admire about you."

She shifted straighter in her seat. "What do you mean?"

"You've faced down challenges and haven't let them beat you. You're courageous."

Her gaze lifted to him. "Nobody's ever said that to me before."

"It's true, though."

The world fell away until it was just the two of them, Serena and him, her green eyes and small smile, and his hopes—and, okay, prayers—wavering in this quiet space between them. Was it worth pursuing someone who had said full-time ministry was not for them? But what she'd said about all aspects of life being ministry resonated too. He liked her perspective and wanted her perspective to be his, too. But if he did get a full-time pastoral position elsewhere, would she want to leave her awesome job to be with him? Or was all this overthinking when they hadn't even gone on a proper date yet? *Lord?*

A crash of a glass snapped their attention across the room, and then back to where Matt and Toni were smiling at them.

Matt placed his empty cider glass on the table. "So, what's this I hear about an upcoming visit to the city?" He glanced at Toni, then back at Joel. "You planning to visit me?"

"He's planning to take Serena to the airport," Toni said, mouth curled up in tease.

God bless sisters.

"Where are you flying to?" Matt asked Serena.

A discussion followed about India, and travel, and food, and exotic sights and experiences. It made Joel wish he'd traveled more, but life and study hadn't panned out that way. Not yet anyway.

But maybe if he was to spend more time with this jet-setting woman, he might see where that could take him too.

~

Serena pushed aside the big, black, furry-legged spider hanging in the middle of her door. Nice. She tossed it in the corner where it sat with the other Halloween decorations she'd salvaged from the storeroom. How to make a classy resort capture the Halloween vibe without heading into Tackyville was a question she'd long pondered.

The end of the Canadian Thanksgiving season meant a few swift alterations in resort décor to showcase the Cranberry Festival, before a very different feel for Halloween. She wasn't a big fan of skeletons and witches and was glad they'd only be hanging around for a few more weeks, until November when the Christmas decorations would go up and stay up until the end of January.

She sat at her desk, pulling up the bullet point list of marketing ideas. Summer and autumn were the resort's biggest seasons for tourists, but once vacation time finished, and the autumn color had mostly disappeared, tourists tended to stay away. A winter festival, then, might prove of interest. Snow was never a problem in Muskoka, thanks to being part of the province's snow belt with its large-scale weather systems and lake-effect snow. Some years Muskoka Shores topped the province for snowfall levels, which could make planning for events challenging. But if they could be events requiring little financial outlay, and independent of the weather or guest numbers, that might work. They could possibly partner with local businesses and showcase produce, and perhaps she could encourage Alphonse to showcase more local meats in his seasonal menu.

Visions of snowmen and ice sculptures, snowshoeing, mulled wine and twinkling lights filled her mind. How beautiful and romantic that could be, especially in the lead up to Valentine's Day. Especially if there was a special someone to share it with.

She smiled, thinking back to the cranberry farm visit last week, and that look of Joel's that still hitched her breath. He hadn't said anything more—they were both still busy, and he'd had another service at Golden Elms last Sunday after church—but she wondered whether something might be said next Monday when he took her to the airport. Two hours in the car had to be long enough for something to be said, right?

Her phone buzzed a message—Jenny Wells, wanting to know about what she'd need to do with the Minimites program when Serena was away. After replying, she scrolled to the photo Toni had sent last week. Serena and Joel standing in a red heart of berries, gazing at each other like Joel might want to kiss her. She shivered.

"You're getting carried away," she muttered, and returned to jotting down more resort ideas. Perhaps something to appeal to the many L.M. Montgomery fans, a mini Anne of Green Gables festival, or perhaps, more fitting because it was based on this beautiful part of the world here, something featuring *The Blue Castle*. They could have talks, or connect it to Bala's Museum, in the converted boarding house near where Lucy Maud had once stayed. That was something to further consider. Winter, spring, summer, fall – it didn't matter the time of year, Muskoka Shores and its surrounds were beautiful, and worth celebrating, worth capturing in books, in film. And...

She opened up the email she'd sent Mr. Jennings about Toni's work, wondering if there'd been any reply. The rebrand had taken a backseat in recent weeks, but perhaps it was time for a reminder. The idea of art classes floated back into memory, and she added that in along with suggestions of local art exhibitions, and the concept of an artist in residence. All things that could happen regardless of the weather, which could set their resort apart and provide income for Toni and other local artists.

She sent that off, then moved to the next thing. Her job

always had something fresh to keep her attention, the juggling of people and time and finances squeezing out long hours every day.

Maybe another benefit of going away, apart from seeing her parents, was taking a break, regaining some of that perspective that allowed for her to have more fun. That thought tracked her thoughts back to Joel and she smiled then sighed. "Come on girl, focus!" The question of Joel might get sorted in their car trip to the airport in five days' time.

"Are you serious? A day's worth of traveling?"

Serena turned from her position in the front seat and smiled at Toni, next to the baby seat in the back. "I think it's actually a little more. We leave midday here, and with the layover in Dubai it means I'll arrive around seven the following night."

"That's insane."

Serena nodded. It kind of felt like it, especially when put like that. "It's cheaper for me to do it than for my mom and dad to bear the cost."

"What do you do on the plane for all that time?" Joel asked.

She shrugged. "Read, watch movies, sleep. I don't mind it too much. I view it as me-time."

"And you don't do a lot of that."

Not really. For someone who lived on her own you'd think she'd do more, but self-care tended to fall by the wayside. "It seems like a long time in a plane, and it is, but it does help provide some head-space so I can leave my stress here and focus on what's ahead."

"So apart from seeing your parents, what are you most looking forward to?"

"Well, it's been years since my last visit, but I can guarantee it'll be warmer there than here."

A dump of early snow flashed past on the highway, having

taken the road workers by surprise, considering the ice-capped safety cones and other equipment. "India really is so different to anything here. The sights, the smells and sounds, the people. It's so crowded, crossing the road feels like you're taking your life in your hands, but that makes it exciting. It's just so different." It was all coming back to her now. "Oh, and the food is amazing. I'll have to cook you some when I get back. It's melt-in-the-mouth delicious."

"We'll hold you to it, won't we, Joel?"

"Yep." Joel's expression was amused. "I don't think I've ever seen you so excited."

Joel's teasing comment made Serena pause as she reflected. "It's been ten years since I was in India. And it might only have been a year or so but it feels like ages since I've seen my folks. I'm really looking forward to it."

She glanced across. She knew from what Toni said it had been only a few years since their parents had passed. This conversation might be bringing up memories, for both him and Toni.

He glanced at her and smiled, easing her concern. "You'll enjoy catching up."

She nodded, holding back her misgivings. Maybe it was uncharitable to have some doubts about her parents' motivations in asking her to come. They wouldn't try to guilt her into focusing on the needy, would they? Or insisting she give up her job and stay? She bit her lip.

"Hey, what's that look for?" Joel asked, as Ethan's protest in the back drew Toni's attention.

"I love my parents, but sometimes we don't really think about things the same way."

"That full-time ministry thing?"

"Yeah."

"I'll be praying for you."

"Thanks." Her eyes blurred, and she had to look out the

window. When was the last time a guy had said he'd pray for her? Dwight had never offered, and even if he had she thought it'd be tokenistic. Joel, she sensed, would actually pray for her. And the thought he cared enough to do that drew greater warmth toward him in her heart.

At the airport she checked in and dropped her bags, and they had time for a coffee while waiting.

"You're going to have such a good time."

Serena looked up from where she was tickling baby Ethan's toes and smiled at Toni. "I'll be sure to think of you, while I'm sipping my mango lassi, enjoying the warm weather."

"Yeah, you be sure to do that." Toni rolled her eyes.

Serena's chuckle met with her coffee and spluttered.

Joel handed her a paper napkin while an amused glint in his eye gave away his real thoughts. "What time do you need to get to security by?"

Serena glanced quickly at her phone. "About now."

They moved to the security gates and she gave Toni a hug, before leaning into the stroller to hug baby Ethan and give him a kiss.

Joel watched the tender moment, before teasing Serena. "Do I get one of those?"

Serena looked up. What did he want? She stared at him, her lips playing with a smile while she considered his words. "Sure, why not?"

She stepped into his personal space, wrapping her arms around him while she gave him a hug, savoring the feel of his arms around her again. Easing back, she looked up at him again —should she? Oh, why not?—then swiftly pushed up and brushed her mouth against his.

Oh. She hadn't realized what she'd started. His initial hitch of breath signaled surprise, but the way his lips firmed and his hands slid to cradle her face closer suggested he liked this too. His kiss was warm and tender, tasting of the coffee he'd recently consumed, and as his chin abraded hers and she wanted to nestle closer she knew she needed to stop. So she did, pulling away from his arms abruptly.

Uncertainty rushed through her. What had she done? But it was too late now. Best to pretend to own the confidence that kiss proclaimed. She gave the open-mouthed Toni a final smile, then turned to depart through to security. "Bye!"

"Have fun," Toni called. "See you in ten days."

A glance at Joel revealed his stunned expression, but he managed a small wave. Serena quirked a tiny smile, heaving out a shaky breath as she rounded a corner and he disappeared from view. Dear heavens. What on earth would happen now?

CHAPTER 15

"*H*ello? Earth to Joel!" Toni waved a hand in front of his face, her mirth barely under control.

He rubbed his lips, sure they must be marked with the imprint of Serena's. He still wasn't sure what had happened, except that might've just been the most glorious moment of his life…

"That was just the funniest thing ever!" Toni didn't bother now to hide the laughter. "My ever-serious brother just got kissed something good."

Yes. He had. Something *seriously* good. His chest pounded with a tumult of emotions. Had that been a dream, or had Serena—sweet, sometimes shy, Serena—just up and kissed him? The tingle rolling through his lips all the way to his heart said yes.

"I wish I'd caught that on camera." Toni chuckled again.

"I don't get why you keep laughing," he grumbled.

"It might have something to do with your expression."

"What about it?" He exhaled, grabbing the handles of Ethan's stroller and pushing it to the exit.

"You looked shocked, then you looked like you could've been in one of those movies. You know, the romantic ones."

"Yeah, those ones I never watch."

"Or those cartoons with hearts for eyes."

He cut her a look.

"Come on. You asked for it. Like, you *literally* did."

"But I didn't think..." Her kiss would taste so sweet. That her skin would be so soft. That her curves—Stop! He wasn't meant to be thinking about that. "I didn't mean for that to happen, though." Although, now it had...just how long until she got back?

"You like her, don't you? Come on, everyone has known for months."

They had?

"Oh, don't look like that. It was obvious." She smiled up at him. "When was the last time you were kissed?"

Joel thought back to Mel. His last girlfriend. The one who had made him swear off dating women in his church. Had he been wrong? Was Matt right and he'd let her determine his future, without really committing such a decision to God? For how could he have questions over Serena and her feelings toward him when it seemed she'd just announced them loud and clear?

What was he going to do?

They pushed outside to the cold air of the parking lot, but even as they drove away, he found it hard to get Serena out of his thoughts. What had made her kiss him? Did she really mean it? She had to, right? A woman couldn't kiss a man like that without it meaning something. But had it just been because he'd virtually dared her? Would she feel the same way when she returned?

. . .

"WHAT ARE YOU WORKING ON?" Toni asked, sitting on the arm of his office's sofa.

Joel pushed his office chair back from his desk and turned to face her. "I'm writing a sermon for a wedding ceremony John asked me to officiate this weekend."

"Ooh. Anyone we know?"

"Just some people from the city who wanted to elope, but decided they'd prefer to marry at a traditional church instead." He took a large swig from his water bottle. "John's dad isn't well, and he needs to be in the city nearby."

"Poor John. He's had a hard time recently, hasn't he?"

"You can pray for them if you think of it." He stretched out his arms, twisting his back to release the kinks.

"Oh, okay," she said, her voice holding sarcasm.

His attention returned to his sister. "What?"

"You know, sometimes I get the impression that you think I don't pray or believe in God anymore."

She still did?

"Wow. Good to know, oh he of little faith. Do you really think I'm that far from God?"

"Toni—"

"What did you think Ethan's christening was all about if you thought that?" she demanded.

"I didn't want to assume."

"Please. You might say that, but I think you still do. Did you really judge me for having a baby outside of marriage and think that's my relationship with God over?"

"I think a Christian tries to do things God's way—"

"And yet sometimes still makes mistakes, right? You do believe that God's grace is big enough to cover mistakes, don't you?"

"You know I do." He rubbed his forehead. How had this conversation escalated so rapidly? "I'm sorry if I haven't given that impression."

She eyed him for a moment then jerked a nod. "You should work on that grace thing, then."

"Yeah, I probably should. That thing about Christians making mistakes?" He raised his hand. "That's me, too."

"Finally," she muttered. "If only others knew you aren't so perfect."

"I'm sure you'll let them know," he said, his tight heartstrings easing at the drop in tension.

"Yeah, well, some seem to know already, and still like you enough to kiss you. They're obvs as weird as you."

He wouldn't comment. He hadn't heard from Serena all week, and knowing she'd be back in a few days was making him edgy, wondering what he should do, what to say. But ask his little sister if she'd heard from Serena he would not do.

"So have you heard from her yet?"

Could Toni read minds? "Heard from who?"

She groaned. "Come on, doofus. Serena. I know you want to know what she's been posting." She drew out her phone and started scrolling.

His pulse hiked. He hadn't dared look at social media, wanting but not wanting to see her. Seeing her—even if only in a photo—only raised longing, and all kinds of questions that couldn't be answered half a world away. But in a few days, she'd be back, and there'd be no more hiding.

"Okay, she's having fun, posted some pictures of mounds of spices, some amazing looking food, an elephant, see, isn't that cute?"—she shoved the phone in his face, then snatched it away—"ooh, a monkey, and a white temple that looks a bit like the Taj Mahal, but I think that's somewhere different. India looks amazing."

"Sounds like it." He wouldn't bite. He wouldn't. He gestured to the computer. "Anyway, I'd better get back to this. For a message that's only meant to be five minutes long it's taking a surprisingly long amount of time to prepare."

Toni snickered. "Is that because of all your marriage expertise?"

"I don't think you need to be married to be able to offer Godly suggestions on relationships."

"No." Her mouth half-curved. "But maybe you need to think about it."

"Uh huh."

Her smirk bored into his composure.

"What?" His eyes narrowed. "Got something else to add? Maybe you want to make suggestions on my hair or my clothes, or—"

"Well, you could do with a haircut." She eyed him critically. "And maybe some new clothes. Especially if you're going to pick her up and want to pick things up from where they left off." She raised her brows suggestively.

There was obviously no point pretending he didn't know who or what she referred to. "You really think so?"

She nodded. "I really do."

His stomach churned at all the unknowns. Awesome.

JOEL CLENCHED his hands and blew on them. Around him, the cold terminal echoed with the shouts and tears of reunions. He shuffled his feet to stay warm, wishing he hadn't been so vain as to get a haircut before he came. Or at least had brought that new scarf instead of leaving it in the car. His neck was cold. But he bet that was nothing compared to how Serena would be feeling. From thirty degrees Celsius down to five?

Toni had insisted he pack some warm items for Serena, and then added her own spare scarf and toque and jacket to make sure she'd be warm.

"But you know the best way to stay warm doesn't need more clothes," she'd teased, puckering her lips.

He exhaled, suddenly feeling a little shaky. What would

Serena be thinking? That her goodbye kiss had been a mistake? He scarcely dared imagine that, as he'd scarcely dreamed of anything else these past ten days. Her kiss. Her hug. Her in his arms. Her…

He tugged his toque down, then crossed his arms, slouching next to a pillar, his eyes peeled as he waited, waited, waited…

There! His heart kicked as Serena finally appeared. Had she missed him? Would she be glad to see him, like he was her?

But as she wheeled her suitcase down the ramp, he noticed her shoulders were slumped, and the way she gazed around, as if wondering if anyone would meet her, didn't exactly shout the same brand of confidence she'd worn when she'd left. Was she okay? Or did she feel nervous too?

He drew closer, lifted a hand and waved. Her mouth fell open. Had she forgotten this was what they'd arranged? He hurried toward her, uncertainty weighting every step. She didn't seem half as vivacious as the sassy woman who had kissed him ten days ago.

"Joel. Hi."

"Welcome back." Should he hug her? Kiss her cheek? He settled for a light hug but didn't linger. Her stiff shoulders suggested even that hug had been a mistake. "How was your trip?" he asked, motioning for her bag.

She passed it to him without protest. "Long."

She was obviously weary. Her glasses were slightly askew and her hair was mussed and her clothes looked rumpled. Such a contrast to the bright, vibrant woman who'd kissed him ten days ago. "Toni wanted to be here, but Ethan was sick, so she's taken him to the doctor's. You'll have to make do with me instead."

She nodded. "Thanks for coming."

"My pleasure." And it was. Even if it wasn't quite the joyous reunion he'd hoped for. He reached out to gently push her bangs out from under her glasses. "Your hair was stuck," he explained at her look of enquiry.

"Oh." She paled suddenly and pressed her hand to her mouth.

"Are you okay?"

She shook her head. Was she regretting their last encounter?

"I think I ate something I shouldn't have. Then I didn't sleep much on the plane. So I feel a little nauseous."

"Do you need the washroom?"

Another shake of her head. "Already been. It might just be the hours traveling. And the cold." She shivered.

Cue his moment of awesomeness. "I brought you a scarf and woolen hat." He drew them from his jacket pockets and handed these to her. "There's one of Toni's jackets in the car, too, in case you're cold. Welcome home."

"Thanks." Her lips tilted, her smile grew shy. "It's nice to see you."

"And you." Was this another moment for a hug, maybe more? But if she didn't feel well, then probably not.

His arms felt twitchy, wanting to hold her, not sure if she'd welcome it, so he gently tugged her carry-on from her, hoisting it over his shoulder. "Do you need a coffee?"

"No. But if you want one, that's okay."

He kinda did, but drive-through would work okay, so he shook his head and led her to his truck. Once they were finally settled, and she'd zipped Toni's jacket to her chin, he cranked the heat and steered onto the highway. He asked about her flight, about the highlights of her time there, but whether it was jet lag, sickness, or something worse—like regret—she obviously wasn't up to answering much. Her replies were half-hearted, and a little vague, and the conversation lagged until he realized she'd fallen asleep before they'd even finished passing Vaughan.

He glanced across at her, head against the window, Toni's

coat snuggled up to her chin. At least she wasn't looking like she wanted to be sick anymore.

A drive-through coffee run later, and he rejoined Highway 400, sipping his caffeine, checking on his sleeping passenger every few minutes. But she was out.

He blew out a breath, wryly amused at his presumption to think this trip would be some type of grand reunion where he could finally gain some answers for the questions her kiss had raised. That obviously wasn't gonna happen. But concern peppered his disappointment with prayers—for her health, for her family, for her work, for their future—so his soul was buoyant by the time he pulled up in front of her house.

"Serena?" He gently stroked her cheek—so soft. "You're home."

"What?" She blinked, then rubbed her eyes.

"We're here. Let's get you inside."

"Where—? How'd we get here so fast?" She peered out the window, then sat up, covering her mouth as she yawned. "Sorry. I'm just so tired."

"I know. You can sleep in your own bed soon." He fought the thoughts those words provoked. What kind of pastor was, having thoughts like that? *Help me, Lord.*

A minute later she stood, hand on her chest, smiling as she glanced around the living room. "Oh, it's so nice to be home. And look! There's a welcome home sign. Wow."

He placed her bags near her bedroom, glad he'd stopped by earlier to turn the heater on and drop off the food and other items that made her place look more welcoming. "Toni stocked up your groceries and the little girls from your Sunday school group made the cards."

"That's so sweet of them." She carefully read each of them.

"They've missed you."

"It's nice to be missed." Her glance was shy, her smile too brief, before her gaze settled on the vase of flowers.

"Who are these from?" She leaned in closer to smell the delicate fragrance.

"Toni mentioned you liked cottage garden flowers so we got them from Annette's this morning."

Her face softened. "Thank you. They're beautiful."

"My pleasure." His heart expanded. Maybe now was the time to talk…

She yawned suddenly. "Sorry, I'm so tired."

Or maybe not. "You'll sleep well tonight. Are you hungry? I know some ladies from church made a couple of casseroles. They're in the fridge. Oh, and Anna and Jackie said they'd give you a call soon."

"I'm feeling the love."

"There's a lot of love out there."

Serena glanced up at him and he caught her eye. A smile flickered on her lips before she glanced away. "I think I'd better first have a shower. I've been wearing these clothes for way too long now."

"Okay."

She gave another big yawn, then stood abruptly, clasped her hand to her mouth and made a hasty exit.

Joel winced. He could hear the sounds of her being sick in the toilet, and he didn't want to embarrass her. But he also knew when his sister had suffered from morning sickness, she'd been grateful when he'd shown he cared and helped in practical ways. He moved closer to the half closed door and knocked gently on it. "You okay in there?"

Serena looked up from the toilet bowl, wiping her mouth. "I feel awful."

"Maybe you should have a shower. You might feel better soon."

She nodded and tried to stand, but her wobbly movements meant Joel had to step in quickly and help her regain her feet.

He pushed a strand of hair behind her ears. "Are you going to manage or should I call Toni or Anna to come help?"

She shook her head. "I'll be fine. I just need a moment."

"Well, if you need a hand, sing out, okay? I'm not going anywhere." Because foolish him still really wanted to have that talk.

"Oh, you should go. I don't want you to get sick."

"Hey, if it's jet lag, it's unlikely. Anyway, I have a cast-iron stomach. I've needed to be with changing a few of Ethan's diapers." Well, look at him charming the woman with his talk of diaper contents. *Smooth, real smooth.* "I'm very happy to stay. But no collapsing on me. That could be embarrassing. For both of us."

Her eyes widened. "For sure."

He closed the door, but stayed listening nearby, relieved when he finally heard the water turn on without any loud thumps to signal a falling body.

The minutes passed, and he wondered what to do. Boil the kettle? Warm up one of those meals? He shivered. Despite turning the heat on prior to the airport visit the house still felt a little cool. Maybe he should light the fire…

CHAPTER 16

Serena grabbed her towel. Thank God for hot showers with good water pressure and all the creature comforts of non-travel-sized shampoo and conditioner. She felt human again, even if slightly woozy still. But at least the shower had dealt with the sweaty grossness of travel that had made her hesitate when Joel had hugged her earlier. She shuddered. Ugh. The fact the man had persisted in staying suggested he can't have been too grossed out, even if she'd felt awful. Maybe he was a saint of Mother Theresa proportions.

All the flight back she'd wondered what to say to him. How to explain that stupid impulsive moment that had lifted her lips to meet his in farewell. What had she been thinking? It wasn't like she was Marilyn Monroe, filled with flirty confidence. And even though that kiss had proved utter bliss now it just made things harder. Oh, what was she going to do about that handsome man out there?

She brushed her teeth, getting rid of her mouth's vileness. Throwing up in the toilet might've cleared her system, but how *embarrassing* to have Joel witness that! So much for making a good impression. She groaned, then wondered if that noise was enough to bring a concerned Joel back in.

A blast of the hairdryer, some hair product, makeup, and she looked far more alive than the half-dead creature she'd glimpsed pre-shower. She looked around for her clothes. Where were they? Oh. No. She normally brought them into the bathroom with her, but had been so tired, and more than a little distracted by Joel's presence, she'd forgotten them, and there was *no* way she was putting her old clothes back on. They were so gross, sticky and stinky with the sweat of a dozen time zones and the odor of sick.

Heart beating fast, she checked herself a final time in the mirror, rewrapped herself securely in her towel, then slowly opened the door. A quick dash to her room. That's all she'd need. And hopefully Joel was elsewhere and wouldn't see…

A peek up and down the hall showed no sight of him. Just to be sure she called, "Joel?"

No answer. The coast was clear. She took a step, then another, then the back door opened and Joel walked in with an armload of wood. Serena gasped, his eyes widened, then she quickly raced into her bedroom, slamming the door. Her humiliation was complete.

Ugh. After the world's quickest dragging on of clothes she sat, heart pounding, wondering if he'd be gentleman enough to leave. Dear heavens. Maybe he hadn't seen anything. Maybe he'd had a really long blink in that moment, and she'd managed to slip across the hall without him noticing. And maybe unicorns were real.

A tap came on her door. "You okay in there?"

His consideration drew fresh self-loathing. The poor man had given up hours to help her today, and she was hiding in her room like a child. *Get it together.*

A tantalizing smell drew her to the kitchen where a cup of tea sat steaming on the kitchen counter, next to a plate of buttered toast, with a pot of cranberry-peach jam waiting nearby. The coffee machine perked a promising aroma. Bless the man.

Joel looked up from where he was stoking the fire in the living room's fireplace. "You're looking better."

The scene from earlier flashed through her mind. "Better than when I just had a towel on?" She winced. Had she just said that out loud?

His eyes crinkled. "For what it's worth, I didn't see anything."

A chuckle worked its way loose from the grip of embarrassment. "Um, thanks for the tea and toast."

"You're welcome."

She spread jam on the toast then carried the plate and tea to the dining table, where she sat, finally able to relax. Oh, how good to be home.

Joel poured himself some coffee before sitting down opposite her. "So how are you feeling now?"

"A lot better. I'll probably feel even better after a big sleep tonight."

He nodded, glancing away, tugging at his collar.

"Thanks for lighting the fire. It makes things feel so much homier."

"You can't beat a nice fire."

True. She took another big bite of the toast. "This jam is so good."

"I got it from the farm the other day."

The conversation felt stilted, like there were words to say she didn't know yet. Talking about jam seemed far safer than asking if she should apologize for kissing him. She lowered her gaze, awkwardness drawing around her like a fog. What to say, what to say…

"So, are you going to tell me anything about your time away?" he asked. "Toni showed me some pictures you posted, and they looked amazing."

Okay. This she could do. Her tension eased as she began sharing, telling of her flights, her arrival in Kolkata, the sights she'd seen, and her parents' delight, which had soon soured into obligation. "I know my parents love me, but I sometimes feel like it's only able to be expressed when it's on their terms."

"What do you mean?"

"I mean, they'll tell me they are proud of me when it comes to me doing things like Sunday school and stuff, but my promotion at the resort barely earned a smile."

His expression softened. "I'm sorry."

"It's okay." She shrugged. "I'm used to it."

He sipped his coffee. "So your time with them was interesting."

"Interesting is a good way to express it. I mean, it was good to see them, but my dad was pretty busy with work stuff too, so I didn't get to spend as much time with them as I thought I would."

She stole another glance at him, then remembered. Winced. How could she complain about her parents when he'd lost his? How selfish did that make her? "But it was good. I'm glad I went, as I did enjoy my time. The food really was amazing. Hey, if you and Toni are free this Saturday maybe you could come over and we could enjoy some Indian food."

"That sounds fun."

She nodded. "I might see if the others are free—"

"Oh wait. Saturday I can't do, sorry, I just remembered. I have an all-day youth group thing. But I'm free for lunch on Sunday, if you think that'd work."

She'd make it work. If the others couldn't come, well, too bad. But if he couldn't, that was a different thing. "That sounds like a plan."

"Great."

His smile beamed sunshine through her chest, spooling warmth between them, daring her to believe that maybe, just maybe, all the embarrassments and missteps of the past few hours could be forgotten. They really needed to talk.

He leaned forward, swallowed, like he was about to speak, but was nervous.

The weight of his gaze—or maybe her own nerves—forced her attention to her phone. "I'll, um, just let the others know."

"Uh, sure."

She sent a quick message to her friends, adding John and Angela, and Jenny and Mitch Wells for good measure, then, conscious he remained, patient as ever, she lifted her eyes to find he remained focused on her still.

Quietness filled the space between them, and her thoughts swung back to the previous topic that still felt too awkward to share. But he didn't seem too inclined to leave, so maybe he was enjoying being here with her. Her heart thumped. Maybe that meant he wasn't so disturbed by her actions on her departure. Or maybe it meant he was.

She sipped the last of her now-cold tea. "Thanks again for all this," she gestured to the food, the flowers, the fire-lit room, "and for coming to get me from the airport."

"No problem."

"No problem? It was hours out of your day."

"Like I said," his gaze remained steady on her, "no problem."

Her stomach swooped at his look. Was this her chance to finally prod this conversation into what they both seemed to be avoiding? "So, um, do you do this for all the congregation?"

His blue eyes didn't waver. "Not really, no."

Her chest squeezed. "So I get the special treatment."

He pressed his lips together then nodded. "You are special."

The tenor of his voice rolled shivers across her skin.

"Are you cold?" he asked.

"No."

"Are you nervous?"

"Yes," she whispered.

He smiled, picked up his mug and took the seat nearer her. He placed his hand on hers, and gently brushed the back of it with his thumb. "Serena, why are you nervous?"

"Because I don't know what to do."

"Do you mean after our last," he paused, as if looking for the right word to say, "encounter?"

If by "encounter" he meant kiss, then, "Yes."

His lips curved to a quarter moon. "Do you regret it?"

Why? Did he? She swallowed. She would be brave and speak the truth. "No."

"Neither do I." He cleared his throat. "So does that mean you've wondered about us too?"

Us.

Another shiver. She pulled back. Told herself to breathe. "I may have. But I thought you didn't want to date congregation members."

"I didn't. Until I met you." He reclaimed her hand. "Serena, you've opened my eyes and changed my mind about so many things. I'm a better person because of you."

Warmth bloomed across her chest. Could any words be sweeter?

He lifted her hand, pressed a kiss on her palm. "So, you're happy to see if this can be real?"

Apparently, they could. "You mean—?"

"Serena, would you go out with me on the Saturday after this one?"

He was asking her out on a date? Joy bloomed across her chest. But, wait. Did he know—"That's my birthday."

"I know."

He did? She blinked away emotion. Dwight had never remembered.

"So is that a yes?"

She nodded. "Yes, please."

His smile lit up his face. "And just so we're clear, I think it's only fair to say that I'm very open to a repeat performance."

"A repeat performance?"

"Of your, um, goodbye at the airport."

She winced, her cheeks aflame. "I still can't believe I did that."

His hand stole up her arm to gently caress her cheek, drawing her attention to his serious expression. "Very open," he repeated.

Breath suspended as he leaned in to brush the softest of kisses across her lips. Oh. My. Her eyes closed, her hand lifted to trace his jaw, as he cradled the back of her head and shifted closer, capturing her mouth more fully. This was heaven. This was bliss. This was nothing like what she'd experienced with Dwight. Joel's kiss deepened, until she started to drown under sensation, and had to pull away, breathing hard.

The wonder in his expression sank into raised eyebrow query. "Did I misunderstand?"

"No." She swallowed. "I just can't believe this is real."

"I really like you, Serena Williamson." His voice held rasp.

"The feeling is mutual, Joel Wakefield."

The space between them pulsed with attraction, anticipation, heat.

As if recognizing this, he sighed, and pulled back. "It's getting late. I should go."

She nodded. This room had witnessed what could happen when a man stayed too late at a woman's house.

She walked him to the door, thanking him once more.

He smiled, said goodbye, then hugged her. "I'm glad you're home."

"Me too." She nestled close, savoring his scent, glad this embrace held nothing of the embarrassment from before.

His lips grazed her cheek. "Have a good day at work tomorrow."

"You too."

He nodded. "See you Sunday."

"Bye."

THURSDAY, Friday, Saturday passed in a dream, where work and weariness and welcome home messages from her friends struggled to compete with this bone-deep thrill. And while at times she might have felt sluggish—between the contrasting time zones, and her father's words, and her struggle to reconcile a five star resort with her recent experiences of uttermost poverty—she was still conscious of this sense of elation. Was this thing with Joel actually real, or just a jet lag-induced dream? A check of her phone to see his sweet messages renewed her confidence, fueling her dreams during her Saturday morning sleep in, energizing her preparations for lunch the next day.

Sunday, she got to church a little earlier, anticipation high as she wondered when she'd see Joel. She was welcomed with hugs by various parishioners on her way to the Sunday school room, where she soon became busy setting up for the day's lesson.

"Miss Serena! You're back!" The little pudgy arms were quickly thrown around her neck as Serena knelt to say hello to Jemima. Soon the room was crowded with children and their parents as they welcomed her back. Serena shared about some of her adventures in India, concluding the lesson by handing out little gifts for all.

The hugs and welcomes continued upstairs in the main auditorium, Jenny Wells drawing forward a young man. "It's been a week for reunions. You remember my son, James, don't you? He's a doctor," she said proudly.

A hot doctor, Rachel would no doubt say, with his muscled build, curly dark hair, five o'clock shadow, and sparkling dark eyes.

"Jem has been working in Africa, and is back visiting with us for Christmas, so I'm afraid I might have to cancel today."

"No problem. Of course you should spend time with family." Although she'd bet Anna and Jackie would be disappointed.

Somehow, as she caught up with other friends in the brief coffee time before church started, Serena was always aware of where Joel was. She looked up a number of times to see his eyes on her. He'd smile, making her pulse rush, before his attention was reclaimed by someone else. This new awareness of him was making it very hard to concentrate on anything else.

"You okay?" Jackie asked.

"I'm still a bit tired." Even if it didn't fully account for her distraction.

"Started work already?"

"Yeah. But we don't have any weddings scheduled for a few weeks. We're quiet for the rest of November, then it's Christmas. Our next big event will be the Valentine's Day Dinner and Dance."

"Valentine's Day." Jackie groaned. "I think we'll need to organize another singles party to compensate for missing out on all the fun. Will you be up for that?"

Serena caught Joel out of the corner of her eye once more and subtly shifted her position again. "Maybe."

"Maybe?" Jackie's eyebrows rose. "Is there something I need to know?"

Serena shook her head—was that a lie? But anything that really needed to be said could be shared at lunch. She hoped. Fortunately, the music that signaled the start of the service began, so Serena was saved from having to answer anymore potentially embarrassing questions.

Joel was leading the service, so after the time of worship he got up to share the announcements and to pray then preach. She tried to pay attention, but couldn't help notice how nice Joel's hair looked—had he had a haircut?—and how smooth his voice was, and… She drew in a steadying breath. Glanced down. *Lord, help.*

When she next looked up, Joel was staring at her and she flashed him a quick smile. He blinked, looked down at his notes, and quickly resumed his sermon. Okay, personal memo time: don't smile and make the preacher lose his place. Even if it was strangely wonderful to think she could.

After the service, Serena was caught in a crush of well-wishers, before finally exiting to reach her home. Aromas from the curry she'd begun cooking last night filled the room, drawing her smile. The warmth inside here would certainly compensate for the cold outside.

Her friends noticed too, sniffing the air appreciatively as they entered, Toni capturing Serena in a hug, whispering, "How are things with you know who?"

Serena's gaze stole to the man, his smile prompting hers.

Toni nodded. "Going well then, huh?"

"Stop it," Serena said, fighting a smile. "Go sit down."

"And watch the Joel and Serena show?"

"There's nothing to see," she protested.

"Yeah, you keep thinking that."

Serena laughed and shook her head, placing the trays of naan breads, dips and chutneys on the counter as they waited for John and Angela.

"Love the flowers." Jackie motioned to the cottage bouquet.

Serena glanced at Joel, then refocused on Toni. "Toni was very kind, filling up the fridge and fruit bowl, and getting those flowers."

"The flowers were Joel's idea, actually," Toni said.

"Joel, huh?" Rachel and Anna smirked speculatively at Serena.

"He was just being kind."

"Dwight was never that kind, was he?" Rachel said.

No.

Later, when she was checking on the rice in the kitchen, Anna came in.

"Correct me if I'm wrong, but is there something going on between you and Joel?"

Serena's cheeks grew hot, but she didn't turn away. That would be too obvious. "I don't know what you mean."

"Come on. All day you've been looking at each other, then pretending you're not looking. What's going on?"

So apparently Toni hadn't felt to share about the airport kiss. Bless her.

"Hey, did you two see the guy with Jenny Wells today? Hello!" Rachel grinned.

Good. Change of topic. "That was Jem, remember him?" Serena asked Anna.

"Oh! He's the doctor who was working for some aid agency in Africa, right?"

Serena nodded, explaining to Rachel that he was a few years ahead of them at school, before turning to Anna. "Looks like the hot doctor you wanted is finally here."

"Hallelujah!" She fanned herself.

Serena grinned, retrieving the bowls she'd use to serve their main course. That'd been close. Maybe Anna would forget—

"Hey, but don't think you're getting away with not answering my question. What's going on with you and Joel?"

Or maybe not. Serena swallowed. Joel might've kissed her, said he wanted to go out with her, and called them an 'us,' but that didn't mean he wanted their relationship advertised to all the world. And telling her friends would proclaim it as real, would invite all kinds of speculation. But what could she admit to that would protect this fledgling relationship and wasn't a lie?

"I like him, okay?"

"Finally." Rachel grinned. "And it seems from the way he watches you that he likes you too."

Happy shivers of anticipation rolled through her insides, and she couldn't help but smile.

"Oh, you're so happy. That's so sweet," Anna said, moving to hug her. "I'm so glad for you."

If this was Anna glad at a mere admission of liking, she'd be delirious if she knew Serena had kissed Joel. "Thanks."

Rachel moved in as well, and they trio-hugged in the kitchen.

Serena's heart swelled. God bless her friends. "I'd better serve this."

She moved out to the living room, her eyes catching Joel's again. He winked, and she swallowed a giggle. Oh, this was fun, sharing this secret between the two of them. Her gaze fell to a smirking Toni. Okay, the three of them.

And while this afternoon was good, she couldn't wait for Saturday night.

CHAPTER 17

*J*oel glanced across the white linen tablecloth at the woman seated opposite. The dinner was delicious, the restaurant chosen for its ambience and well-deserved reputation for fine dining. But was she enjoying it?

"I hope you don't mind that I brought you here. I didn't realize when I Googled top Muskoka restaurants that Alphonse's was at the place you worked," he admitted.

Serena chuckled. "It's not the first year I've come to work on my birthday."

Yeah. Not exactly what he'd been aiming for. "I hope you don't feel like you're working, anyway. Even though you've probably eaten here lots of times before."

"I have eaten here a few times, but never on a date." Her eyes sparkled as she leaned forward. "So thank you so much for bringing me here."

Phew. "The food is good, eh?"

"So delicious." Her head tilted as she eyed him. "And the dinner companion's been great, too."

"Especially the dinner companion."

Her lips curved, and she swallowed another mouthful of beef. "This is so good. Alphonse is a master."

"They seem to like you here." When the server had recognized Serena and discovered it was her birthday, she'd led them to a special reserved table for two before the fire, seating them, before he noticed the server place the original reserved sign on a table nearer the window. Then they'd been supplied with all kinds of treats, petit fours the waiter had called them, that nobody else here tonight had received. Alphonse himself had come to check on them, later personally bringing out their mains. Joel could tell Serena was touched.

"You can see why I like working here. Everyone treats each other like family."

That reminded him. "Did you talk with your parents today?"

She nodded. "Just a quick call. Dad was busy." She wrinkled her nose. "But it was good to talk." She sipped her cider. "My sister called too, so that was nice."

He asked her about her sister, and they talked about families, about memorable birthdays, about the best and worst presents they'd received as kids. He wondered what she'd think about the gift he had stashed in the car, a set of expensive soy candles he'd bought at Annette's to go with the flowers he'd given Serena when he'd arrived to pick her up for their date. He hoped she liked them. Annette had said she would.

The server returned and enquired about dessert, and they ordered from the leather-padded dessert menu. He wasn't hungry, but he was keen to extend the date, even if he'd be doing double runs for the next week to work it off.

The server departed, and they talked some more, and Joel held her hand, admiring everything she did, from the way she'd styled her hair, the elegant jewelry she wore, to the way her eyes sparkled as she told a funny story about something at the resort.

His heart swelled. This ease, this shared laughter, this friendly comfortable feeling was like nothing he'd experienced with Mel. How could he have let her actions dictate his for so long?

"Are you okay?" she asked.

See? Her kindness, her solicitude was yet another reason he loved Serena. He blinked. Loved *about* Serena. He liked her. A lot. And he suspected his feelings could easily tip into something more serious and committed the longer he spent time with her. Like maybe even tonight.

"Joel?" she asked again.

"I'm fine. I'm great. I'm loving that I finally got the chance to go out with you."

"Finally? Have you been thinking about this for a while?" she asked shyly.

He nodded, his gaze distracted as a flame-lit cake was carried their direction.

She followed his gaze and laughed, as Alphonse and several other waiting staff drew near and began singing 'Happy Birthday', which caused other diners to pause and soon join in.

"Happy birthday, dear Serena, happy birthday to you." Joel called. "Hip, hip—"

"Hooray!"

This was repeated twice, then the restaurant broke out into applause, as Serena blew out her candles and wiped away a couple of happy tears, then stood to thank and hug the chef.

"Alphonse, you're so sweet," she said. "I wasn't expecting this at all."

"You deserve it," Alphonse said gruffly, before eyeing Joel. "Treat this one good, eh?"

"He is," Serena said, patting the chef's arm then resuming her seat. "Joel is a good man," she said, her gaze soft on him.

Yet another reason why he lov—*liked* this girl. She recognized and appreciated what he tried to do, even though he might fall short. Melanie never had.

"Don't stay too late," Alphonse said with a wink.

Joel nodded. "Thanks for making tonight special."

"She is special," Alphonse said.

"I know." Joel threaded Serena's fingers with his. Cake and birthday wishes from departing diners soon dropped into insignificance as he stared into her eyes. "Did I tell you how beautiful you look tonight?"

Her lips lifted. "Maybe once or twice when you collected me. Then another few times on the way here."

"Just wanted you to know for sure."

She squeezed his hand, then released, picking up her dessert fork. "I wouldn't have ordered dessert if I knew cake was involved too. I'll have to diet this week."

So maybe she was still working on knowing she was attractive. "You don't need to diet at all," he assured. Her clothes fit every curve just right.

"You're sweet."

"You know it."

Her chuckle ended on a hitch of breath as a shadow fell over their table.

"Serena?"

He'd heard that voice before. He shifted in his seat and squinted up. A skinny woman, who looked like she might be anorexic, except for the swell in her stomach, eyed Serena with a sneer. Just as she had last month at the Muskoka running event.

"I couldn't believe it when he said you were here. And it's your birthday." She flashed a hand in Serena's face, the large diamond twinkling in the candlelight. "Happy birthday."

Serena's lips pressed together, her gaze falling.

No. No, no. Serena couldn't still hold feelings for the weedy dude standing behind the pregnant stick insect. Not when Joel was starting to consider all kinds of commitment—

But wait, this wasn't about him. He reached across the table to grasp Serena's hand, but after a quick squeeze she released his fingers, pushing back in her chair before quietly performing introductions.

"Well, aren't you going to congratulate us?" the woman demanded.

"Just happened tonight," the Dwight guy mumbled. "I figured with the baby on the way I'd better do the right thing."

Serena took a sip of cider, her gaze swerving up to meet her ex. "You figured, huh?" Her words held as much warmth as the snow falling outside. "Well, congratulations."

Her gaze faltered, snagging Joel's eyes in what looked like a desperate plea for help, which drew him to shift in his seat. "Congratulations. A baby deserves to be raised in a happy home. Even better if it's in a family with a husband and wife who love each other." Something he wasn't sure these two did. Hence the not-so-subtle reminder. "You should come to the church and go through pre-marriage counselling."

Hope's lip curled. "With you?"

Interesting. Despite only just being introduced these two clearly knew what he did for a living. "Nope," he said. "That'd be weird, especially as I care for Serena and wouldn't want to know stuff about you two that would make things hard for her. She doesn't need anyone else making life difficult for her, does she?" Joel smiled. "I can talk to John and Angela McPherson about it for you if you like." He shot a look at Dwight. "I think you know who they are, don't you? I met your parents there, anyway."

"Uh, thanks." Dwight glanced at Serena then back at him. "See you around."

Joel nodded, noting the way Hope's features had tightened as she glanced at Serena, whose fake smile still hadn't altered, before tossing her hair and stalking off.

"Pleasant couple," he murmured.

The tightness on Serena's face said she wasn't ready for jokes yet.

"Are you okay?" he asked, reaching for her hand.

She moved it away. Shook her head. "How could you talk to them like that?"

"Like what? Oh, you mean suggesting they get pre-marriage counseling? They're going to need it, that's obvious, and—"

"She was enjoying flaunting her ring, her pregnancy in my face—on my birthday!"

"She needs Jesus," he said softly.

"That's not all she needs," she muttered. "I can't believe they decided to come here. That should be my baby, that should be *my* ring."

All amusement fled. So she was still hung up on the guy. He pushed past the hurt, past the disappointment, daring to ask the question that really mattered now. "Have you forgiven them?"

She bit her lip. Her gaze fell to the tablecloth.

He'd take that as a no, then.

"I thought I had, but apparently not," she murmured.

He repossessed her hand. "I know it's not easy, but until you do, the bitterness won't ever really leave."

"I don't know how," she murmured, finally meeting his gaze again. "How do you forgive people who flaunt their sin in your face? I think I'm better, then something like this happens and it stirs it all up again."

He caressed her fingers. "I remember when Matt challenged me about forgiving the drunk driver who killed our parents. The guy didn't show much remorse, and while the jail sentence seemed fair, it kept on eating me up inside. Matt challenged me to pray for God to bless the drunk driver."

"What?"

He nodded. "I know. Sounds crazy, right? But doing that, even though I didn't want to, helped release some of the poison inside. Doing that helped remind me that that person's actions didn't change God's love for me. I found focusing on God's love really helped me too."

She studied him, her forehead furrowed, then glanced away. Yeah. Look at him bringing the birthday fun.

"Besides," he gently squeezed her hand, "would you really want an engagement ring from a man who can't be faithful?"

Her lips pressed together as she paused, then shook her head. "You saw how gorgeous Hope is. I can't compete."

Joel's brows rose. "Really? You think Hope is gorgeous?" At her nod his gaze softened as he looked at her with compassion. "Serena, she's too skinny. I think there's something wrong with her. She might even be anorexic." He sighed as he recalled being duped by Melanie's outward beauty. His former girlfriend really was as shallow as Toni had always painted her to be, with a depth of character about as thick as the oil Toni used on her canvas. He found himself telling Serena some of that story. "Hope seems to be like Mel. Outwardly appealing, but inside they've got nothing. Serena, they've got nothing on you."

Judging from the way she was looking at him he wasn't so sure his explanation had helped. What was it with women and their insecurities about their looks? Then he remembered his first comments about Serena and understood a little more.

"Serena, you are more than just the shape of your body," he said. Even though he found her shape immensely sexy. "Just because some foolish people have made stupid comments doesn't mean you need to worry about your own attractiveness." He took her hands. "I guess I don't tell you enough, but I think you're one of the most lovely women I know, inside and out."

He noticed her bite her bottom lip as she looked down. "Thanks."

"No, I mean it." He leaned across the table and tipped her chin up so she couldn't avoid his gaze anymore. "I haven't wanted to get involved with any woman until I got to know you. I like you, Serena. I like your sense of humor, your kindness, your work ethic, your hospitable nature, your willingness to serve God." He reached forward and touched her hair. "I also like your hair, it's so pretty, especially in the sun. And I love your eyes, your beautiful, mossy-green eyes that tell me more than what words ever could." He touched her lips. "Your smile makes me feel like the sun got brighter."

"You're starting to sound a bit like Solomon from the Bible," she murmured.

He raised his eyebrows.

Her breath hitched, and her cheeks pinked, forcing him to swallow a smile. Yeah, there were certain aspects of Solomon's love poem he'd avoid tonight. But other poetic images suited his purpose. He reached across to touch her face. "Her cheeks are like pomegranates, or is it tomatoes?"

A giggle escaped as Serena pushed his hand away. "Thank you very much. Next, you'll be saying my nose is like a tower."

"Well, no, I wasn't actually going to *say* that." He waggled his eyebrows, eliciting another laugh. "But seriously, Serena, I do find you," he searched for the word. Better than attractive, better than appealing, more like, "alluring."

"Alluring, huh?" She arched her eyebrows. "And are you sure an assistant minister is allowed to be 'allured'?"

He stared steadily at her, his voice growing husky. "I'm pretty sure this one is."

"Oh." Her smile blossomed into fullness.

But even as he wooed and teased, he sensed that wasn't really what she needed to hear right now, not when the issue went much deeper. He drew his chair closer to hers, folded her hands in his. "Serena, I could spend a lifetime telling you how beautiful you are. But what's most important is that you believe what God says about you. You need to know what He says about you, to *know* it, rather than just live on the rise and fall of circumstances or other people's opinions."

Her lips pressed together, her gaze fell.

He winced, wishing he had better words, but still feeling a

sense to speak this now. "I know I can sometimes be a people pleaser—"

"You?"

He smiled. "I think we all can be at times."

"I know that's me for sure," she whispered.

"But I've learned the danger of paying attention to what others say and letting that become more important than what God says."

"You have?"

"I have. But I'm learning to speak what God says." He tucked a strand of hair behind her ear. "You are loved. You are chosen. You are precious in God's sight."

Her eyes, her beautiful green eyes, filled, shimmering like the lakes in spring.

"God has equipped you with the power to fight those thoughts, to take them captive, but you're the only one who has the power to actually do that. So in one sense, it doesn't matter what others say if you keep saying it to yourself."

She looked away and exhaled. "I don't know why you bother with me."

"Because I," he paused. Was it too early to say, 'it's because I love you'? Again, he felt that sense to back up, to not say things she might latch onto rather than allow the truth to sink deep into her soul.

"Because I care about you very much." He swallowed. "And I don't want to see you held captive anymore to the lies of the enemy."

Her gaze lifted to his, and he was sorely tempted to kiss her, but again that sense held him back. Then she nodded. Wiped at tears. Smiled.

"You know, I kind of knew that, but I don't think I ever really heard it put quite so well before. Thank you."

"You're welcome."

She exhaled heavily, her shoulders straightening. "I'm not a victim."

"Not at all." He squeezed her hands.

"And it's up to me to fight those thoughts."

"You, and the Holy Spirit. He'll help you, that's his job, so ask for help when the thoughts get in there."

"I will."

He lifted her hand, pressed his lips to the back of it. "Can we pray?"

"Yes please."

He kept his eyes open, though she closed hers, gifting him the opportunity to appreciate her long lashes. "Lord, thank You that You love us, that You regard us as Your children. Help us to really know this, to live knowing we are loved by You, and to treat others the way you want us to. Thank You for giving us the Holy Spirit to remind us of this truth. Bless Serena on this special day, and every day. Amen."

"Amen," she whispered. "And God bless Joel, too."

"Amen."

She opened her eyes. "Thank you."

"My pleasure."

Her smile lit the corners of his heart. Yeah, this he could do. Being yoked with a woman who believed with him, believed for him, this was both pleasure and privilege. And an answered prayer as well.

Their mutual smiles and stares continued for a weighty moment, until she sighed. Glanced at the cake.

"What's up?" he asked.

"Mmm?" Her gaze lifted to him. "Oh, I was just thinking about dessert."

"Really?"

"Yes. I don't like how Dwight and Hope killed the atmosphere before and took away my appetite."

"You still really want dessert?"

She smiled sweetly at him. "It's my birthday, right? And between your reminder about forgiveness and your prayer I think you've just given me the best present of my life."

"Really?"

She nodded, and his heart was full.

A little later, she pushed the chocolate torte aside, confessing herself unable to eat another bite. A nod to a server drew him near, with a request to box the remainder.

"Would you like anything else?" the waiter asked.

"Just the check, please."

Serena excused herself, murmuring something about needing to powder her nose. The waiter returned with the check and the torte in a takeout container, his manner holding something of relief.

"I hope you'll get home safely, sir."

"Safely?"

"Were you aware of the blizzard warning for tonight? Most people cancelled their reservations for tonight, so we've been much quieter than normal."

So that explained why they were the last couple remaining in the restaurant.

After finalizing the check—way less than he'd expected, leading him to suspect Serena's friends had given a substantial birthday discount—Serena returned, and he pushed to his feet. "We need to get going. Apparently, there's a blizzard warning."

"A blizzard? That's a bit early in the season, isn't it?"

"I've been so busy this week I haven't had a chance to check the weather forecast," Joel admitted.

The waiter's brow creased. "Well, I'm sure if you're staying onsite that you'll be fine."

Joel scratched the side of his jaw. "Actually, we're driving back to town tonight."

Serena nodded. "But we'll be fine. Besides, I can't stay out all night with you. Not with the assistant pastor. Imagine your reputation."

Her tease said she wasn't as worried as the waiter, so Joel smiled at him. "Thanks for the warning though."

Joel helped Serena into her heavy coat before assisting her down the steps to Toni's sedan. He'd borrowed it for tonight, feeling it was way more date-worthy than his truck, even if it did boast a baby seat in the back, but now he wasn't sure the sleek vehicle was best equipped for the snow. He'd put snow tires on two weeks ago, but he couldn't help regretting the car didn't have the heft and muscle of his Ford. Already the increased amount of snow falling and bite of wind suggested tonight's drive home wouldn't be fun.

After settling her in the car, Joel turned up the heater and faced her. "Are you sure you want to go home? We could see if there's a room and just head back tomorrow." As Serena opened her eyes wide Joel realized how that sounded and felt his cheeks heat. "Two rooms, of course."

"Just take it slow and steady. We'll be okay."

"Okay, then."

The road from the resort was fairly clear, earlier traffic having helped to disperse the heavy snow that had fallen in the last few hours. But as they neared the halfway mark, in the depths of dark forest, the road became more treacherous, the tires slipping and sliding. Exactly why had he insisted on taking his sister's nice sedan rather than his much safer, reliable truck? Who cared about appearances, when all they really needed was to return home safely. At least he'd ensured Toni had good snow tires.

As they rounded another bend, Joel fought to keep the vehicle on the road, the tires slipping on another stretch of ice. A quick glance at Serena revealed her strained features and the way she gripped the door. The trip was proving to be anything but serene. A violent gust of wind pushed the car into another skid. Joel gritted his teeth. If only he had the superior handling of his truck.

"I've never seen anything like this." Serena's voice held an undercurrent of fear.

Joel had never driven in anything like it either. He couldn't see in front of him more than a couple of meters and the situation was proving dangerous. "I think we may need to pull over for a while. These conditions are terrible."

"That might be wise."

It was basically a whiteout, making the need to pull over increasingly urgent. He slowed, veering to pull over on the right when the car suddenly slid and spun completely around. Serena's cry filled his ears as he wrestled for control, images of trees, snow, darkness flashing before his eyes. The car slammed into a huge snowbank, jerking them forward, thuds accompanied by a scream. His chest hit the airbag, drawing a hiss of pain. He glanced across to see Serena inching back from the window, blood trickling from a small cut on her forehead.

No. No, no. Panic clawed up his throat as he leaned across and touched her face. She slowly blinked. "Serena? Oh, I'm so sorry. This is all my fault. Are you in pain?"

"I...I'm fine. My head hurts a bit, but I'll be okay. Are you hurt?"

"I'm fine." He would be, anyway. "Here, let me get the first aid kit." He pushed past the deflating airbag and leaned across her to rummage in the glovebox and draw out the plastic-cased medical kit. "Here." His chest tightened as he gently dabbed at the wound and applied a sticking plaster. He finished, and she grasped his hand and pressed a kiss to his palm and thanked him.

"Let's get this show on the road, huh?" he said, to her nod.

But despite gunning the engine, Joel couldn't move them. A walk around the vehicle revealed that they had plowed into a low-lying stump, that no amount of rocking eased. Even laying out grit for traction and revving reverse at top speed didn't see the car budge.

"Looks like we might be stuck here awhile. I'm really sorry. Must be the city boy in me. I should've checked the weather but I was excited about coming."

"So this wasn't part of your surprise?"

He grasped her hand, gently squeezed. "I'm sorry."

"It's not your fault."

Except it kinda felt like it was.

"We should call someone to help us."

Of course. Hello, city boy and doofus. But his phone had no signal. "You got any signal?"

She shook her head no, swiping at a spilled tear. "I'm sorry. If I hadn't insisted on coming home tonight—"

"Hey." He wrapped his hands around hers and blew on them to warm them. "You didn't know this would happen. We couldn't have stayed anyway. You know how people talk."

She bit her lip. "So now they can talk about us staying the night together here instead?" She choked off a hysterical-sounding laugh.

"I think they'll understand. And if they don't, well, there's not much we can do about it, right?"

She nodded and he noticed her chin start to quiver.

"Aw, don't go there. You're not responsible for what other people think," he reminded her. "So don't take it on board, remember?"

Another nod, and a tear trickled down her cheek.

"Hey, don't cry." Joel reached out to hold her hand. "Especially not on your birthday. There is an upside. We get to call this an adventure, and I get to spend more time with you."

He got the smile he was hoping for, the tension dissipating as they continued to talk, and he periodically restarted the car to keep the fuel line from freezing.

After a while, Joel noticed Serena was starting to shiver and he reached into the back to the emergency pack that always lived there. "I know we've got some extra clothes, blankets, food, and things to help in situations like these. Let's see what we've got."

Joel pulled out some thick heavy sweaters, handing the smaller one to Serena. "I don't know why Toni insisted on keeping this. At least it's warm. Put this on under your coat. You might not be quite so stylish but at least you won't freeze."

"Thanks." She unbuttoned her coat and slipped into his old college sweater. It was too big for her but he knew from experience it would at least keep her warm.

"Hope it doesn't smell too much."

Serena took a delicate sniff. "It just smells like you."

"I hope that's a good thing."

She reached out and squeezed his hand. "I like things that remind me of you."

Joel squeezed back before releasing her hand. Whilst she struggled back into her coat he rummaged through the rest of the bag. "We have flashlights, some fruit bars, chips and cookies. There are some bottles of water as well, although we might want to go easy on that. Toni did a good job packing supplies—oh, wait, that was me."

"No false modesty, eh?"

"It's good to know your strengths," he said meekly.

She chuckled. "And we have the leftover chocolate torte. What Toni doesn't know won't hurt her."

Joel grinned. "I like how you think. Oh, that reminds me." He pushed his chair back and reached into the back for his gift. "I should give this to you while it's still your birthday." He handed her the gift bag.

"You didn't have to get me something. You gave me flowers, and a lovely meal—"

"That was mostly Alphonse. He was pretty generous," he admitted.

"God bless him. But you're the one who gave me an adventure." She smiled, lifting the bag. "It's heavy."

"I hope you like it."

"I'm sure I will." She lifted the envelope, read the small card, smiled at him again, then unwrapped the beautifully packaged present. "Candles. Oh!"

She lifted them to sniff them, her lips pressing together, before she blinked rapidly.

"What is it? Don't you like them?"

She shook her head.

Oh. His heart dipped. Another fail.

"I love them," she murmured.

"Really?"

He caught her nod in the darkness. "I had a similar set, and, uh," she swallowed, "something happened to them."

"Annette said you liked the frangipani scent, so I hope that's true."

She nodded. "It's beautiful. Thank you."

She leaned across and their cold noses bumped before she kissed him.

Once again, he felt that stirring, that desire to open his heart and share all of him with her. Even tonight with all its drama had only solidified his feelings for her.

"Happy birthday," he whispered, his breath mingling with hers.

"It is. It has been. Thank you." She kissed him again. "Thanks for tonight."

"My pleasure. Sorry about the end."

"Not your fault."

She was too generous. But he'd take it.

"We could light the candle," she said. "Did I see a tin can in your emergency pack back there?"

A minute later the soft glow and scent of her expensive gift wafted through the interior, the can acting as a mini heater as well as a light in case rescuers needed a sign.

He restarted the engine, and they checked their phones again but the signal still wasn't there. After a quick check to unblock snow from the exhaust pipe he hurried back inside, joining Serena in pulling on thick socks and gloves and wrapping the blankets around them.

"All set?"

She nodded.

"We might as well try and get some sleep while we can. Who knows how long we'll be here."

"This is certainly an adventure," she said.

Sure was. God bless her for regarding it as so.

"I like you, Joel Wakefield." Serena's sleepy smile made his breath catch.

"I like you too, Serena Williamson," he replied huskily. "Goodnight." He leaned over and brushed a kiss on her cheek. "See you in the morning."

Serena smiled sleepily at him a moment longer. "See you then." She held his hand and closed her eyes, and he watched her until he too finally fell asleep.

CHAPTER 18

*W*hat the—? Serena blinked open her eyes, struggling to gauge her surroundings. The sound came again from the huddled blanket next to her. A slight snoring sound from… Joel!

She rubbed her eyes as memories flashed from the previous night: delicious food, laughter, candles, snow… a car crash? She pressed her forehead, wishing she could push the headache away, feeling a Band-aid instead.

Her stirring must have woken Joel because he shifted and opened his eyes to look at her. "Good morning."

The rasp in his voice tightened her midsection. It wasn't right that an assistant minister should be that good looking, especially first thing in the morning after a shocking night's sleep.

"Good morning." Could he smell her morning breath? If only she could brush her teeth.

"How did you sleep?"

"In a car seat, next to you."

"Very funny." He smiled. "You feeling okay? How is your head?"

"There's a bit of an ache, but it's okay. How are you? How many times did you get out to check the exhaust?"

"A few." He yawned. "What time is it?"

Serena glanced at her phone. "Unless there's a miracle, I think you'll be late for church."

"Miracles do happen." Joel stretched and yawned again before finding his phone. "Do you have any signal yet?"

"Not yet."

"Maybe my provider will work again, now that the snow and wind have died down." He switched it on, and a persistent buzz announced the arrival of dozens of messages. "Guess I've got a signal then."

He pressed the numbers, then he looked up at her and winked, before speaking.

Relief rushed through her. Someone would be coming to help soon.

He ended the call and exhaled. "They said the truck will be here in an hour."

"That's great!"

"Give me a moment to check these messages. I bet Toni is worried."

Of course. She listened as he went through his missed calls, replied to messages, spoke to Toni and assured her they were okay. Toni insisted on talking to Serena which meant she had to assure her too. Then he called John and said he'd likely miss today's meeting, and she called Anna and asked her to take the Minimites today too.

"So you're okay?" Anna checked.

"I, um," Serena glanced at Joel. "I had an eventful night, but I'm okay now."

"Does that mean you weren't?" she demanded.

Between Hope and Dwight's bombshell, and the car crash, yeah. "There were a few things that weren't in the plan, but I'm definitely okay."

"And can you tell me why you're calling on Joel's phone?"

Ah. That. Had she explained her date with him? Maybe not. She filled Anna in, which met with cries of "No way," and "That's so romantic," and "Oh, so that explains it!"

"It's probably best you don't say too much," Serena warned.

"My lips are sealed," Anna promised. "I'll just say you had a big night last night for your birthday."

"And make it sound like I'm drunk?"

"Okay, then I'll come up with something else. Sounds like we've got lots of catching up to do."

Serena ended the call soon after, handing Joel back his phone. Worry teased his brow. "What is it?"

"Will your friends be okay with you and me? You're a pretty tight-knit group."

"As long as you treat me right then you have nothing to fear."

His lips curled to one side. "Oh, I plan to."

Her heart fluttered at the deep look in his eyes. She didn't have to work in a doctor's office to diagnose that look.

He exhaled. "So, I guess that means there's one thing left to do."

"What's that?" She hoped he didn't have kissing on the brain. Much as she loved kissing him, between her headache and her morning breath fears, it might be best to refrain.

"We need breakfast."

"Of course you do."

"Hey, a man has to eat, and after the excitement of last night, I find I'm hungry." His gaze slid to her lips.

"Hungry for what?" she dared.

"Hungry for some of that torte that you're still wearing."

"What?"

He leaned across and kissed the corner of her mouth, his lips focused on a smear of chocolate. She wriggled away, laughing. "Stop it. I don't want you to die from my morning breath."

"Honey, I can't smell anything but the delightful aroma of

that candle you insisted we burn all night. I think the scent is singed on my nostrils for eternity. Look, it's still going."

"It's good to see a twelve-hour candle living up to the promise." She touched the rasp lining his cheek. "You chose well."

"I sure did," he said, his voice low, his eyes not moving from her.

Her heartbeat stuttered, and a second later she was sinking into his embrace again. So much for fears about morning breath. Or for needing blankets to keep warm. The car was heating quite nicely, thank you.

A tap on the roof saw them break apart and see the grinning face of Alphonse at the window. "You two happy in there, or do you want to come back to Muskoka Shores with me?"

Home had never looked so good.

She opened the front door and sighed before turning to face Joel. "Thanks for a great night. Certainly was one of the most interesting dates I've been on."

"It didn't exactly end the way I'd planned."

"Oh." Her smile grew bigger as she tilted her head to one side. "You like to plan how your dates end, do you?"

"I like to have some idea, yeah."

"And how exactly did you plan this one ending?"

Joel stared at her a moment, then bent down until he was only a breath away. "Something like this." He closed the small gap and kissed her.

Oh. My. Goodness. The man could kiss.

It wasn't like her sassy kiss at the airport, or those ones stolen in the car. The intent and care behind this kiss made Serena's head swirl. Dazed, she blinked her eyes open and drew away, breathing haphazardly, her pulse pounding. The last time she'd felt like this had been…never.

Serena pressed her lips together as if to hold onto the sensation for longer, but his look now sent butterflies racing through her stomach. She tried to think of something to say. "You need to be careful, Mr. Wakefield. You kiss me like that and I'll think you might like me a little bit."

"Maybe I do, Serena. Maybe I do."

She drew back, filled with thankfulness for snowplows that had helped clear the way for them to return to Joel's in Alphonse's truck, which had passed the tow truck.

"Well, thanks again, for everything."

Joel smiled at her again, causing that now familiar tug on her heart. "It turned out to be a date and a half, didn't it? I promise to make the next one far less exciting."

"You better." She smiled at him, before giving him a final hug. "Thank you."

"Serena, may I have a word?"

"Of course, sir."

She closed her computer, grabbed her iPad and followed Mr. Jennings to his office. Along the way she passed Angela and Jenny—at the resort coffee shop after their Pilates class, no doubt—and gave them a wave. The general manager's office held a sweeping 180 degree view of the resort. She could see snow covered tennis courts and the treetops adventure course, and beyond that, the snowed-over golf course greens.

"I trust you're all recovered from your birthday misadventure."

It hadn't taken long for her extended date to hit the resort gossip. "It was certainly an unexpected way to finish the day."

"I'm glad you're all right." He gestured to a chair and she sat. "Now, I wanted to talk to you about this art proposal you had."

The art—? Oh. Her chance to help Toni.

"I see the young woman you mentioned has the last name as the, er, young man you are seeing."

"Toni is Joel's sister."

He nodded, his brow creased. "We don't normally encourage such things, as we like to avoid what might appear to look like favoritism, but my understanding is that your relationship with the young man is a relatively new thing."

"Sir, I'm afraid I don't really see the relevance—"

"It's just that the board has been inspired by your proposal, and are interested in both her tree picture's image for our branding—"

Really? How wonderful!

"—and wish to consider an art gallery here."

"Oh! I didn't think I put that in my proposal."

"We've seen other resorts with ideas like this, and there's something about showcasing the beauty of Muskoka through local artists. She is local, isn't she?"

"She lives in town, yes." Even if she'd only lived there for a few months.

He nodded. "It's just at the trial stage, but we were wondering about reclaiming the old sports office and using that space for an art gallery."

"Really? What a fabulous idea!"

"Well, it is mostly your idea. We just tweaked it a little. But it helps set our resort apart from others in the area, especially if we can incorporate the idea of art classes as well." He glanced at his notes then back at her. "Do you think this young woman would be able to manage that?"

"I think she'd jump at the chance. She does have a baby, though."

"And we have a small onsite childcare facility employees are free to use."

Of course. She'd forgotten that. "I can call her if you like."

He nodded. "I'd like to set up a meeting soon. If this winter is anything like what we've seen so far, then it would be good to get our winter options up and running before too much more time passes."

"Yes, sir. Thank you."

He smiled. "I'm excited about what you're bringing to the table, Serena. I hope your friend is as full of ideas for going forward as you."

"I think you'll find she is."

They discussed more details then she thanked him again and moved back to her office, settling at her desk. Going forward. Leaving the past behind. She was doing it. And Joel was right. It didn't matter what others said or thought, she had to know and believe it for herself.

Mr. Jennings' validation might provide a momentary lift to her spirits, but what she thought about herself was what really mattered. And she *knew* now, from the birthday gift that Joel had given her, that she was loved by God.

Loved. He was making her paths straight.

Loved. He sustained her through it all.

Loved. God had placed supporters around her, cheering her on.

She was loved.

God's love was like a buoyancy vest, something she had to choose to put on, but it would hold her afloat. No matter what happened with Hope and Dwight. No matter what her parents said. No matter what her circumstances were. She was loved.

Her eyes pricked. God bless Joel for opening her eyes to recognize this truth, for praying for her in that fog-lifting way. What a good man he was. How blessed she was. Her heart bubbled with joy, with gladness, with tender affection. These feelings were nothing like what she'd ever felt before. She loved—

Her phone flashed with the picture taken by the server showing her and Joel grinning at her birthday dinner. She answered. "Hello. I was just thinking about you."

"Were you now? And here I was thinking about you." Joel laughed. "Hey, are you free?"

"Right now?"

"Tonight. For dinner."

"Um, sure. Hey, will Toni be there? There's something I want to talk to her about."

"She wasn't going to be, but she can be now."

"Thanks." She smiled.

The day passed in emails, meetings and more plans, the thought of driving home to see Joel weighting each hour with impatience. She visited the space Mr. Jennings had talked about, took pictures on her phone, and was relieved when five o'clock hit and she could make her careful way home.

The roads were still slippery, and even with her snow tires and years of experience, she had to watch her driving and take it slow but steady. A quick change at home, comfortable jeans, boots and warm top, and she was driving to Joel and Toni's.

She didn't have time to knock on the door as Joel opened it, drawing her inside. "You didn't have to bring anything," he said, eyeing the pie she'd dug from the freezer, before kissing her, "but I'm glad you did."

She laughed, put the pie down on the hall table, and wrapped her hands around his neck. "I think you should say hello properly."

"I think you're right."

He removed her glasses then took his time kissing her, his arm behind her back, one hand in her hair, and she kissed him back, melting into him.

A clap of hands and a baby giggle drew them apart. "Nice to see you two have figured out the kissing thing."

"Hello, Toni," Serena said, her arm slipping around Joel's waist, her head on his shoulder. "Did you have a good day?"

"Well, the highlight so far has been the evening entertainment."

"Ha. Well, I think that's about to get better."

"Why?" Toni glanced between Serena and Joel. "Are you going to give her mom's ring? I told you that's okay—"

"Stop it kiddo, you're embarrassing yourself."

"I don't think I'm the only one embarrassed here, am I right?" She winked at Serena, which drew her laughter.

"I don't know what your brother plans to do or when, but I wanted to talk to you about your art."

"Oh. Is this one of those conversations? When I have to be all serious? Because I really think—"

"Toni, listen. Better yet, sit down. I am serious. This is important."

Toni obeyed, to Joel's murmur to Serena, "See why I need you in my life? She does that for you but not for me."

"I like her more," Toni said, obviously overhearing.

Serena eased from Joel's arms and sat at the dining table with Toni, drawing out her phone. "I was talking with the general manager at Muskoka Shores today, and he wanted to know if there was anyone interested in running an art gallery at the resort. For some reason, I immediately thought of you."

"What?" Toni shook her head. "I'm barely an artist these days, let alone know anything about running an art space."

"But you do know about creating evocative art pieces, something the resort is interested in too." She smiled. "They actually want to use your maple picture as part of the new logo and branding."

"What? How?"

"I took your picture to work and the GM saw it and loved it. He basically pushed it to the board, and they said yes."

"You can't be serious. That little picture I gave you from here?"

"That's the one," Serena said.

Toni slumped in her seat. "Wow."

"And because of your skills, Mr. Jennings is wanting to talk to you about the possibility of opening an art gallery, and potentially a studio, where people could come and learn."

"From who?" Toni asked.

"You."

"But I'm not an art teacher either."

"You would be, if you taught others." Serena glanced at Joel then smiled. "I've learned a lot recently about being careful about what we think. Don't say no without thinking through what the possibilities could be."

"But even if I wanted to, what would I do with Ethan?"

"I don't think we'd be talking full-time, not at first, anyway. But on the days that you'd work there are childcare facilities he could go to. And from what I understand from what Mr. Jennings was saying, it seems you could do your own work there."

"What—even if no customers came?"

Serena nodded. "Even if no customers came. So basically, you'd be paid to do your art and have your child looked after for free. I'm sorry if that's not something you'd like to do, but I kind of thought it might be of some interest."

"Are you serious? Like, you're not pulling my leg or anything?"

"I don't pull legs," Serena said.

Toni pressed her lips together, glanced at Joel, then pushed up and raced to her bedroom. A minute later they could hear loud sobs coming from Toni's room.

Serena glanced at Joel. "I thought she'd be happy."

"Give her a moment," he said, holding her hand. "This is legit?"

"One hundred percent."

"You're amazing," he said fondly.

"Not really. I'm just passing on a message."

The sound of an opening door drew their attention to Toni again. Mascara streaks dripped down her cheeks but her smile said she was all right. "You really are for real?"

"Yes."

Toni wrapped her arms around her and squeezed, fresh tears soaking through Serena's hair and shirt as she wrapped her in a hug.

"Hey, it's okay. Why the tears?"

Toni wiped her nose with tissues Joel handed her. "Because for so long I've been wondering what to do, and I started asking God what He wanted for me with my art. I was getting so desperate that I said on Sunday that if I didn't hear something this week that I'd start looking for work as a cleaner, or maybe even go back to the city. But I didn't want to. I love it here, and love being with you, and Joel, and Jackie and the girls. But it seemed I was out of money and out of options until now."

Serena squeezed harder. "God has the right time frame, doesn't he?"

"Always," Joel's voice came from behind, as he wrapped the two of them in his hug.

The next half hour passed with more explanations, showing pictures, and Serena giving pointers for Toni's meeting with Mr. Jennings. "They'll want to get the rights for your image, so you need to get someone who knows about copyright to help you get the best deal." She glanced at Joel. "I don't know if you know—"

"I'll ask Matt. He probably knows a lawyer type or two."

She nodded. "And I suggest you go through all your paintings and find a selection of ones more indicative of Muskoka so you can look at selling them." A memory from several months ago flared into awareness. "In fact, now I remember there are some people who might be very interested in seeing your work, especially if we tag them on Instagram, and say how much we love Muskoka Shores."

"Who?"

"Oh, I happen to know a certain hockey guy who has a house nearby which is big enough that it probably requires more art. I also heard he likes to give his wife art. And his wife just so happens to follow me on social media."

"No way. Really? Do you mean Dan Walton?"

"It's worth a shot."

Toni's excitement meant she took some persuading to not ignore her Bible study with Jackie and Anna, but she was soon out the door, along with Ethan.

Joel wrapped his arms around her waist. "Well, look at you, being amazing."

"You know it," she murmured, taking a leaf out of his confidence playbook.

He laughed and kissed her cheek. "I can't remember the last time I saw my sister so excited. It seems like a miracle."

"God is into doing miracles," she said. "So somebody wise told me not so long ago."

"Wise, huh?" He grinned. "Wise enough to know when I've found a good thing."

His kiss was sweet and thorough, causing her to draw back with a gasp. "Now, did you say something about dinner?"

"Hmm. I much prefer dessert."

"Stop." She laughed, pushing him away. "Is that chili I see in the slow cooker?"

"I figured it's time to compare those recipes."

"Is that so?"

"It is indeed," he said, removing the lid to release a delectable aroma.

"Well, I hope you'll serve it soon because I'm hungry."

"Bossy. I like it."

"Not bossy," she corrected. "Just a woman who knows what she wants."

"And that is...?"

She smiled. "You."

"Hmm. That's a relief," he said, moving back to hold her again.

"And why is that?"

"Because I happen to want you too."

"Is that so?"

"It is, most definitely."

She laughed, and he pressed kisses on her throat.

"So was there anything else you wanted to say?"

"Ah, that. Let me serve dinner so you don't eat me."

She set the table, trying to not think about what had sobered him so fast. Was he in trouble with John and Angela? Had someone complained about them being out all night? Was he—?

No. *Holy Spirit, help me to stop worrying.*

She sucked in a breath, and finished setting the table for two, her heart edged with more peace.

Joel served the bowls of chili, said grace, and she took the moment to enjoy the meal. To enjoy his company, his presence. "This is delicious."

"I agree."

She grinned and used the bread roll to mop up the sauce. "So that thing you didn't want to say before?"

He exhaled. "I hope you won't be mad, but I got a call today from John. You'll never guess who has asked him to marry them."

"Dwight and Hope."

He nodded, studying her seriously. "Is that okay?"

"You ask that like you think I mind that they're getting things right with God."

"So you don't mind?"

"No." And it was true. Now. *Lord, bless them.*

Dwight and Hope getting married *was* a good thing. Truly. Because she knew God loved her, her heart remained at peace.

See? Not a twinge. *Thank You, God.* "The other night, I

might've acted like I minded, but I've come to realize that their words and actions don't need to poison me. It's like darts from the enemy that fall short because I've wrapped myself in God's love."

"Really?"

She nodded. "Really."

"Can I say that I'm relieved?"

She smiled. "You know that Dwight can't hold a candle to you, even if you have the same taste in candles."

"Please explain."

So she did, and he laughed at the story of the thrown candles. "Honey, you constantly amaze me."

"That's a good thing?"

"That's a great thing." He nuzzled her neck. "You know what else?"

"What?"

"I love you," he murmured.

Her chest grew tight. "Are you the one pulling legs now?"

"Not about this," he assured, before swooping in to kiss her.

He took his time, and she returned his affection fervently.

"You know what?"

"What?" he murmured.

"I love you too."

"Is that so?"

"That is so."

"Hmm. Well, in that case we might have to one day go talk to John and Angela too. And then, maybe talk with this great wedding coordinator I happen to know."

"One day."

"One day soon," he murmured.

And as the last of the sun's rays slowly sank into the depths of Lake Muskoka, he cupped her cheek, leaned close and stole another kiss.

THE END

Want more romance on Muskoka Shores? Then check out *Muskoka Christmas* and discover whether a real hero can live up to Staci's fictional man of her dreams.

A NOTE FROM THE AUTHOR

Thank you for reading *Muskoka Shores,* the first book in the Muskoka Shores Christian contemporary romance series. This book is based on my visit to the beautiful Muskoka region of Ontario, Canada, and springs from Muskoka Blue, the sixth book in the Original Six contemporary romance series, that enters on Sarah and Dan's romance story (grab your copy of *Muskoka Blue).* If you've enjoyed this book, please check out the pictures from my visit to Muskoka on my website at www.carolynmillerauthor.com

Reviews help other readers find new-to-them authors, so if you can spare a moment to write a quick review at Goodreads / your place of purchase, I'd be very grateful.

Enjoyed this taste of Muskoka? Then make sure you read *Muskoka Christmas,* part of the Muskoka series that continues with *Muskoka Hearts.*

If you enjoy Christian contemporary romance you may want to check out the books in the Original Six hockey romance series, a sweet & swoony, slightly sporty Christian contemporary romance series.

The Breakup Project
Love on Ice
Checked Impressions
Hearts and Goals
Big Apple Atonement
Muskoka Blue

Romance and hockey fans may also want to read *Fire and Ice*, the first book in the new Northwest Ice series, releasing in 2023.

I'd love for you to check out my other books and to sign up for my newsletter at www.carolynmillerauthor.com where you can be the first to learn all my book and contest news, and discover more behind-the-book details and photos.

A huge thank you to the following people for their encouragement and eagle eyes: Ros, Jacqueline, Bea, Brittany, Rebekah, Kaye & Becky - I appreciate you all so much! Big thanks to the ladies in my Facebook group, Carolyn's Books & Friends, for all your support in helping promote my books.

ABOUT THE AUTHOR

Carolyn Miller lives in the beautiful Southern Highlands of New South Wales, Australia, with her husband and four children. A long-time lover of romance, especially that of Jane Austen, Georgette Heyer and LM Montgomery, Carolyn loves to write contemporary and historical romance that draws readers into fictional worlds that show the truth of God's grace in our lives.

To find out more about Carolyn's books, and to subscribe to her newsletter, please visit www.carolynmillerauthor.com

You can also connect with her at

ALSO BY CAROLYN MILLER

<u>The Original Six hockey series</u>

The Breakup Project

Love on Ice

Checked Impressions

Hearts and Goals

Big Apple Atonement

Muskoka Blue

Muskoka Shores

Muskoka Christmas

Muskoka Hearts

<u>Northwest Ice hockey series</u>

Fire and Ice

<u>Trinity Lakes collection</u>

Love Somebody Like You

<u>The Independence Islands series</u>

Restoring Fairhaven

Regaining Mercy

Reclaiming Hope

Rebuilding Hearts

Refining Josie

Historical:

<u>Regency Wallflowers</u>

Dusk's Darkest Shores

Midnight's Budding Morrow

Dawn's Untrodden Green

<u>Regency Brides: Legacy of Grace</u>

The Elusive Miss Ellison

The Captivating Lady Charlotte

The Dishonorable Miss DeLancey

<u>Regency Brides: Promise of Hope</u>

Winning Miss Winthrop

Miss Serena's Secret

The Making of Mrs Hale

<u>Regency Brides: Daughters of Aynsley</u>

A Hero for Miss Hatherleigh

Underestimating Miss Cecilia

Misleading Miss Verity

'Heaven and Nature Sing' from the Joy to the World Christmas
novella collection